A TEMPEST SOUL

Gray Door Ltd.

Copyright 2018 Oliver Phipps. All rights Reserved.
ISBN 978-0-9908034-5-4

To: Rachelle and Tabitha,

I love you both so very much.

CONTENTS

Chapter One: A Soul of Desire 1

Chapter Two: No Great Loss 32

Chapter Three: The Winds of Change 72

Chapter Four: The Ascension of Serena 86

Chapter Five: A Past that Waits 109

Chapter Six: Life in Vista 132

Chapter Seven: A Lonely Cry 155

Chapter Eight: Flower of My Heart 181

Chapter Nine: Autumn Arrives 208

Chapter Ten: A Legendary Dance 231

Chapter Eleven: A Dark Stage 260

Chapter Twelve: The Closing Curtains 299

CHAPTER ONE:

A Soul of Desire

"You're really going to wear that?" Lois sounded astonished as she gazed frightfully at the swimming suit Gina held up to herself.

"Yes, I'm really going to wear this! It's 1920 Lois. Women don't have to wear ballroom dresses to go swimming." Gina smiled with a little satisfaction after saying this, then rolled the swimming suit up and put it back into her bag.

Although the suit would cover most of her body, it was made to fit snug and the legs were cut above the knees, allowing for her calves to show.

Lois shook her head a bit, indicating she didn't really agree with the young woman. "I know it's 1920, but I don't think a young lady such as yourself should be showing off so much skin. What would your mother say?"

When Lois said this Gina's face immediately grimaced as if in pain.

"I don't care what she thinks, or where she is for that matter" the young woman replied quickly with disdain in her voice.

She grabbed several plates of food from a window leading to the kitchen area and walked briskly into the large restaurant to waiting customers. Then, carefully, Gina made her way back with a handful of dirty dishes.

Lois regretted her comment and as the day went by she watched for a chance to make amends with Gina.

Finally, before their shift ended Lois found an opportunity to talk with the young waitress.

"I'm sorry about earlier Gina. I was told by some of the other girls not to ever mention your mother; it just slipped out… I just can't believe she…well, it just seems hard for me to believe. But, maybe something happened that she couldn't come back."

Gina glanced at Lois and then sat down at the table she had been cleaning. She stared at her hands for a few seconds. She examined her fingernails as Lois stood by waiting for a reply. Finally, she spoke in a soft tone.

"Lois, I don't want to talk about this after today. I realize you don't understand, so I'll tell you this, one time." The young woman took a deep breath and clasped her hands together in her lap. She stared out at the floor ahead of her as if it helped her recall memories. Then she slowly began again.

"My father died when I was very young. I don't think my mother ever really wanted me. If she did at one time, I don't think she did after my father died. My mother and I moved here to Jacksonville four years ago, when I was thirteen. We moved into the same small apartment I live in now. She got me a job here washing dishes. Then after about a month, she disappeared for several weeks. I didn't know what to do. She left me a note telling me to work every day and she would be back."

Gina paused a few seconds and wiped her hands on her dress. Lois watched her with sadness. Then she went on.

"My mother came back with a man. She asked about my job and how I was doing. Then after a few days, she said, 'I'll be back later, in a week or so; keep working and pay the rent dear.' This time, she didn't come back for over a month. After a few days, she left again, and I've not seen her since."

Lois now ran the palm of her hand along the side of her face and tried to think of something to say. Gina glanced at her again and Lois decided she needed to say something.

"Well, you know sweetie, maybe she feels bad about leaving you and she's afraid to come back. Maybe she would like to come back… but she's afraid you won't forgive her."

Gina's mouth twisted a little as she considered this.

"She should be afraid. She abandoned me, and I'll never forgive her for that."

Lois's eyes squinted slightly in discomfort as the young woman said this.

"Gina, I realize I'm probably not the best person to be giving advice, and I don't know why your mother left you the way she did, but I really feel you should forgive her. It's not good to keep something like that inside."

Gina continued to stare blankly at the floor. Then she finally replied.

"I'll never forgive her. I would never do anything like that. I don't care if I ever see her again. She abandoned me; her thirteen-year-old daughter. She should never come back. I hope she never does."

Lois couldn't think of anything else to say. She placed her hand on Gina's shoulder for a second.

"I've got to go take care of this table. Thanks for telling me about that. I'm sorry I brought those memories back; I won't mention your mother again." She then went to wait on a customer.

When her shift ended, Gina gathered her things together and walked out the door of the kitchen and through the waitress area.

"You have fun sweetie, be careful now, you hear." Lois smiled and waved as Gina passed her.

"Thanks, I'll be careful." She went through the restaurant and out the front door. As she moved towards the bus stop, she checked her bag to make sure she had everything.

The busy streets of Jacksonville were noisy, dusty and laden with heavy exhaust fumes.

After a lengthy bus ride, Gina stepped off at the beach boardwalk. She made her way to a changing room and anxiously put on her new swimming suit. It was a maroon color and fit her body like a glove. She liked the way the suit looked and thought it was a shame most young women had to wear those big, baggy dresses to swim in. Besides being uncomfortable, they absorbed so much water a woman could drown by simply stepping into the water wearing one.

She strolled onto the beach in the new suit that showed much of her legs. Heads turned and one poor guy who watched her too closely as she passed by was knocked over by a large beach ball being thrown to him. This caused Gina to giggle with a bit of delight. If anything, she enjoyed the fuss over her.

The shapely young woman found a spot on the beach with an available public umbrella and put down a large towel. She grabbed her book from her bag and took it with her as she sprawled her body across the towel on the warm sand, to get some sun. Not too much, though. She positioned herself so that the umbrella blocked some of the rays from her face and head.

1920 had developed into a good year for Gina. She had moved into a waitress position after she turned sixteen and with a year of better pay and tips, the young woman felt more confident and independent than ever.

She enjoyed being in active places and had lately become keen on people noticing her and giving her attention. Gina felt pretty and as she developed into a woman she began to have a desire to be artistic. The way to do this however eluded her.

She knew nothing about acting, but lately that's what preoccupied her thoughts. She also liked the idea of being a dancer or some other type of performer.

Perhaps the bathing suit was an attempt to attract some assistance in becoming artistic. Maybe someone would notice that might help her reach her dreams.

Gina casually read her book on the warm sand as the sun basked her body.

"Hi, doll."

A young man suddenly dropped down beside her and smiled in a cavalier way.

She glanced over at him as if she cared little. With a quick look, Gina perceived a young and husky young man; not bad looking, though somewhat rough in appearance.

After a brief pause, she gave him a little smile and immediately turned away in a manner to express she wasn't very interested.

"You sure are a sight. What's your name beautiful?"

Gina now looked at the young man suspiciously.

"I just want to know your name doll... or I can guess. Let's see, you must be, Venus?"

She couldn't help but giggle about this but stared in the opposite direction to camouflage the fact he'd entertained the giggle from her. She tried to turn her attention back to the book.

"It's not Venus?" The young man persisted. "Then it must be Lilian, as in Lilian Gish maybe?"

This became too much for Gina and she turned to face the man.

"It's Gina, if you really must know." She then turned back to her book but smiled to herself in satisfaction of handling the situation.

"Gina... what a beautiful name, and so fitting for a beauty like you." The young man lay back on the sand, putting his hands behind his head.

She loved this type of attention, though she'd also learned to be wary of such flattery.

Being a waitress necessitated a quick learning experience for the attractive girl. She had simplified the process in her mind after several close calls. A little clever flirting can reap larger tips from men. Too much flirting seems to give them license to try anything they want.

After a year as a waitress, the young woman knew when to smile and when to frown. She knew how to use her eyes and what body movements could get a glance and which ones would get an unwanted slap on her behind. She now slyly glanced at the young man.

"Well, you have my name. Would you kindly return the favor?"

"Oh sure, sure doll, I mean Gina. My name is Rodney. My friends just call me Rod for short, though."

She intentionally waited before replying. When she felt the pause had been long enough to indicate she was only slightly interested in him, she replied.

"I'm pleased to meet you Rod."

Rod was instantly revived as he sat back up and leaned on his arm.

"It's a pleasure to meet you, Gina. So, you must be an actress, right? I mean, I'm sure I've seen you in a movie. . .or two."

This caused an instant flutter throughout her body, causing her to giggle loud enough she was sure he must have heard.

"You better quit that," she said and turning slightly hit his arm.

"What do you mean? Are you saying you're not an actress?"

"No... I'm not an actress; you're being...silly." She smiled and felt excited by the flattering words.

"Well, then you must be a dancer, right, like a chorus girl, in the stage shows?"

This caused another uncontrolled giggle, and now Gina could feel herself blush.

Rod knew he'd said just what she wanted to hear and continued to play the charade to perfection.

"You better stop," Gina said without much conviction. She now appeared to glow from the attention.

Rod paused with a sly smile. He had no doubt she loved the attention and he also knew what she wanted to hear. He lay back on the sand, staring up at the sky.

Gina waited for him to continue. Then she turned and glanced at him with an expression of anticipation. When Rod felt he'd kept her on the hook long enough he continued.

"Well, if you're really not an actress or a chorus girl, you should be."

Gina now relaxed a little; as if glad he'd saved at least one more compliment.

"I would love to be an actress. But I think it may just be a dream." She replied, as she laid back on the sand next to Rod.

"I knew it! You see, I knew you had to, at least, be an aspiring actress." He sat back up quickly.

She rose back up on her elbows.

"Aspiring actress? What does that mean?"

He leaned over closer to her as he began to explain.

"You know an actress in the making. In other words, you're an actress, but you're still in training."

Gina became obviously excited as she contemplated this.

"Really, you mean I can do that? I can be an actress in training?"

"Sure, you can Doll." Rod lay back down on the sand, confident he had her right where he wanted her.

Gina stared at him. She wanted to know more about this "aspiring actress" thing but didn't want to appear ignorant. Rod opened his eyes slightly and glanced up at her.

"But I should probably leave now. Your Pop is likely around here somewhere and will pound me into the sand when he finds me talking with his little girl." After saying this, Rod sat up a little and looked around apprehensively.

"He's not." She quickly replied.

"Then, where is he?"

Gina continued to stare at Rod. Then seeming a little reluctant she finally answered.

"If you really must know, my daddy died when I really was a little girl." She then lay back down and turned slightly, as if upset.

"Oh, I'm sorry Doll. I didn't mean to bring up anything that would make you sad. I only want to see that smile."

She looked back at him with a pouting face but then smiled a little just before turning away from him again.

Rod now lay back down for a moment without saying anything.

Seeming to think of something he sat up quickly again and said. "Well, your Mama is probably around here somewhere ready to skin me." He then looked around again seeming a little frightened. "I know you're not old enough to be here by yourself, Doll."

Gina sat up quickly after hearing this. Obviously upset, she stared at Rod and replied with frustration in her voice.

"I'm twenty-one."

"Twenty-one? I don't believe that. More like seventeen, eighteen maybe."

Gina's face became a little twisted as if he had indeed come closer to her actual age. Then, seeming to realize she hadn't convinced him of being twenty-one she stated gruffly.

"I'm nineteen, and I am so here by myself. I take care of myself quite well, thank you."

Rod chuckled. "Alright, nineteen it is. But your Mama will still kill me when she finds out a twenty-five-year-old man is flirting with her 'nineteen' year old daughter."

Gina retorted gruffly. "That's not likely. I've not seen my Mother for four years. And why are you being so nosey anyway?"

"Nosey?" He appeared hurt. "I call it interested. Can't a man be interested in a beautiful woman without being called nosey?" He then leaned away from her and drew in the sand with his finger.

Gina appeared to calm down. After watching him for a few seconds, she laid back on the sand. Then Rod also lay back down beside her. Neither one spoke for a few minutes. Rod glanced over to see what she was doing. She just lay there staring up at the sky. Then after another moment of silence, Rod spoke.

"You know Gina, when I look at that beautiful face of yours, I can see your future."

She turned her head and stared at him with suspicion again.

"You can not. Why would you say such a thing?"

"It's an easy thing to do, Doll." He sat back up on one arm and looked her over. "Yes, you are destined to be a great actress."

Gina giggled, seeming happy to return to the compliments.

"You'll travel to exotic places," he studied her face, as if discerning a map. Gina stared up at him with an excited smile. Then Rod went on, moving his arm out as he spoke.

"You'll be on world stages, entertaining officials and dignitaries. Men will fall helplessly in love with you and women will envy you. You'll be in newspapers and photographers will all want to take your picture."

Gina now felt as if she were on cloud nine. She smiled and her eyes gleamed.

"You really think so?" She asked innocently.

Rod smiled slyly. "I know so, Doll. You're going places I can tell."

She stared up at the clouds as she lay in the sand, intoxicated by the things he had said.

"I sure hope you're right," she finally said.

Rod now lay back down and waited for the right moment. After a brief pause, he reacted as if just thinking of something.

"Hey, you know what?"

Gina became a bit startled when Rod said this.

"What?" she replied as she sat back up quickly.

Rod also sat up.

"I'm in really good with a man that has connections in the entertainment world."

"You are?" she asked with surprise.

"Yeah sure, Hal, why didn't I think of this sooner?"

"Hal?" Gina still seemed to be having trouble keeping up.

"Yeah, Hal, he knows a lot of people in entertainment. He has a big yacht and I'll bet he can get you a job as an actress or a chorus girl maybe."

This information appeared to almost overwhelm the young woman. She sat with her mouth slightly open staring at Rod. After a few seconds, he realized she needed a nudge.

"Did you hear me, Doll?"

"Yeah, I heard you." She replied, still seeming to be in a bit of shock.

"Well, anyway he has a yacht and we're all going out on it tomorrow. I can invite you along and you can meet Hal. He'll love you. I'm sure he can find you a job. He's a great guy, you'll love Hal. This is great!"

Rod rubbed his hands together almost as if he were making a fire. Gina still appeared to be in disbelief.

After briefly watching him rub his hands together she said. "I am not that sort of girl Rod. I don't just go out on yachts, with people I don't know."

Rod acted a little hurt again.

"What do you take me for, Doll? No… don't answer that. I know what you're saying. I'm trying to help you and you make me out to be some guy that does, the things you're thinking." He hung his head down but still managed to glance at Gina.

"No, I didn't mean you were, bad or anything. I just meant, well, I just met you today."

"Yeah, but I feel like I know you, Doll. I knew you was an actress, right?"

She liked the sound of being an actress so much, she couldn't bring herself to deny it.

"Well, I guess so."

"You see there. It's just as if we've known each other much longer."

Gina struggled with the logic. She really wanted to go.

Rod continued with a renewed energy, now that he had her on the fence.

"Besides, there are several other girls going along. You won't be the only girl there. We're just like a big family."

Now Gina looked at him with an obvious desire in her eyes.

"Really, there are other girls going?"

"Sure, Doll you won't be the only girl. Like I said, we're just like one big happy family."

After considering this for a minute, Gina asked with a cautious tone.

"So, how long are you talking about, all day long?"

"Oh no, at least three days, Hal doesn't take the boat out unless it's for three days at least. It's a large, engine powered yacht, not a small boat."

She thought about this some more.

"Well, I've got to work. I can't just take off."

"Hmm," Rod's mouth twisted as he considered this. "Isn't there anyone that could cover for you?"

"I guess Lois could," she replied after a few seconds.

"Alright then, just ask Lois to cover for you a few days.

Besides, Doll after you talk to Hal you may not need that old job anyway."

She liked the sound of this as well but still wasn't sure about going on a yacht with strangers.

Then again, if this guy had enough money for a yacht, surely, he must be a decent person. She could barely sit still now and went over these things again and again in her mind.

After some additional discussion, and with some reservations, Gina finally agreed to go on the yacht and meet Hal. Rod would pick her up the following afternoon.

That night she sat alone in her cramped apartment. She heard a baby crying from the apartment beneath her.

She sat on the edge of the bed and stared at the floor. The decision of going on the yacht concerned her. She thought about it repeatedly.

Then Gina noticed the picture that lay face down on the small table beside her bed. She slowly reached over and picked it up.

The old and faded photograph was one of the few things her mother had left her. She studied the faces in the picture as the baby continued to cry. She pulled the picture closer. Her father held her in his arms. She appeared to be two, maybe three years old. Her father smiled and looked happy.

Then she moved her eyes to her mother. She didn't smile. She seemed disappointed to be there. As Gina stared at the photo, a tear fell from her eye and splashed onto the glass.

Gina quickly wiped the picture off and placed it back on the table face down. She wiped her eyes with the same urgency, as if someone might notice her crying. She then stood up and began gathering some clothes for the trip.

The next morning Gina arranged for Lois to cover her a few days at work. She knew Lois wouldn't like her going on a yacht with strangers, so she neglected to tell her the exact reason she needed time off. Instead, she just told her she needed to go meet a man about an acting job. Lois was excited about this and quickly agreed to cover for her.

She met Rod at the designated place with her bag in hand. He drove a nice car and she became even more impressed when they arrived at the dock. The yacht was long and luxurious. The wood trim had a deep shine and elaborate ornamentation decorated the exterior as well as interior.

Inside a spacious lounge area, two young women sat on a couch talking to each other.

"Hello Ladies," Rod said as they approached the women.

"Hello Rod," they both replied in unison.

"Vivian and Rebecca, this is Gina."

Gina said hello and the two women greeted her rather nonchalantly.

"Follow me Doll, I'll show you to your room. We'll be shoving off soon, so it'll be tomorrow before I can introduce you to Hal."

Rod led her to a small but tidy room. She put a few things in the closet and got comfortable as the large boat moved out to the open ocean.

That night Gina slept a little restlessly as she wasn't accustomed to being away from her small apartment. She awoke the next morning to find they were far out to sea.

In the lounge area, she found a small group of people consisting of Rod, Vivian, and Rebecca. Next to them sat another well-dressed man that appeared to be in his early forties. As she entered, Rod stood up.

"There's the sleeping beauty."

Gina smiled.

"Good morning," she said with a little wave.

"Gina, this is Hal McBride."

Rod pointed to the man sitting. Hal had a drink tipped up as Rod said this. He pulled the drink from his mouth and stood up quickly, putting out his hand to her.

"I'm pleased to meet you, Gina." He winked at her and said, "You're right Rod, this one is a beauty."

Gina blushed as she shook Hal's hand.

"Thank you and I'm pleased to meet you too, Mr. McBride."

"Please call me Hal; Mr. McBride still sounds to me like my father."

"Oh, alright then, Hal it is."

"You met Vivian and Rebecca last night." Rod turned to the two young women who both waved a little and then went back to sipping their drinks. Vivian then leaned over and whispered something to Rebecca.

"Please sit down, Gina. I'll have Walt bring you breakfast." Hal waved towards someone standing behind Gina where she hadn't noticed him.

A man dressed as a waiter or perhaps a butler, came up from behind Gina and asked what she would like for breakfast.

She sat down after giving him an order. It all seemed very pleasant to her as she drank some orange juice and gazed around the large room.

"Please excuse us, ladies." Rod and Hal stood up in preparation to leave.

Rod then turned to Vivian and Rebecca, "You girls behave around our guest, unless you both want to swim back to Florida." He then winked at them.

The two young women turned to him and again, almost in unison said, "Yes Sir."

Hal and Rod then moved out the door and onto the deck of the boat.

Walt brought breakfast and Gina ate it, struggling to watch her manners. She tried to get a good look at Vivian and Rebecca without seeming to stare. They were dressed in the finest fashion. Both were very pretty, and Gina couldn't help but feel a bit out-of-date in her plain clothes.

The two girls continued to sip their drinks and talk amongst themselves about people and places Gina had no knowledge of.

When she finished her breakfast, she waited for a lull in their conversation. She considered going outside but felt her best bet would be making friends with Vivian and Rebecca. Though still young, she had no misconceptions about the nature of some men. Rod and Hal seemed to be nice guys, but she felt safer around other women right now.

"So, how long have you known Rod and Hal?" she asked as soon as there was a pause in their conversation. The two young women gazed over at her as if she were speaking a foreign language. Then after a few seconds, Vivian spoke in a somewhat slow manner.

"Gina, it is Gina, right?"

She nodded yes.

"Gina, I'll give you a bit of advice, Sugar, you know, woman to woman, and all that. Just do as you're told, and you'll be alright."

Gina wasn't sure what she meant.

"You mean, acting? Are you both actresses?"

The two girls looked at each other and laughed a little, almost under their breath.

"You might call it acting," Rebecca said. Then they began to sip their drinks again.

"Well, thank you for the advice." Gina said a bit meekly.

"You're welcome, Sugar," Vivian replied now and gave her a strange look.

Not wanting to leave, Gina tried to think of something else to talk about.

"Is Rod in the entertainment business too?"

With this comment, Rebecca almost spewed a mouthful of her drink out. An obvious effort and a hand to her mouth enabled her to restrain herself and eventually swallow her drink.

Vivian laughed out loud at the comment, then when she had calmed some she tried to answer Gina.

"Oh, I'd say he likes to entertain, Sugar, but Rod and Hal are both Bootleggers, you know Rumrunners. In fact, we're on our way to pick up a load right now."

Gina thought about this for a few seconds.

"Bootleggers… is that a shoe business?"

Now Vivian and Rebecca almost became hysterical with laughter, due to this obvious naivety. Gina felt embarrassed about her lack of knowledge and wasn't at all sure about being on the trip.

"Oh, my Sugar, you really are fresh off the farm, aren't you?" Vivian replied as she tried to stop laughing so hard.

"You better stop Vivian, or we'll be swimming," Rebecca put a hand on Vivian as if to restrain her.

"You're right," she replied and then continued with a stifled laugh.

"Well Sugar, let's just say they're in the… 'beverage' business."

Gina smiled apprehensively.

Meanwhile, on the deck of the yacht, Rod and Hal were having a conversation of their own.

"She's a bit young don't you think? I mean she's definitely a sweet little dish, but she can't be more than eighteen or nineteen." Hal spoke with obvious concern.

"She's perfect," Rod said with a sly smile. "I don't think she's even eighteen. But her Pop died when she was a little girl and her Mama left her several years ago. She's got no one, and that means no one to look after her. Like I said when you hired me Hal, you're going to get some benefits. Before long, we'll have a bevy of beauties to go with your yacht."

Hal smiled and took a sip of his drink. "I see why you say she's perfect; young, beautiful and all alone. So, when are you going to start breaking this new filly in?"

19

Rod turned and leaned back against the rail beside Hal. He thought about the question for a few seconds.

"I think I'll start tomorrow. I believe the farther away from her home we are, the more cooperative she'll be. In the mean time though, remember, you're in the entertainment business. Or at least, you have connections in the entertainment business."

Hal considered this.

"Sounds like you have everything under control. I'll just brush up my movie producer look." He ran his hand on the side of his face, as if he was working on it already.

In the lounge, Gina had little luck making friends with Vivian and Rebecca. After listening to their chat, a while longer, she tried once more when an opening presented itself.

"Rod and Hal seem like nice guys."

The two girls turned to Gina with a condescending look. Rebecca sipped her drink and gazed at her from over the rim of her glass. Then she replied.

"They're Rascals, and I mean that in an affectionate way. Rod is very feisty you'll find. And Hal is, well, not as feisty. But that can be a good thing. You know, give a girl a bit of a break."

Gina tried to understand what Rebecca meant. Then when the two began talking together about a jazz band that she knew nothing about, she decided to take her chances out on the deck.

"Hello, Doll," Rod greeted Gina with a smile. Though she'd become a bit apprehensive by the things Vivian and Rebecca said, the warm greeting was a nice change.

"Hi," she replied with a smile. "It's really beautiful out here."

"Yes, it certainly is," Hal said turning around to face the young woman. "Calm seas and smooth sailing!"

She laughed a little, then walked over to the rail and leaned against it peering out to the expansive sea.

"I told Gina you could help her out, Hal. She's an aspiring actress."

Hal smiled a bit at Rod's remark and then cleared his throat before replying.

"An actress you say? Well, that's something. I thought she had the look of an actress or a dancer maybe. Sure, I can help her."

Gina thought Hal sounded as if he were fibbing.

"The girls say you're in the beverage business, Hal?"

The two men glanced at each other, seeming surprised.

"Oh, yes well, that is one of my businesses," Hal replied. Then Rod jumped in.

"In fact, Hal supplies many entertainment establishments with beverages and such."

"Yes, Rod's right, I meet a lot of important people through that process alone," Hal added, seeming eager to clear things up for her.

"I see," she said, examining the two as she might a suspicious salesman. She then turned back to the ocean and pulled several dark brown strands of hair from her face.

"Well, we can talk about this later. I think we should just enjoy the day right now. Would you like a drink, Gina?"

Hal asked, seeming concerned that Gina had become apprehensive.

"Do you have a soda?"

"Yes, we certainly do," Hal replied.

"I'll have Walt bring one out to you, Doll," Rod darted back towards the lounge.

"There are lounge chairs aft of the boat," Hal pointed to the back of the boat. "You can get some sun if you like. Just beware though, a pretty thing like you will likely get some attention from the crew. I hope you don't mind a few admirers."

Gina shook her head, indicating she didn't mind. "Thanks, Hal." She then moved in the direction he had pointed. As she walked along the rail she tried to reassure herself the two men were nice enough.

After examining the lounge chairs, Gina went to her room and put her swimming suit on. She then returned and relaxed with a cold soda.

As Hal had warned her, several men of the crew were spotted lingering around on the upper deck trying to get a view of the sunbathing beauty below. She didn't mind though and acted as if she wasn't aware of their presence. As the large boat cruised along, the concerns of the morning began to wane.

Later, Walt brought lunch out to her and she dozed off not long after eating.

Vivian and Rebecca came out while she slept and were also getting some sun when she woke. The suits they wore exposed even more leg than Gina's suit. She wondered if they were simply trying to outdo the guest.

Nevertheless, they didn't bother her and with all three laying under the partly cloudy sky there was soon a steady flow of crew members around the upper deck, trying hard to pretend they weren't watching the three pretty young ladies on the lower deck.

Evening came, and the group ate a fantastic dinner. The conversation, for the most part, consisted of Rod and Hal directing topics and the three women commenting from time to time. Gina preferred this however to Vivian and Rebecca's method of discussing things she obviously knew nothing about. By the time she went to bed, Gina had become somewhat relaxed again and considered that she may have simply inflated her concerns.

As she lay in her small cabin, she felt maybe Vivian and Rebecca were being mischievous to the newcomer. They must be somewhat bored, she thought. These and other excuses helped explain the earlier meeting. Perhaps they just wanted to stir up trouble for the fun of it. She slowly drifted off to sleep with this thought in mind.

The morning brought very little sunshine. The sky presented a gray day and Gina felt a bit disappointed by the lack of sun as she ate her breakfast with the others. Later, on the deck, the wind blew her hair about and she finally pulled it back and tied it to keep from constantly removing it from her face.

She then changed into her swimming suit and laid on the lounge chairs, even though the sun constantly struggled to break through the gray clouds.

The arrival of crew members along the upper deck signaled once again she must, at least, be a pleasant sight. This increased her confidence and she began to wonder when she could speak seriously with Hal about a job somewhere.

She thought of the restaurant where she waited tables. Though her job as a waitress paid for her small room along with a few other necessities, she could care less about ever returning to it.

Soon Vivian and Rebecca joined Gina in their swimming suits. With all three girls laying on the deck a constant parade of admirers assembled on the upper deck.

Gina sleepily glanced up to where three crew members leaned over the rail, trying to get a better view of the beauties below. This caused her to smile slightly as she closed her eyes and slowly dozed off.

When she awoke, the sky had become very dark. The wind blew aggressively, and the boat rocked due to much larger waves. She stood up and stumbled to gain her footing. No admirers were on the upper deck now. She made her way towards the lounge feeling a little startled by the change in weather.

Passing under the upper deck, on her way to the lounge door, she spotted several life vests hanging on the wall. They were rather odd-looking devices with two, large round, canvas covered floats on the front and back. She patted one before entering the cabin area as if to reassure herself it was there. Regardless of what the devices looked like, she felt glad they were available.

"Hi, Doll," Rod greeted her as she entered the lounge area. The others sat on the couches as if in a recent conversation. The two girls still wore their swimming suits and a phonograph played a current jazz hit.

"Hello, everyone, how long did I sleep?"

"Well, you slept a couple of hours at least," Hal stated in a rather loud voice. "I thought about waking you, but Rod told me to let you sleep."

"Did I?" Rod appeared surprised by this statement.

"Of course, you did," Hal then chuckled a little as if he'd wanted Rod to go along with a joke.

"I'm sorry, I didn't mean to sleep so long," she then pulled the hair tie out.

"Nonsense Sugar, you should get all the beauty sleep you want," Vivian spoke sarcastically, causing Rebecca to laugh.

The group ate dinner and afterward they all became even louder and more animated as everyone, but Gina drank what appeared to be champagne or maybe wine.

Rod filled a glass for Gina and after she took a drink she realized it did indeed have alcohol in it. She didn't want it anymore, but Rod and Hal kept trying to get her to take another drink. She sipped a little and then acted like she was drinking more. They seemed happy about this and she smiled graciously.

Meanwhile as the afternoon set in, the boat began to sway more and more. Soon the rain came down.

Rod wanted to make a toast about Gina becoming a star of the silver screen and she felt inclined to take another small sip. Then Hal had to toast something as well. Another drink found its way into her stomach.

To Gina, the other two girls seemed immune to the effects of the beverage. They drank more and more. They laughed out loud. Vivian then got up on a small table and danced around barefoot. The boat swayed, and she fell on the couch laughing.

A long scratching sound came from the phonograph as the needle moved across the record. This caused a continuous clicking and scratching sound as the needle continually played the sounds of the centerpiece on the record.

Again, the group laughed at this and it seemed to encourage them to drink more. Rod moved around the room pouring more of the alcoholic beverage. Gina began to feel dizzy.

Things began to move faster as her head started to swim. Rod again came around and almost demanded she take another drink. She declined but Hal came over and prodded her to drink. Reluctantly she took another small drink.

The rain came down harder and she could see lightening out the windows. The boat rocked more, and she began to feel ill and dizzy both. Getting up carefully, she started to move towards the hall leading to her small room.

"Hey, where're you going, Doll?" Rod appeared strangely evil to Gina as he yelled out to her. With everything spinning around and the odd feeling of the floor moving under her feet, she was in no mood for his flirty antics. She waved him off and continued towards the safety of her room.

Rod turned to Hal and smiled slyly.

"You're up Tiger," Hal said and then took another drink. "I think I'll go up top and check our status. It seems this storm is getting worse."

Rod grinned and nodded.

"You'll know where to find me if you need me," he pointed towards Gina's cabin. "But I'm hoping you won't need me, because I'll be busy." He then half stumbled towards Gina's room as the two girls laughed in drunken delight.

Gina made it to her cabin and began to feel very ill now. The room wouldn't stop spinning. She held herself up by holding onto the wall. Then she went to the bed and sat down.

Suddenly Rod came in. He had an obvious air of mischief about him.

"It's about time for you and me to get better acquainted, Doll." He sounded drunk and looked out of control.

Gina suddenly realized she shouldn't have trusted him. He moved closer to her. He stared at her, but not her face. He smiled ominously as he closed in and appeared more like an animal now than a man.

Gina felt a shot of panic run through her body. She stood up, but the room was too small for her to get around him. He realized this and smiled even wider, knowing she was trapped.

The situation became overwhelming. The fear inside her, as well as the effects of the alcohol and swaying of the boat, caused an immediate reaction. As Rod took hold of her arms, she vomited all over him.

He stumbled back as if being hit with a punch. "Ahhhh, eww, you stupid......!"

Gina started to apologize out of habit, but realized she wasn't sorry at all. She knew what he'd planned to do to her. Rod opened the door and stumbled out, still cursing her.

The boat was swaying almost violently now. She began to cry as the stress of Rod's aggressive attack and being sick began taking a toll. She needed to get out. She wanted to escape the situation and went out the door just as something could be heard falling to the floor. She tried to walk but the movement of the boat caused her to stumble several times.

Entering the lounge, she heard the phonograph needle slide slowly back across the record, causing the strange mix of music and scratching sounds.

Vivian and Rebecca appeared out of their minds as they laughed and rolled on the couch with the swaying motions. Rebecca held her drink in the air and then Vivian's head and upper body fell onto Rebecca's lap, which caused more laughter. The lights had been dimmed to conserve power and this presented an ominous picture to the young woman. Something else fell from a shelf causing a crash.

"Are we going to sink?" Gina shouted, but her words came out weak. The two drunken girls turned to Gina, as if she were the one drunk.

Vivian shouted back. "Yes, I think we may be sinking, Sugar." They both laughed hysterically again.

Gina wiped her eyes. She began to cry even more as she was having trouble seeing due to the tears, dim lights and effects of the drinks. Knowing nothing about beverages with alcohol in them, she thought the girls were telling the truth, but simply didn't care due to the contents of the bottles. She moved on her hands and knees to the door leading out to the deck.

When she opened the door the wind and rain greeted her.

As she stood up and made her way to the life vests her heart seemed to fall inside her. She took one of the vests from the wall and pulled it over her head. The swaying of the boat forced her to catch herself from being thrown against the cabin wall.

She frantically tied one side of the life vest. Everything became a blur now as a hopeless feeling came over her. Tears mixed with rain, ran down her face. She started to tie the other side of the vest when a violent movement from the boat threw her away from the cabin wall. She fell onto the water drenched deck and slid across it, only stopping when she reached the short wall and rail around the boat.

Lying in the rain, she reached over and with much effort tied the other side of the life vest. Fear again took hold of her and she glanced back to the lounge. She tried to spot a crewmember on the upper deck, but the darkness was too thick.

She crawled towards the lounge door, but a deck chair slid in front of her almost hitting her. She attempted to move it but didn't have the strength. She stood up and began to climb over the chair.

The boat swayed; a wind hit the side of her, forcing her to fall back, she tripped over the railing that caused her to immediately fall overboard into the ocean. She was barely able to close her mouth before taking in the salty seawater. In this instant, Gina felt she would surely die.

The life vest pulled her to the top of the water. She struggled to catch her breath as the dim lights of the yacht moved away from her. She yelled out and then screamed in desperation towards the disappearing boat. Slowly the lights faded until there was nothing but darkness and water all around her.

Although the life vest kept her head above water, the waves continued to splash her face forcing water into her mouth and nose. She struggled to remain calm, but inside panic and fear tried to break out. Her heart pounded so hard she could hear it and feel it in her head.

Then a new fear developed. The fear of what might be in the water around her. She cried hopelessly as the rain on her face merged with tears.

Time seemed to stop as the darkness and storm continued without restraint. Completely alone, Gina grasped in vain at the dim lights from the lightning in a desperate hope of spotting anything other than the vast violent ocean.

She became angry with herself as she struggled with the violent sea. The young woman fought the storm and herself for becoming careless and allowing a man like Rod to deceive her. Inside Gina, something slowly changed. In anger, she began to isolate the person that believed Rod. She decided at this point, she would rather die as a no-one than that foolish girl. It was no wonder her mother had left her, she thought to herself. Now she became angry with her mother as well as herself. Floating in the immense, enraged waves, all alone, as if a tiny particle of flotsam, she felt worthless and thought it would be best to die anonymously.

In the eye of the storm and the intense darkness, something unseen had occurred inside her. She sensed it, along with the overwhelming fear, but she ceased to care. Why be concerned about anything when death would take her at any minute? She slowly gave into the violence inside as well as outside of her.

Eventually, she became exhausted by the conflicts that consumed her and yielded to the death she felt was inevitable. With all fear and strength gone, she faded out of consciousness.

CHAPTER TWO:

No Great Loss

Gina slowly opened her eyes to wet sand and the sensation of a hot sun beating down on her back. A sudden involuntary cough brought the taste of saltwater up from her lungs. More coughs and more of the nasty saltwater came out as the waves moved methodically around her feet and legs, keeping her lower body soaked.

Sitting up caused her body to object in pain. She felt as if a truck had hit her. She slowly crawled farther up on the beach.

Her immediate concern was if she were to pass out again and possibly float back into the water. Once the distance from the waves was enough, Gina laid back down.

She may have slept more after this, or maybe she just faded back into a semi-conscious state. After more time had passed she sat up again and looked around. There were no houses or signs of civilization anywhere.

The saltwater made her feel sticky, as if she'd not bathed for days. Standing up required much effort as her muscles were sore from struggling with the ocean.

Laboring in the sand, she moved inland and away from the beach. Only a vast area of shrubs and small trees presented itself to her. With no house or building in sight she tried to decide which direction to move.

Miles off in the distance she could see large hills and even farther away what appeared to be mountains.

After some thought, she felt the most logical direction to go would be inland. Due to a night of floating in the sea, she had a strong urge to move away from it. Slowly she walked forward straining to see any sign of a building, or anything to give her hope of being found.

The life vest became hot and heavy. She tried to untie it, but her muscles were so sore she resigned to deal with the discomfort of the vest rather than the sharp pains in her arms when trying to remove it.

After stumbling in the sand and brush for what felt like hours, Gina spotted something off in the distance. The thing in question moved slowly and in her general direction. She attempted to wave but couldn't move her arms high enough. She then tried to yell but her mouth and throat had become so dry and parched she couldn't utter any sound other than a screeching cough.

She moved as quickly as possible to intercept the moving object. As the apparatus came closer she identified it as a small donkey pulling a two wheeled cart. A man sat in the cart and appeared to be paying little attention to his travels.

A closer examination revealed that he appeared to be asleep as his head slumped down and bobbed with the movement of the cart.

Gina moved to a point where a small road lay, not much

wider than a trail. She imagined this to be what the man traveled on and she fell to the sandy ground exhausted; waiting for the cart to arrive.

Slowly, the little donkey labored along the dusty road bringing the man and cart to where she sat anxiously awaiting its arrival.

When the man came close enough, she stood up and tried to yell but only a hoarse voice came out.

"Help! Can you help me please?"

The man, who had dozed off, awoke suddenly with the unfamiliar sounds of English. Startled and sitting up quickly he almost fell. He pulled the reins tight to stop.

There stood Gina with the odd-looking life vest. She waved her arms at her side and spoke a language that he knew wasn't Spanish.

The man she stood in front of was Manuel Flores. He and his wife owned a small store in the sleepy little town of La Gordo Mexico.

Owning the store meant he and his wife were among the wealthier of the population in town, but it also meant he must travel to the larger city of Tantico to obtain wares and goods for the store.

Mr. Flores had traveled this little road so many times over the years he'd become somewhat complacent.

Although there had been cases of robbery on the road, they were rare, and he wasn't really worried since the goods he carried were not actually worth the risk of being shot.

He carried a small muzzle-loading pistol with him and

though he wasn't even sure if it would still fire, he felt somewhat secure in the knowledge that any bandits desperate enough to rob him would likely not even possess a gun.

Manuel quickly searched beside him for his pistol, while keeping his eyes on this apparent threat. With his heart pounding hard in his chest, he found the pistol, raised it up and held it pointed at the strange person.

He then exclaimed in a nervous voice, "Who are you? What do you want?!"

Now Gina became frightened as Mr. Flores held the pistol pointed at her and spoke a language she wasn't familiar with but knew it not to be English. She held up her arms as high as she could before the pain forced her to stop raising them.

"Please, I need help. I fell from a boat out there," she pointed to the direction of the ocean.

Mr. Flores was now awake enough to realize this to be a woman and not a bandit. He gazed in the direction she pointed and then back to her.

"You came from the sea?" He asked in Spanish.

Gina tried again to communicate through her parched mouth and throat.

"I fell from a boat. I'm lost. I need help."

This time, she spoke slowly and louder to hopefully make Mr. Flores understand her situation.

Manuel stepped down from the cart still holding the pistol towards Gina. He scanned the area in search of anyone in the bushes hiding.

"I'm sorry, but I must be sure this isn't a trick."

She had no idea what he said.

"I don't understand you. Where am I?"

He, in turn, had no idea what she said as he'd never actually heard any language other than Spanish.

"Where are you from?" he asked her as he put the pistol in his worn belt for quick access if needed.

"Where is this? Where am I, Germany? Am I in Germany or France?"

Mr. Flores shook his head "no" trying to indicate he didn't understand her.

"I don't understand," He said. Again, he asked. "Where are you from?"

Gina continued.

"What language are you speaking? What country is this, Switzerland, Italy?" When she said 'Italy' Manuel recognized the name.

"Italia, you are Italiano?"

Gina stared at Mr. Flores in shock. She tried to raise her hand up as far as she could in disbelief and placed it on the bottom of the life vest.

"Italy? I'm in Italy?"

"Oh, you are Italiano?" Mr. Flores shook his head up and down as he mistook her response as an indication of her being Italian.

Gina, in turn, mistook this response as an affirmation that she had in fact washed up on an Italian beach.

"Oh God, I'm in Italy," she said softly to herself.

Mr. Flores seemed unsure of what to do now. The young

woman appeared quite attractive and dressed in what he thought to be her underwear. Yet he also could see she'd been in the water for some time and he realized she must be hungry and thirsty. He took a hollowed-out gourd that he carried a small supply of water in and gave it to her, so she could drink.

Although the water container seemed strange to Gina, she'd become so thirsty she drank the water without caring about the appearance.

Then he gave her some of the lunch his wife had prepared for him and she ate the food quickly. She thanked him, and he understood her to be grateful though he didn't understand the words.

After some additional thought, he considered that there must have been a shipwreck and surely someone would be searching for this attractive young lady.

Being a businessman, he then considered there should be some form of reward. Or at least, if he and his wife cared for her, they could ask for compensation once her family located her.

So, with thoughts of a big reward or large compensation, Mr. Flores decided to take Gina to his house. He also realized she wouldn't survive alone on the road. He led her to the back of the cart and she sat down with a renewed feeling she may survive after all.

As the little cart bobbled along the road, she wearily laid back. The life vest now worked as a pillow and she soon fell asleep.

The trip from Tantico along the sandy coastal road to La

Gordo required the best part of a day. Although Mr. Flores had come upon her about halfway back to his home in La Gordo, the remainder of the trip still took several hours. She slept most of the way, being exhausted from her night on the stormy sea.

Mr. Flores turned back to check on her occasionally but otherwise kept an eye ahead in case other survivors should materialize.

No other survivors would be found though and the travelers slowly made their way into La Gordo that afternoon.

Mr. Flores had considered a possible reward for finding Gina. He also thought of payment for taking care of her until her family came. He had even considered what he might do with the large sum of money and how they might spend the reward.

However, the thing Manuel Flores neglected to consider was how his wife Duena might react to this situation. This lack of foresight on his part became apparent shortly after he brought Gina into the house via the back door. He thought this would be a good way to keep the neighbors from noticing he had a foreigner in the house.

Most people of La Gordo didn't have a back door on their house. None that he could think of had ever seen a foreigner. Should they notice Manuel had one, he knew a commotion would certainly follow as everyone would want to meet the stranger and stare at her for a while.

"Who is this?" Duena Flores asked snidely as Manuel walked in with Gina. It was at this point he suddenly realized his woeful neglect to prepare for this instant.

"She is, well... She's an Italiano."

Duena eyed Gina from top to bottom with suspicion. The bathing suit she wore must have also appeared to Mrs. Flores as underwear.

"She's your mistress? I cannot believe you brought your Italiano mistress home and tried to sneak her in here without me knowing about it! Do you think I am stupid Manuel?"

Mr. Flores tried to get a word in; "No Duena listen." This only seemed to infuriate his wife more, and now she began to speak very loudly.

"You do think I'm a fool, don't you? I'm not stupid, Manuel. You're the fool for bringing this tart home with you. Why would you do this to me?"

She paced back and forth in obvious anger.

Manuel tried again to speak. "Duena, please, listen."

"No, Manuel. I'll not listen to your excuses anymore. You think you can fool me? Do you think I don't know what kind of a woman this is? I can see how she's dressed; I'm not a fool Manuel!"

Gina had no idea what Mrs. Flores said and could do very little one way or another. She moved to the corner of the room and stood meekly by the wall, watching the scene in silence.

Outside the Flores's house, which had a small store connected to the front, a crowd began to gather. They'd been attracted by the sounds of Duena loudly denouncing her husband's apparent infidelity.

As Duena continued to rant about Manuel's 'Italiano mistress', more and more people gathered around on the small street outside an open window. And, as the crowd grew larger, the congregation of people in turn, attracted more people.

Soon, most of the small town's population stood, sat and even lay reclining outside the house listening to Duena. This new development in town quickly became more interesting than anything else.

Everyone considered this to be public information as Duena had, after all, left the window open.

A few enterprising persons even brought fruits and snacks to sell. After a short time, there were almost no people in town that hadn't stopped their activities to find out about Manuel Flores and his fancy "Italiano mistress."

In the meantime, Duena never allowed Manuel to get a word in. She concluded rather loudly that perhaps times had become difficult in Tantico for his Italiano mistress and she'd somehow talked Manuel into bringing her to La Gordo. She then moved over to Gina.

"You slut, you should be ashamed of yourself!"

Gina, not having a clue what Mrs. Flores said, simply replied the best she knew how.

"I'm sorry, I don't understand Italian."

Mrs. Flores perceived this as something of a bold move on the young woman's part since the only word she understood was "Italian."

"Yes, I know, you're a fancy Italiano whore! I can see your fancy underwear and your, what is this anyway?"

Duena now took notice of the life vest Gina wore. She pulled the front of the vest, examining the device. She'd never seen anything like this and instantly thought the strange item to be some form of fashion accessory.

"What is this for? Is this to make your breasts appear larger?"

When Duena asked this, she made a motion right below her own breasts with both her hands, as if lifting them upwards. Gina, seeing this motion mistook it as Mrs. Flores asking if the device were for floating.

"Yes," she replied and made the same motion as Mrs. Flores. "This is a floating device. It helps you float in the water."

With this, Duena Flores almost fainted. Somehow, she managed to stay standing and walked briskly over to Manuel.

"Duena please," Manuel again tried to speak.

"Really, Manuel, you want to kill me? How can you do such a thing as bringing this tainted woman home, with her, breast-lifting device? I think you must be trying to stop my heart."

Then she sat down, seeming exhausted from the marathon of excited speech. Now Manuel seeing his chance moved beside her.

"Duena, she's not my mistress. I found her on the road from Tantico. I believe she's from a shipwreck. The device she wears must be to help her float in the water."

Now Mrs. Flores appeared instantly relieved. And in a much quieter voice, she replied, "Why didn't you say so?"

Manuel simply gave her a frustrated expression, as if to bring to his wife's attention her own overreaction. Duena looked over at Gina with a different attitude now.

She then turned back to her husband and asked for more details.

As the Floreses spoke with each other about the situation, Gina spotted the open window.

She had no idea there was a crowd outside. Nor did she know this crowd had been whipped into a frenzy of excitement by Mrs. Flores's exuberant overreaction to Gina.

The mention of some type of "breast lifting device" caused so much excitement for men and women alike that at the very moment she noticed the window, a few were contemplating flinging themselves into the house to see this person and her enhanced breasts.

Before this happened though, Gina noticed the open window and thinking she may see something outside that might be helpful to her situation, innocently strolled over to it.

At a point of almost uncontrolled excitement for the crowd outside the window, Gina stepped squarely into it.

Now the mysterious woman appeared to them, and perfectly framed by the window they could see her upper body, life vest and all.

Immediately they shouted with a burst of joy in finally getting to see the Italiano mistress and her fashionable breasts.

Gina became shocked and stumbled backward, falling onto the floor. The Flores' also were shocked by the roar of the crowd outside.

Manuel cautiously stood up and moved over to the window. As soon as he arrived at the window a voice cried out.

"Manuel, show us the fancy Italiano mistress with the big, you know." The man motioned to his chest as if lifting large breasts.

"What are you all doing? Go home. I don't have an Italiano mistress!"

Then the same person replied. "Don't try to lie to us Manuel, we just saw her. Come on, we just want to see her again."

With this, the crowd seemed to make a unanimous sound of agreement to the man's logic.

Mr. Flores spent over an hour in an effort of disbursing the crowd. When they finally went away, he and Duena sat down again to discuss the situation.

"Why did you bring her home?"

Manuel expressed surprise by his wife's question.

"You think I should have left her to die?"

Duena grimaced as if she'd not considered this.

"Surely someone is searching for her," she said, glancing over to Gina; who had by now been able to get the life vest off and sat quietly, appearing lost and dejected.

"I think someone must surely be searching for her. However, by the time they found her out there by the sea she would be dead if I had left her. Besides that, if a bandit had found her who knows what would have happened to her by now?"

Duena appeared to accept her husband's reasoning.

"You know, I think there may be a reward for persons lost at sea."

After hearing this, Mrs. Flores perked up some.

"You think so?"

"Surely there will be. And if not, then we should get something to pay us back for the care we give her until she's found."

This appeared to change the matter for Mrs. Flores who now saw Gina as a possible asset.

"I'll help her get cleaned up and I believe I have an old dress I can alter for her. Then I'll prepare a dish of food."

She went over to Gina and managed to communicate she wanted to help her. Gina finally relaxed some and after getting cleaned up and eating she slept soundly that night.

The next several weeks were unusual for everyone in the tiny Mexican town. Gina had a lot of time to reflect upon her situation and realized she now resided completely in the mercies of her hosts. No one in Florida would look for her. Lois was the only one that might miss her and even she had no idea where Gina had planned to go.

Considering what Rod tried to do to her before she fell from the boat, she knew he wouldn't bother to report the incident to the authorities. So, she concluded her only hope lay in these Italians who were now trying to assist her.

As the days moved slowly by, she considered her survival as something of a rebirth. Everything from the time she awoke on the beach began to feel as a second life to her.

In the meantime, the Flores' store experienced an instant boom in business from the time Gina arrived. Mrs. Flores, being an extraordinary entrepreneur realized an opportunity when she saw one.

She placed Gina strategically at an angle behind the counter and in a chair at a small table. The only way the customers could see her clearly would be to stand in front of the counter where payment for purchases was made. If someone stood at the counter to see Gina, Duena Flores would ask. "Are you going to purchase something?"

If they were to purchase something, Duena would allow the person to stand and chat with her a while. Often the discussions were about Gina and both would gaze at her while talking. Gina sat silently at the small table as the people came and went.

During this time, depression slowly tightened its grip on the young woman, as she would quietly sit while others stared at her and talked about her in a language she didn't understand.

After several weeks, things became even more complicated as one night at the Flores' store a drunken La Gordo man tried to crawl into the window of the tiny storage room Gina slept in.

Gina screamed, and Mr. Flores came in to quickly dispatch the man.

The Flores's began to consider the long-term situation due to this event.

After the initial weeks of booming business, the new had begun to wear off in La Gordo and slowly life was returning to normal.

Manuel and Duena began to realize there might not be anyone coming for Gina soon or ever. Since she had apparently originated from an Italian ship, the area to search for her and other passengers must be very large. Though neither one had any idea where Italy was, this seemed the reasonable thing to them.

"So, what are we to do with her?" Duena asked Manuel one evening as they ate dinner.

"We need help," Manuel said after some thought. Duena considered this for a few moments.

"You're suggesting the Federals?"

"No, no," Manuel replied quickly. "I don't trust the Federals and besides they would try to get money from us regardless of whether they helped the young woman or not."

"Then what are you thinking?"

Manuel took a drink from a rough gourd cup and then replied, "I was thinking of your cousin, Olivia."

Duena gazed over at Gina who sat at a small table eating in silence.

"I've not seen Olivia in years." She then took another bite of food.

Neither one said anything for a few moments. Finally, Manuel continued.

"I think Olivia may be this girl's only hope for getting home."

Manuel now paused and looked at Gina.

"She's the only one I know of that may be able to help. I know we can't afford to take care of her much longer."

Duena nodded her head indicating she agreed with her husband.

He turned back to his plate and ate a few more bites. Then after seeming to give the situation some thought he continued.

"I'll take her to Tantico Thursday and speak with Olivia."

The following Thursday Manuel and Duena woke Gina up before daybreak.

Soon she once again sat in the back of the two-wheeled cart.

They traveled back over the same road Manuel had found her on weeks earlier.

Gina sat quietly, either dozing or watching the scenery. Manuel checked on her from time to time and on one occasion noticed that with her dark hair she did sort of look like a Mexican girl.

Duena had found one of her old dresses and altered it to fit her. The dress seemed to be not much more than a sack with holes for the head and arms, but Gina graciously thanked Duena. Even though she didn't understand the language, she knew well enough that without the dress she could cause a commotion simply by being noticed as a foreigner.

Gina had also become keenly aware of the fact that she could disappear at anytime and no one would know. She resolved herself to somehow get back on her feet and be as little trouble as possible for those who were trying to help her.

As she rocked about in the little cart she also contemplated the change in her life and wondered if she would ever return to Jacksonville again. Survival must be the first thing. She had no idea where she may be going. She had no idea exactly where she was. All she knew for certain was that she had somehow survived what many have not. Whatever lay ahead, she still had hope, which is more than she had floating alone in the darkness on the open sea.

After traveling most of the day and only stopping at strategically located bushes, the two quietly rolled into Tantico.

There would be no mistaking this for a sleepy little town like La Gordo. Tantico vibrated with life as they moved farther into the city.

She hunkered down and viewed the lively atmosphere from the security of the wooden cart. The sights and smells were new, and she tried to take everything in.

Music could be heard as the cart bobbled through the narrow streets. Small boys and girls would run up to Manuel and even Gina to offer small items for sale. She would shake her head no and say nothing.

On one occasion a small girl noticed Gina didn't look quite right. She asked Gina something and several times tried to get an answer. Gina just shook her head no. Finally, Manuel said something to the girl to cause her to stop following the cart.

Considering her hair color was slightly lighter than those around her, Gina pulled the piece of cloth being used as a scarf tighter over her hair in the hopes she would avoid any further instances.

Finally, around dusk, they pulled up to a building and stopped. She looked up at an old and faded sign that read "Cafe Flamenco."

A man came out and briefly spoke with Manuel. He then led the little donkey and cart around the back of the Cafe as Manuel ushered Gina into the building.

Inside, a wonderful smell greeted them. Once her eyes became accustomed to the dimmer light, she could see the Cafe Flamenco must be an entertainment and dining facility.

Along the right side, a long table ran with a kitchen area behind, covered by curtains and racks containing cookery items. Straight back along the wall stood another table that appeared to be more of a bar. Several men stood along this bar with drinks in hand and a man behind the bar was tending their needs. In the middle sat numerous tables and chairs. At a few of these tables, people sat eating and drinking.

Right after she had looked around, a guitarist began to play, and her attention turned to the left side of the building. To the far left a stage stood, several feet high from the floor. Gina could see there must be other rooms behind the stage area but could identify nothing more from her current view.

Manuel directed her to a table and they both sat down. Then something happened that changed everything for the young woman. It was as if a tiny beam of light found its way through all the darkness and lit upon Gina's weary heart.

A beautiful young woman stepped gracefully onto the stage in a brilliantly colored dress. As the guitarist played, the woman danced about in a way she had never seen.

The dancer seemed to float about on the stage, holding the edge of her beautiful dress in her hand. Then, she would pull it up slightly to reveal her feet as she tapped out quick rhythms with the music.

Again, she would twirl and move about and tap her feet intermittently with the music. The scene was so unfamiliar and yet beautiful to Gina that she couldn't look away. Everything else disappeared and only this beautiful dance existed.

For these few moments, Gina lost track of all her concerns and became so involved in this beautiful display that she forgot about everything else.

When the music stopped, and the young woman left the stage, Gina thought of how wonderful it must be to dance so gracefully. Then, her concerns came rushing back, as if an invisible yoke once again pressed down upon her soul.

A waitress came to the table and spoke with Manuel, then left. A few moments later a well-dressed woman approached the two of them; she appeared to be in her forties. She sat down at the table and spoke with Manuel.

He and the woman then stood up and directed Gina to follow. The three moved past the stage and into a hallway that ran along the area behind the stage.

In a room located at the corner of the building sat a woman at a table; she directed Manuel to sit at the table across from her and the first woman pulled a crude chair from along the wall for Gina to sit in. She now sat almost in the middle of the room and felt a bit exposed in the open.

The woman Manuel sat at the table with was also well dressed, very pretty, and appeared to be in her mid to late thirties.

Manuel and the woman smiled and spoke together for several minutes as if they knew each other.

Then the woman looked at Gina and again began talking to Manuel, seeming to be speaking about the young woman in the middle of the dimly lit room. Manuel, in turn, spoke to the woman as Gina sat in silence, not understanding anything the two said, yet aware of the fact they spoke about her.

"You found her on the side of the road to La Gordo?" Olivia could barely believe what Manuel told her.

"Yes, she said she is Italiano and I think she may have been on a shipwreck. She wore a floating device."

"Do you have the device?"

"Yes; she gave it to Duena after she gave her that dress."

Olivia looked at Gina and appeared thoughtful. Then Manuel continued.

"We hoped someone might come looking for her, but after almost three weeks no one has. A drunken man tried to crawl in the window one night. My guess is he just wanted to look at her. Nevertheless, this frightened the poor girl very much. I suspect she is very stressed and scared. Yet she's not complained once. She has remained quiet and calm throughout the time we've kept her. Do you think we should take her to the Federals?"

Olivia turned to Manuel quickly. "No, no, you did the right thing to bring her here. I don't trust the police or the Federals. There's no telling what might happen to an attractive young woman in their hands."

She turned back to Gina. She seemed to study her for a few moments before continuing.

"I don't have the money to send her back to Italy. We can't trust the government officials to get her where she needs to go either."

Olivia paused again and then continued with a concerned tone.

"I've not heard of any shipwrecks. I wonder if she may have fallen from a ship. This might explain why we've not heard of a shipwreck. Also, if she fell from a ship during a storm then the ship wouldn't know where to search for her and by now must believe she's dead."

Manuel appeared impressed.

"You know, that makes sense Olivia. And I believe there was a storm the day before I found her. If this is the case then she has likely been given up as lost by now, and no one will come for her."

Now Olivia considered the situation with a renewed effort.

"I'm afraid there may be little hope for this girl to get home very soon. Until we can find some way to get her home, I'll keep her safe, here with me."

Olivia again paused in thought.

"She can work around here to earn her way, but that won't be enough to get her home."

Manuel now seemed to think of something.

"Could you teach her to dance? A good Flamenco dancer might earn enough for a ticket to Italy."

She thought about what Manuel suggested and then after slowly standing up walked over to Gina.

"I don't know... she's already too old I think. But this would be the only respectable way she could earn enough money for a trip back to where she came from."

She walked around Gina, seeming to examine her closely. She then motioned for her to stand up.

After Gina stood up Olivia pulled the back of her plain dress together to reveal the shape of Gina's figure.

She examined her from top to bottom and front to back. Then she let the dress go and reached down, grabbed the bottom of her dress and lifted it up past Gina's knees to examine her legs.

Gina protested a little as she felt like an animal being looked over before purchase.

"Relax, I wish to help you," Olivia told her.

To Gina however, this sounded as if the woman had scolded her for protesting.

Then Olivia gently grasped Gina's mouth and pulled her lips up and down to see her teeth.

Now Gina became worried even more. She wanted to run away but knew she had nowhere to run to.

"She has the beauty and the figure for the Flamenco. Good teeth also, which won't hurt matters."

She motioned for her to sit again and Gina did as Olivia asked.

The two walked back to the table and sat down again.

Olivia stared at the young woman for a moment as if deciding. Then she pulled a small purse from an unseen pocket in her dress. Opening the purse up Olivia pulled a few silver coins from it.

"Here's what I'll do Manuel," she then handed Mr. Flores the coins.

"I can give you this much to help cover what you've spent to care for this girl until now. I'll take full responsibility for her. She can earn that much back I'm sure.

"I may try to teach her to dance. She may have no talent though, so this may or may not work. I'll have one of the girls help her learn Spanish so that we can communicate."

"If by chance she can learn the Flamenco, she may be able to earn enough for a fare back to her home. Or maybe we can figure out a way to contact her family in Italy and they can come for her.

"In the meantime, if I should hear of her family searching for her here in Tantico, I'll get her to them safely. This is all I know to do."

Manuel pocketed the coins Olivia handed him.

"That's the best thing that can be done, I'm certain, Olivia. You may wish to keep the fact that she is Italiano a secret though. We had quite a commotion in La Gordo once everyone became aware of it."

She smiled and laughed a little as if imagining the situation. Manuel then continued.

"Thank you so much, Olivia. I'm sure she'll be safe here and have the best possible chance to get home."

He stood up, smiled and after waving bye to Gina, quietly left the room.

Gina now felt terrified as Olivia walked over to her.

"Did you just buy me?" she asked with a nervous voice.

Olivia didn't understand what she said and expressed this with a questioning look.

"Do I," Gina put her hand to her chest, "belong to you now?" She then pointed to Olivia.

"*Si,*" Olivia said, then nodded, mistaking what Gina had said.

"You," Olivia pointed to Gina, "stay with me now," Olivia then pointed to herself.

Gina felt her heart fall inside her.

"I'm a slave," she said in a soft voice to herself. She then remembered the few silver coins Olivia gave to Manuel. "And it seems I'm not worth very much at all."

Olivia smiled and nodded again to Gina, not actually understanding any of what she had said.

She then took Gina by the arm, helping her to stand up and led her out the door and down the hall behind the stage.

Gina felt weak and as if she was outside of herself. She couldn't quite grasp the situation she now found herself in.

The first well-dressed lady she'd seen in the cafe came up to them in the hallway.

"Elisa, this young lady will be staying with us for a while. Can you take her to the spare room and try to make her comfortable? She doesn't speak Spanish by the way."

Elisa gave Olivia an odd look.

"What does she speak then?"

"Well, she's Italiano. We believe she may have fallen from a ship several weeks ago. Let's not let this get out though. We'll try to keep the lid on it until everyone has become more accustomed to her. According to my cousin's husband, there was quite a commotion in La Gordo after everyone found out she was a foreigner."

"Oh my," Elisa replied. "I see your point."

Olivia then motioned for Gina to go with Elisa.

After a short walk, the two arrived at a small room with a bed and a tiny table in the corner. Gina had seen closets back home larger than this room. She sat down on the bed as Elisa left, closing the door behind her.

Alone, she now fell into despair as she considered the recent events and her apparent situation. What would become of her?

Then, a terrifying thought came to her. The way the woman examined her figure and made an extra effort to view her legs, would she use her as a prostitute? The more she thought about this terrible possibility the more depressed she became.

What could she do? Maybe she could escape. But where would she go? She couldn't speak Italian. She might find a good person to help her. She might also find a bad person like Rod who would do terrible things to her. She seemed to be without options.

Gina tried to tell herself that at least she was still alive. This however didn't help as much as it did before.

As she sat on the bed in the tiny room, a heavy feeling of darkness lowered onto her; even the fragile hope she had held onto with the Flores's slipped from her grasp.

Elisa walked into the room with a dish of food and a drink.

"Here's something to eat. I'll bet you're starving. Olivia said you came all the way from La Gordo."

Gina accepted the food and thanked Elisa and after she left, Gina tried to eat. The food smelled and tasted wonderful. Though she wanted to enjoy the meal she instead ate slowly and methodically.

After a while, Elisa came back in and took the dishes. Gina wasn't sure what to do. The noises of the cafe had slowly subsided. Sleep beckoned her, but she felt too depressed and restless. The terrible thoughts of what might lay ahead for her consumed her. She couldn't release herself from this feeling of anxiety.

She thought this must be as low as she could ever get and wondered where any hope could come from. At this very instant, Olivia entered the room with a warm smile. Elisa followed behind her.

"I hope you enjoyed the food," she said to Gina. "I'm sorry you've been here alone but I am generally busy until the cafe closes."

Olivia studied the young woman as she tried to communicate with her. Gina sat quietly and appeared a bit frightened. Olivia continued.

"Elisa and her husband are my partners in this cafe. They operate the food and drink side and I manage the entertainment. I teach the Flamenco dance and as part of the tuition payment, the girls must perform here at the cafe."

Olivia felt as though she couldn't communicate with Gina at all. She studied the silent girl sitting in apparent despair on the edge of the tiny bed.

"What's her name?" Elisa asked.

"I don't know. It seems Manuel and Duena made no real effort to communicate with her."

Olivia turned to Gina.

"What's your name?"

To Gina, the two well-dressed and distinguished women were a little intimidating. She understood none of what they said and felt as though they may be discussing their newest acquisition.

"My name is Olivia." She pointed to herself. "This is 'Elisa'." She pointed to Elisa. "You are?" She pointed to Gina.

Now Gina understood what Olivia had asked her.

"Gina," she replied in a soft voice.

"Gina." Both women repeated the name with a bit of excitement.

"Well, it seems we are making some progress now," Olivia smiled as she said this and looked at Elisa.

"We wish to help you Gina. But we're somewhat limited in what we can do. You're fortunate to be in a prosperous area of Mexico. Tantico has a small port and Vista Cruz has a much larger port and is only a half-day away by bus. Money flows much easier around here than in some areas of Mexico.

"But to purchase fare to Italy is more than most people around here could ever do. You wouldn't be safe with the authorities either. The best we can hope for is that your family somehow gets a message to Tantico or you can help us get a message to your family. In the meantime, you can perhaps learn to dance or work in the restaurant."

Olivia turned to Elisa.

"I don't think she understands anything I'm saying, do you?" The two women gazed down at Gina as if attempting to read her thoughts.

"She seems frightened," Elisa finally stated.

"Hmm, yes she does appear to be frightened. Manuel said a man tried to crawl into her window one night. Maybe she just doesn't feel safe anywhere."

Again, the two studied her.

"I know, bring Hernan in and have him bring his club."

Elisa nodded and left the room. Soon she returned with her

husband Hernan. Gina realized this was the same man Manuel spoke with in front of the cafe. He was a husky man and carried a large club.

Gina's eyes widened when she saw him. She was sure she was about to be beaten.

"Gina, this is Elisa's husband, Hernan. He protects this place and is very good at it. You needn't worry about your security."

Gina sat silently, watching Hernan.

"I think she may understand." Olivia said and continued, "If someone tries to come into the window." Olivia pointed at the small window. "You call out and Hernan will come and knock them out." She glanced back to him. "Show her the club Hernan."

Hernan stepped up and beat his hand several times with the large club.

At this point, Gina completely broke down.

"I won't try to escape." She gazed up at Olivia with tears in her eyes.

"Please don't beat me. I'll do what you want. Please don't make me a prostitute. I can wait on tables or wash dishes, whatever you want. I won't try to escape. You don't need to beat me."

She expressed great emotion and this to Olivia and Elisa appeared to indicate she had in fact been scared. Now that she saw Hernan with the club she was relaying her fears to the women.

Elisa turned to Olivia with a puzzled look. "Is that Italiano?"

Olivia also appeared puzzled." I don't know, I've only met

one person that has ever been to Italy, and he only spoke Spanish around me."

"It does seem she understands the situation now." Elisa stated.

"Yes, I think she does." Olivia replied and now continued to try reassuring her.

"You'll be fine here, Gina. We'll watch over you and you'll be safe."

Olivia then told Hernan he could go.

When Hernan left the room, Gina calmed down some.

"Well, that must have been it. She's been worried about her safety."

Olivia nodded affirmation to Elisa's comment.

"I'm afraid you'll need to work while you're here, Gina. I wish we could simply care for you or supply you with a ticket home to Italy, but we all must struggle every day for food and other necessities."

Gina understood none of this but felt she had communicated enough to have the man with the club removed.

Now she listened intently to Olivia, to show her she would be good.

"I don't know what you're saying but I'll do as you ask. Please don't make me a prostitute, though. I can do anything else, if you just find anything but that. I'll work hard I promise you."

She felt she had only this one chance to persuade Olivia.

"What is she saying?" Elisa asked in bewilderment.

Olivia studied the young woman again before replying. "I wish I knew."

Then, appearing to think of something she said, "I'll be right back."

She quickly left the room and after a few minutes returned with a framed photograph. She held the picture up for Gina to see.

A much younger Olivia posed in a Flamenco dress, as if dancing. Her youth and beauty displayed a confident woman at the peak of her dancing career.

After studying the photograph and then studying Olivia's face to be sure the two women were one and the same, she pointed at the photograph and then pointed to Olivia.

"Yes, it's me when I was a little older than you." Olivia turned the photograph around, so she could view it.

"I mastered the Flamenco when I still had my youth," she said this in a reminiscent voice.

"I now teach the dance and perhaps I could teach you also if you would like to learn."

As she said this, Olivia pointed at the photo and then to Gina.

When she did this, Gina's heart almost leapt from her chest. She pointed at the photo and then to herself to be sure she understood what Olivia meant.

"Yes, yes. Do you wish to dance? I hope you can learn if you want. This may be the only way for you to find your way home."

Gina smiled now that she felt sure of what Olivia said.

"I would love to dance. If you show me how, I promise you I'll be the best dancer ever."

Olivia understood that Gina did want to dance. She smiled.

"It seems you've said something she understands," Elisa said as she noticed the immediate change in Gina's demeanor.

"Yes, it seems so," Olivia added with a smile.

After the two women left, Gina finally laid down. She felt better now that there was a new hope. She thought about being able to dance as opposed to the things she'd worried might happen to her.

She decided that night to be a great dancer for Olivia. No matter what else, if she became a great dancer, Olivia would not toss her aside or send her somewhere unsafe. Surely, she would keep Gina safe if she could be a magnificent dancer for her.

Then she remembered the young woman dancing after she had entered the Cafe. She tried to imagine herself dancing as the young woman did. With these thoughts in mind, she drifted off to a restful sleep.

The following day Olivia gave her several dresses that wouldn't have been worth much in Jacksonville, but certainly were a step up from the sack with holes she'd received from Duena.

She also brought a young woman that worked as a waitress to meet Gina.

"Gina, this is Alicia." Olivia stood beside a pretty young woman about Gina's age.

She appeared to be a simple girl and didn't overdress as

some of Olivia's students did. She was about the same height as Gina, but her hair was a little darker.

From her rather plain dress, Gina could assess this girl must have duties other than dancing. The young woman smiled at her and at that instant Gina felt it was the most beautiful smile she'd ever seen.

"Alicia will be working with you. She'll be helping you with everything until you can communicate better."

Gina understood little of what Olivia said to her, but Alicia put her hand out to Gina and she shook it.

Alicia showed her everything to get her started helping around the cafe. She learned quickly and soon had a daily routine.

As the days went by, they became good friends, regardless of Gina not speaking Spanish, and over the next few weeks she became more relaxed in her new environment.

While Gina quietly worked throughout the day, dancers would step up on the stage. The guitarist would play a wonderful tune and she couldn't help but marvel at the beautiful dance.

The youngest dancer appeared to be about twelve. Later Gina learned that Olivia wouldn't take a dancer younger than twelve because she felt the Flamenco was something of an adult styled dance. "You must feel the energy of the dance flow through you," she would tell Gina later.

Olivia's oldest student looked to be around twenty years old. Some of the dancers were obviously from wealthy families and acted as if Gina were beneath them. This moved Gina even closer to Alicia who was from a family that wasn't poor, but not wealthy either.

The best dancers always performed when the cafe had the most business. Less experienced dancers would dance in the mornings and during the times when there were fewer customers. When Gina realized the most popular and experienced dancers always held the prime spots; she set her sights on someday ruling these dancing periods.

As she picked up dishes and cleaned tables, she studied the performances with a focused interest. Every day she'd memorize several moves that Olivia would show the students. When the day ended, Gina would practice the moves in her tiny room backstage.

Olivia seemed to forget about teaching her to dance as time went by. Gina thought this to be a result of having trouble communicating with her and doubled her efforts to learn Spanish. She refused to let go of the offer Olivia had presented to her that first night.

She became very proficient around the cafe and earned her way. Yet this reinforced to the dancers and everyone else that she would only amount to a waitress and dishwasher.

However, Gina strengthened her dream every day and focused all her energy on being ready for any opportunity Olivia might give her.

One night, about six months after Gina came to the Cafe Flamenco; Olivia had stayed late to work on one of her student's dresses. As she left her workroom and walked down the hallway that ran behind the stage, she heard something.

She walked slowly around the corner towards Gina's tiny room and could see a candlelight burning from behind the slightly open door. She sat her small oil lantern down and moved quietly up to the doorway.

Peering into the room through the cracked door, she became amazed as Gina quietly practiced Flamenco moves in the cramped area.

Olivia's heart swelled in her chest for the young woman whom she'd almost forgotten about. Yet here she was, alone in a small, candle-lit room, dancing Flamenco moves that she must have viewed the students performing on stage.

A tear erupted and slowly slid down Olivia's cheek as she put her hand to her mouth and stifled a heartfelt moan. Without letting Gina know she had seen her, she silently left the cafe. But Olivia vowed to herself that night she would begin teaching Gina to dance.

Later, that same week, Olivia instructed several of the younger dancers. The oldest of these was around fifteen and the youngest, twelve.

One of the girls that belonged to a wealthy family in the area was obviously more interested in her new dress and talking with her friends, than performing dance moves in the manner Olivia instructed her to do.

Olivia then noticed Gina watching the lesson as she cleaned a table. Perhaps in frustration from her student not giving her full effort, Olivia decided to try something.

"Clareta, you're not going low enough. I know you can go lower."

The teenage girl made a face to her friends but was turned in a way that Olivia didn't see it.

"I can't bend back any lower, Teacher," she whined. "I'll fall over if I go farther back."

"You won't, if you place your feet and legs in the position I instructed you to." Olivia took a deep breath and continued. "I'll give you one more try to get it right, Clareta. You're testing my patience, because I know you can make the move if you do as I tell you."

Clareta expelled a heavy sigh, as if she were tired of trying. Once again, the guitarist played and once again Clareta danced.

Then, as she was supposed to bend back further, she rather obviously pretended to fall.

Gina shook her head a little as she wiped the table with a rag. She'd made that move just last night in her room. She knew if Clareta placed her feet and legs the way Olivia told her to, she could go back far enough.

"Are you alright, Clareta?" Olivia asked with concern, even though she had little doubt the fall had been staged.

"I'm alright, Teacher." She whined as she picked herself up.

Olivia moved around to the front of the stage and rubbed her hands together slightly, as if in thought.

"So, you've been my student for almost two years Clareta. I took you on as a student because your mother asked me so persistently and she also told me you would work hard to learn the dance. Is this not true?"

Clareta sat down with her friends.

"This is true Teacher but I'm not Nina," she said this referring to Olivia's most prominent dancer.

Olivia walked back to the side of the stage, still in thought.

"Perhaps I should have Gina come over and show you girls what can be done with a little desire and determination."

All the girls laughed snidely at this statement, as if their teacher was joking.

"Gina," Olivia called out.

Gina stopped her work and looked up, a bit surprised. She quickly folded her rag up and placed it on the table, then walked over to Olivia.

With some finger pointing and using words she knew Gina had learned; Olivia made it clear to her that she wanted Gina to try the move.

This shocked Gina initially. She immediately felt nervous. The other girls were in fine Flamenco dresses and had their hair made-up.

She nervously rubbed her hands on her faded white waitress dress to remove the sweat.

She cautiously climbed the steps onto the stage. The students now giggled freely as if they were in for a funny show.

Gina knew inside this may be her only chance to show Olivia she could dance.

She put everything out of her mind and told herself; "I'm a dancer."

Then, she stepped back and let out a deep breath. The guitarist began to play. As if a completely different person had appeared upon the stage, Gina began to move almost effortlessly.

Olivia had only asked her to do the one move, but Gina danced all the way to that move.

She then made the move and froze in it immediately as the music stopped.

Everyone stood or sat in shock. Even Olivia, who had been somewhat aware of Gina's potential stood in awe of what had just happen. The other girls had their mouths open and eyes wide in obvious shock.

Olivia quickly regained her composure.

"You see where her feet and legs are?" She lifted Gina's faded dress to expose the taught leg muscles holding her in the position.

"Alright Gina, very good, you may come down now."

Gina stood straight and then slowly stepped down from the stage and returned to her waitress duties.

The effect was immediate. Olivia now knew she must begin to train Gina without any further delay. The other students quickly became jealous of Gina; but considering her performance began to work harder to avoid being "shown up" by the waitress.

Gina wasn't initially sure how well she did, but after the cafe closed that night Olivia called her over to a table where she and Elisa sat.

"I want to begin your dance training right away Gina. Do you understand?"

She did understand and replied with a soft-spoken "*Si.*"

"I'll be right back," Olivia walked to the back. She soon returned with an old pair of shoes in her hands.

"These are a pair of shoes I used when I danced. Please try them on. You'll need dancing shoes if you're to learn the Flamenco."

Gina put the old pair of shoes on.

"Do they fit?"

Gina smiled and replied to Olivia in broken Spanish. "*Si,* they do."

Olivia smiled also and at this time something happened inside her heart. She felt a love for this girl that she didn't feel towards her other students. She loved her students, as any teacher would love their students. But when Gina put the old, worn-out shoes on and then smiled as if Olivia had just given her a very expensive gift, Olivia's heart melted with affection.

Olivia fought back a tear as Gina turned the shoes from side to side and then glanced up again with a warm smile.

Gina then stood up and lifted her stained waitress dress to move in a dancing motion, while still marveling at the worn dance shoes.

Olivia knew at this moment she could never see Gina as just another student. For the first time in her career as a dance teacher, a student had become more important to her than the other students.

She put her hand to her mouth as she watched Gina and considered how to handle this new situation.

"Sit down for a moment, Gina. I would like to talk with you."

She sat down but continued to smile and glance down to the dance shoes.

"Your Spanish is getting better. I'm glad we cleared the misunderstanding up of this being Italy. I think we should keep the fact that you're American to ourselves however, it'll save confusion. Also, it may be safer for you. Most Mexicans believe all Americans have money. There are bad Mexicans that wouldn't believe you have no family back in America or money somewhere and may try to kidnap you. The misunderstanding about Italy may be a good thing for you after all."

"I think so," Gina said softly, again in broken Spanish.

"Gina, I believe you have great potential as a dancer. You'll face much opposition though. You can overcome this if you focus on the dance. Few have mastered the Flamenco as it should be. If you focus on the dance and believe in yourself then I feel you can be one of the few that does. Do you understand?"

She nodded again that she did somewhat understand.

"Good, you may go to bed now, good night."

"Good night," Gina replied and almost floated off to her small room.

"There's something different about this girl." Olivia said to Elisa after Gina had gone.

"You mean besides the fact she's not a Mexican?"

Olivia stared at the stage as if recalling Gina's earlier dance moves.

"Yes, that's what I mean. I can't put my finger on it, but this girl is special."

Elisa took a drink and sat the glass down.

"How do you mean?"

Olivia appeared to consider her friend's question in depth for a few seconds.

"I'm not certain what it is exactly, but I know the other girls want to dance the Flamenco; Gina however, seems to 'need' to dance the Flamenco."

Both women thought about this for a moment. Then Elisa asked.

"Did Alicia tell you Gina's father died when she was young, and her mother abandoned her?"

"Yes." Olivia replied with a sad tone.

"Do you suppose this could be why there's a difference in Gina?" Elisa asked.

"Possibly, it could be she needs something such as the dance in her life, perhaps to help fill a void. Whatever the case may be, I believe this girl will go far, if we can get her on the right path."

Olivia then took another drink and both women sat in the dimly lit Cafe, reflecting on this new development in their lives.

CHAPTER THREE:

The Winds of Change

"They're just jealous. Because you learn the moves so easily. And the fact that you've become Ms. Olivia's favorite doesn't help."

Gina looked across the table at her friend, as if she didn't understand her. Alicia however knew she did.

"You know what I said, don't pretend you don't."

Gina acted slightly surprised that Alicia knew she was acting.

"If they really tried, as Ms. Olivia tells them to, they could learn the moves quickly also. And who says I'm Ms. Olivia's favorite?" Gina replied, pausing several times to find the right words.

"Oh please, don't play ignorant with me. I'm your only real friend, there's no need to act naive about it."

Gina scrubbed the glass in her hands harder, as if there were an invisible spot she couldn't get off. Then she put the glass on the table with the others and picked another one up to wipe off.

"So, what if Ms. Olivia likes me. I do as she asks, and I learn quickly is all. And I know you're my only friend Alicia. I don't want to mess that up."

Alicia smiled. "Oh, don't worry. Where else could I find another 'Italiano friend'?"

Gina laughed about this and then threw her rag at Alicia.

"Hey," Alicia said as she ducked. They both laughed.

It had been around nine months since Gina washed up on the Mexican beach. She'd completely embraced her new home and all aspects of it.

Since Olivia began teaching her to dance, an entire world of hope opened for the young woman.

She knew the meaning of being completely alone, without anything or anyone. She understood how it felt to have no hope of even waking up the next day. Now suddenly she had hope and this was like a treasure she would hide deep in her heart and protect with an unwavering effort.

With help from Alicia, she spoke Spanish well, though still somewhat broken.

Since Olivia had placed her in a class she'd quickly advanced to higher levels, causing the other girls to envy her.

And now to top everything, Ms. Olivia had made it obvious she planned on taking Gina to the annual Music and Dance Festival.

Though she explained that Gina would be an assistant; the other girls knew well Ms. Olivia had never taken an "assistant" before. This seemed to be another case of her having a soft spot for the Italiano girl.

Even though she acted as if her relationship with Olivia was not special, Gina knew in her heart it had become very special. Olivia had begun to treat Gina almost as if she were her child and Gina had come to feel a love in her heart for Olivia that she'd not felt for anyone else, even her real mother.

Though she realized after a short time she was not in fact any kind of slave; the resolve to become a great dancer remained deep in her soul.

To do this, Gina knew she must listen to Olivia and commit herself completely to the dance. This commitment to the Flamenco was in turn something Olivia had been seeking for a long time.

Now the two were becoming almost like a mother and daughter pair. Yet, with the creation of an "assistant" position for Gina, the other students became even more abrasive towards her.

Gina expressed little concern about this. She now felt as though she belonged somewhere, and finally had a genuine goal in her life.

Dancing had become her love and it strengthened her bond with Olivia. This made all the other small obstacles appear irrelevant in the young woman's mind.

The following day Gina stepped up on the stage to dance. She now danced in the early afternoon rather than morning. This, she found out from Alicia, seemed to the other dancers as another case of Olivia playing favorites.

But the Flamenco teacher never considered this as playing favorites. Due to Gina's initial practicing at night in her room, she had quickly passed the more novice dancers and now had no problems dancing at the intermediate level.

Olivia observed closely as Gina seemed to almost eat, sleep

and breathe the Flamenco. She watched all the other dancers with zeal. She listened closely to every word Olivia told her. She practiced the moves she learned over and over every night before going to bed.

Gina only thought of the dance and of making Olivia proud of her. This began to pay great dividends as each day passed.

Olivia also realized Gina was exceptional and began to work with her more. Often, after the cafe closed, Olivia and Gina would spend time together as she had an unquenchable thirst for Olivia's knowledge of the dance. And Olivia knew well this was a necessity for any dancer that wished to master the Flamenco.

As the guitarist began to play and Gina began to dance, she let the music flow through her. Every time she danced, the moves became more natural. Several of the other students clapped their hands beside the stage.

While dancing, Gina felt all her cares flow from her. She felt free in an odd sort of way. Though she moved with memory and practiced efforts, she still had the sensation of being in the clouds and floating on air.

She loved this dance and now she and the dance were slowly becoming as one. As her skill increased she knew in her heart she would make Olivia proud someday.

A slight smile broke over the young woman's face as a new calm flowed through her.

That night Olivia stopped by Gina's room to say good night, as had become her custom. She would also give Gina pointers on her dancing from time to time.

"You're doing very well, Gina."

"Thank you, Teacher," she replied.

"I did notice you smile today while you were dancing. Gina, as you're dancing, you're expressing many complex emotions with your feet as well as the rest of your body, but smiling is not something a Flamenco dancer generally does to express these feelings."

Gina lowered her head a little, "Yes Teacher, it just makes me happy."

Olivia put the palm of her hand on Gina's cheek.

"Don't worry. I sense you're happy when you dance. I don't want to change that. I just want you to express that happiness with your entire body."

Olivia studied the young woman's face briefly. This brought an example to mind. She spoke to Gina softly and with tenderness.

"The Flamenco is like a fantastic and beautiful storm. The audience observes your beauty as lighting and feels thunder with your graceful but forceful moves. Other dances may rely on smiles to express emotions, but not the Flamenco.

"You have a beautiful smile dear. I fear that if you smile, they're sure to see that and it will cause a distraction from the wonderful talent being displayed."

Gina looked into Olivia's eyes with fondness.

"I understand. I won't do it again."

"Good night, Dear," Olivia replied with a smile also and left.

The day finally arrived when Olivia and the small select group left for the annual Music and Dance Festival. As the crude wagon rocked them about, Gina turned to Olivia.

"Has anyone from our dance school won first place at the Dance Festival teacher?"

Olivia turned to Gina. She appeared to be in thought for several seconds but then answered her question.

"I won first place at the festival twelve years ago. None of the students from our Flamenco school has won yet."

Olivia appeared sad after she said this.

Gina felt sad now as well and had to turn away from the sight of Olivia.

"I'm hopeful Nina can win this year. She knows all the moves and dances well."

Now Olivia's voice lowered as she turned and seemed to be talking only so Gina could hear.

"She just doesn't seem to have...Well; she doesn't seem to have the fire in her soul."

She then said something to Gina that the young woman would never forget.

"I see the Flamenco flowing through you Gina. Even though you still have much to learn. I believe the dance flows from deep in your soul. That's where the dance must come from to win first place at the festival."

Gina felt her heart leap when Olivia told her this. Without thinking Gina looked into Olivia's eyes and replied.

"I'll win first place at the festival for you, Teacher. I promise you; I'll win it for you some day."

A tear immediately welled up in Olivia's eye when Gina told her this. She lovingly put her palm against Gina's cheek.

"I believe you will do that some day."

As they came closer to the Music and Dance Festival, the small group became enveloped by people moving towards the event. Gina watched the faces of the people passing by them.

She noticed that there were lighter skinned people and darker skinned people. Although her hair was dark brown, and her skin had taken on a darker color from her duties outside, she wondered where she fit in at her new home. She decided to ask Olivia.

As a child would ask her mother Gina presented a question to Olivia.

"Teacher, I see there are people with dark skin and others with lighter skin and hair that is lighter. Why is this?"

Olivia glanced at Gina. She considered her question and replied.

"There are Mexicans that are of Spanish descent and Mexicans that are descendant from the original peoples of Mexico and those are darker in skin and hair color."

Gina nodded, but she didn't smile her usual smile.

After answering her, Olivia watched ahead again as they wobbled along. She then glanced back to Gina. Perhaps sensing the reason for her question, Olivia continued.

"You my dear, would be considered a Mexican of Spanish descent."

Gina now smiled with glee; feeling that she really did fit in.

Soon music could be heard, and the little wagon pulled into a large open area. Gina marveled at what she thought to be thousands of people all gathered in small groups.

Makeshift tents were set up and around these the people had campfires with food cooking. Women practiced dancing and men played guitars. Many different styles of Mexican folk dance could be seen.

The wooden wagon bumped along until a spot was found to set up their campsite. By the time they were situated with a campfire, the sun relinquished the last of its light for the day.

The group sat around the fire and warmed some food. Then after eating, the guitar player began to play. Nina danced to the music and Gina clapped along with the others.

She wasn't jealous of Nina, even though Nina often showed jealousy towards Gina and Olivia's close relationship.

Nina had worked hard to get here. Deep inside though, Gina could barely wait for her chance to dance at the festival. Her new goal was to make Olivia proud by winning at the festival and to also be the best Flamenco dancer in the world.

With this new thought in mind, she smiled and clapped even harder while she imagined herself dancing at the festival.

During the two-day event Gina infused her heart and soul with the Flamenco and other Mexican Folk dances. Although Olivia taught the Spanish Gypsy style of Flamenco, Gina absorbed many different aspects of the beautiful dances.

During one dance Gina turned to Olivia and said, "I would like to learn how to use those." She pointed to the dancer on stage.

"You mean the castanets?"

"I guess. Is that the things in her hands?"

"Yes, they're called castanets. I have some I can let you use.

None of the other girls have expressed much interest in learning to use them. I'll teach you how to play them and use them in your dance if you're sure you wish to learn." Olivia smiled after telling Gina this.

"Yes, I'm sure I want to learn." She became even more excited as she watched the young woman dance. She tried to take in every move and every method used by the dancers.

She also fell in love with the tambourine as some of the folk dancers made exceptional use of the unique instrument.

For Gina, the two-day festival became the catalyst for her new life as a Flamenco dancer. By the time the event ended she had no doubt as to what she needed to do and how to do it. She would dance at the festival the following year. She would work harder than ever to win first place.

Olivia seemed to sense Gina's newly found inspiration and reassured herself in the knowledge of Gina being exceptional. She considered the situation as the wagon wobbled along and the group moved wearily back towards the Cafe Flamenco. Even though Nina didn't win at the festival, Olivia knew Gina had the potential to reach places no other student had reached.

As the days passed at the Cafe Flamenco, Olivia began to shower Gina with more and more affection. She continued to spend more time teaching her. She also allowed her more time to dance and tried to get her away from washing dishes and waiting tables.

Gina however almost refused to stop working around the cafe. Her days were spent almost entirely waiting tables and washing dishes, only to stop and dance, eat, or practice.

Olivia thought she might stop working as hard as a waitress and dishwasher if she bought her some nice dancing dresses and new dance shoes.

"Where's the dress I gave you Gina? Why aren't you wearing it?"

Gina still wore her faded and stained waitress dress as she stepped up on stage for her turn to dance.

"And are you still wearing those worn-out shoes I gave you last year?" Olivia lifted Gina's dress as she stood on the stage and exposed the faded and worn shoes

"Yes Ms. Olivia, the new ones are too nice. I want to save them for the festival."

Olivia tried not to smile at this answer but couldn't help it. She turned away to keep Gina from seeing her obvious delight.

While the other girls primped and strived to be fashionable, Gina focused her efforts on the dance or on assisting in the success of the cafe. She already danced as well as almost every student Olivia had.

As Gina closed in on matching Nina's skill level, the contrast became apparent. Nina strove to outshine Gina by wearing elaborate dresses and her parents paid to have her hair fixed beautifully. Yet Gina brought the people into the cafe more and more wearing only her old shoes and faded waitress dress. She continually focused on the art rather than fashion.

In Olivia's heart, she felt a desire to express her feelings for Gina in a more appropriate way, and now in a final flash of inspiration she knew what she would do.

When the cafe closed at the end of the day, Olivia and Elisa sat talking and watching Gina diligently clean in preparation for the following business day.

"Are you absolutely sure you want to do this?" Elisa studied Olivia intently after asking the question.

"I'm sure, Gina has become like a daughter to me. If she will accept me, I want her to be my daughter."

Elisa smiled a little smile. "I understand. I just want you to be sure before you speak with Gina."

"I'm sure, and the time is right. As I said before, this girl is special. She's filled a void in my life and I'm hoping I can fill a void in hers."

Olivia turned to the young woman. "Gina, can I have a word with you."

Gina stopped her work. She wiped her hands on her apron and hurried over to Olivia and Elisa.

"Yes Ms. Olivia?"

"Please, have a seat and talk with me, Gina."

Sitting down in a chair beside her teacher, Gina became a little concerned about the tone of the situation.

"Did I do something wrong, Ms. Olivia?"

Olivia smiled and placed the palm of her hand on the young woman's cheek, as she now had a custom of doing.

"No, child you've done nothing wrong. In fact, you've worked harder than any of my other students. What I want to talk with you about has nothing to do with dancing."

Gina appeared puzzled.

Olivia sat up and became even more serious.

"Gina, you've lost your real mother and father. I've always

wanted a daughter, but now with my age, I suspect I'll never have one naturally. You've become like a daughter to me in the short time you've been here."

When Olivia said these things, Gina began to smile in anticipation of what Olivia was saying.

"If you would like, I would very much like to adopt you as my daughter."

Gina could no longer contain her feelings. She almost leapt into Olivia's lap to hug her and wept as she held her arms around Olivia's neck.

"Yes, I would like that very, very much." She replied through the tears.

Olivia put her arms around Gina and began to also weep tears of joy.

At this moment a bond between them took hold. It would rival many mothers and daughters' natural bond.

The following day Olivia and Elisa began planning for a celebration to mark the occasion.

Preparations for the event took several weeks. A big fiesta would take place at the Cafe Flamenco to publicly celebrate Olivia adopting Gina, and everyone in the area would be invited. It would be held outside and all around the restaurant to accommodate the many expected attendees.

Hernan and several other men hammered outside as they assembled a stage for the dancers.

Gina sat down beside her newly adoptive mother as she worked on putting the special invitations together.

"How does this look?"

Olivia handed a paper to her. The paper read, "You're invited to the fiesta celebration for Gina Falcone becoming the adopted daughter of Olivia Frisco."

She stared at the paper for a few moments as Olivia worked on another invitation.

"If you'd given birth to a daughter, what would you have named her?"

Olivia looked at her, a little puzzled by the question, but went back to work as she considered it for a moment. Then she finally answered her adopted daughter.

"I think I would have named her… Serena. I've always been very fond of that name. Why do you ask?"

Gina wasted no time answering. "From now on my name will be Serena. I want to be the daughter you always desired."

She then picked up a pencil and marking out "Gina" wrote "Serena," over the top of it. She handed the paper back to Olivia.

"Now it looks good."

Olivia looked over the invitation closely and seemed a little sad.

"Gina, you don't need to change your name to be my daughter. I love your name and who you are, just as you are."

Gina's head lowered slightly.

"I want to change my name. I want to be the daughter you've always wanted."

Olivia felt torn. She felt joy that Gina would feel this way but also sad that she might feel the need to change.

"Gina, you don't have to change anything to make me

happy or to be the daughter I've always wanted. You're already perfect, just the way you are."

Now Gina turned away from her. She looked down at the floor to her side.

"But I want to change my name."

She then turned to Olivia and looked into her eyes. "I want to change my name. I want to be Serena Frisco. It would make me so happy. Mother please let me."

When Gina called Olivia mother, her heart leap with joy, she looked back at the card and then to Gina, who watched her with the eyes of a child.

"I want you to be happy. But you do understand that you don't need to change anything for me to love you."

Gina again lowered her head meekly. "I understand Mother. I want to be Serena. It'll make me so happy and I'll feel like the daughter you've always wanted. I know I don't have to change my name for you, but I want to. I want to be Serena Frisco."

Olivia paused and looked at Gina closely as she considered this.

Gina glanced up at her in anticipation.

After a long pause, Olivia finally caressed Gina's cheek and asked. "Are you sure you want to do this?"

"I'm sure Mother."

Olivia again looked at her carefully, as if making a final decision.

"Alright then, Serena it is."

Serena smiled with delight and then almost floated away.

CHAPTER FOUR:

The Ascension of Serena

The Fiesta brought many people to the Cafe Flamenco and Serena finally wore the new dress and shoes her mother had bought for her.

After the large meal Olivia formally announced the adoption and papers were brought out that would make Gina Falcone officially Serena Frisco, daughter of Olivia Frisco.

Then music and dancing erupted. Serena became so thrilled that when the time came for her to dance she felt as though she were on a cloud. As she stepped onto the stage she told herself this would be the dance that would express to her new mother how happy she was at this moment. She would dance as never before and make Olivia proud and glad she had adopted her.

The guitarist began to play and people around the stage started clapping to the beat. Serena began to move as if the music flowed through her.

Then, as her feeling and movements merged together, something extraordinary happened. She felt herself becoming one with the dance.

The music, the moves, the audience all became as one, fusing together through her body and soul. She no longer had to put forth an effort to make the moves. The dance moved and flowed through her naturally, as if she was the conduit and the Flamenco was the power.

Olivia and everyone at the Fiesta couldn't turn away as they all suddenly realized this to be the birth of a Flamenco star.

Something almost supernatural was taking place on the stage. Serena performed every tap and every step perfectly and with an unreal energy and beauty. She embraced the dance with her very soul and made it a part of her.

When the music stopped, silence settled all around the gathering. She stood motionless and waited as the audience appeared unsure of what to do.

Then, someone came out of the trance and began to clap and as if a floodgate opened, the entire audience went wild.

This would be the official introduction of Serena Frisco's Flamenco career.

Everyone that witnessed the dance realized she would become a star. Even Nina felt her heart sink slightly as she had no doubts now that Serena was the best dancer at the Cafe Flamenco.

The next morning before the cafe opened Olivia called Serena to sit and talk with her.

"My child, last night you moved into a level of Flamenco dance I had begun to feel none of my students would ever achieve. The dance flows through you now."

Serena smiled with joy and felt happier than she could ever remember. It was a wonderful feeling to have a loving mother and for this mother to be proud of her.

Olivia put her hand on Serena's and then looked towards a window.

"There was a time when the dance flowed through me. It was intertwined with my soul. When you danced last night, I recalled how I felt back then."

She seemed saddened as she recalled memories long faded from the back of her mind.

"What happened? Why are you sad when you speak of dancing?"

Olivia smiled for her daughter and then shook off her melancholy appearance.

"It's not important right now my dear. What's important is for me to tell you how you must deal with this new ability you have. You must listen to me very carefully, do you understand?"

"Yes, Mother. I'll listen carefully."

Olivia now spoke as she often did while teaching her dancers.

"Few dancers ever achieve what you have achieved. Even fewer still in such a short time. You are without a doubt, what we would call a natural born artist. Of those who achieve this level of dance, many are not able to maintain it for any great length of time.

"I'll tell you what you should do from now on and you must not fail to follow these instructions. I know these things because I learned the method to protect myself many years ago and without this method you may lose yourself."

Olivia gently put her hand on Serena's cheek. "Do you

promise you'll follow my instructions, Serena? I don't want to lose you now that I have a daughter of my own."

Serena clasped the outside of her mother's hand and held it to her cheek. She moved her face to kiss her hand and then moved it lovingly back to her cheek.

"I promise you, Mother, I'll do exactly what you tell me to do. I love you."

Olivia almost began to cry now and found she had to wipe a tear from the corner of her eye with her free hand. She smiled softly, "I love you too, Serena. I believe you'll do as I ask you to." She then became even more serious and moved into a position of teaching her daughter.

"To dance the way you danced last night, one must be completely connected to the dance, as well as the music and finally the audience. You give yourself away during the dance and the audience, perhaps, briefly has a small piece of you in their possession. This is necessary, because part of the reason you dance is to display the beauty of the art.

"The problem however is that the audience loves you. They must fall in love with you if you dance the way you did last night. They fall in love with the beauty you represent. And because they love you, they want to possess you. And, as an artist you also have the need to give yourself in small portions to the audience."

Olivia stood up and walked around the table as if gathering her thoughts again. She paused and glanced up, seeming to pull an idea from the air. She then came back to where Serena sat at the table, watching her mother closely. Olivia glanced down to her and continued.

"Now, this is where many dancers fail. Before they realize what has happened, they've given themselves to the audience rather than remaining true to the dance. The dancer begins to 'perform' for the audience, and in this way becomes something of a puppet for them. When the dancer becomes a 'performer' for the audience, they'll not retain a level of the art that you now have. These dancers may be good dancers, but they can't dance the way they could if they knew the secret to prevent this from happening."

Now Olivia sat down again in front of Serena. She took her hands in her own and spoke to her face to face to be sure Serena understood her.

"Serena, here's what you must do every time you dance, no matter what. You can allow the dance to flow through you just as you did last night. You can connect with the audience and the music just as you did last night. When the dance ends however, you must not face the audience as you did last night. Always end the dance with your side to the audience.

"When you dance as you did last night, you'll find there is always a very brief period when you hold the entire audience in a type of mild trance. This brief instant is the key."

Olivia gently squeezed her daughter's hands to emphasize the point, and then continued.

"While you're dancing, you're in the palm of the audience's hand. They watch you and marvel at you. They think they have you as a possession, which they can play with when they want; that you are doing this dance only for them. That it is you who needs them. Yet in this brief period right as the dance ends, you'll give them one last thrill and save yourself at the same time."

She moved even closer to Serena, as if someone other than her daughter might overhear this vital information. Her daughter in turn lowered her head a little to close the gap and make sure she heard the precious words.

"You end the dance with your side to them. Then, when the music has ended, you turn your head slowly and look out over all of them. This is 'your' audience; you are not 'their' dancer. This is the instant of truth and to prove this to yourself and the audience, once you've looked over them all, you quickly turn and walk briskly from the stage, as if you want nothing more to do with them.

"It's like magic. Just as the audience has fallen in love with you and believes they have you in the palm of their hand, that they own you, you prove to them and yourself that it is you that has mastered the art and by having control of the dance you also have control of their desire to see you dance. You must always keep the relationship with the audience in this framework Serena, or the audience will try to consume you with love. They will go to great lengths to make you their dancer. Because they love you and cannot help themselves. Do you understand?"

Serena considered Olivia's words for a few seconds.

"I do understand, Mother. I felt what you speak of last night. It seemed almost as if I stood on the stage naked at the end of the dance. I felt free, but also as if the audience wanted to hold me with their eyes."

Olivia smiled gently. "Yes, that's exactly what I speak of. It's a thin line you must walk when you dance at such a high level. You display something marvelous and you must enjoy the art of the dance. Yet, if you ever let yourself fall in love with the feeling of giving yourself to the audience, you'll lose yourself to them and your ability to dance at such a high level. So, you must always pull yourself from their grasp at just the right time. You must remain true to the dance because it's your real love, not the audience."

She paused briefly and then continued.

"This will cause two reactions from the audience. First, they'll be shocked that you can detach yourself from them so easily. And secondly, when they do realize you have that power, not them, they'll desire you even more. It's like a child watching a butterfly dance about in their hand, and then the child realizing they cannot possibly catch the beautiful butterfly. It is something that is free and will not allow itself to be possessed for the amusement of the child.

"The audience immediately wants you to dance more, so they can have more of you. The fact that you control that, not them, helps them to realize the beauty and true nature of the art. They'll want to sense this beautiful thing again. It's the true and pure endeavor as an artist and this will increase your desirability as such."

Serena squeezed her mother's hands. "I'll do as you say, Mother. I promise you that I'll make you happy, I'm your daughter; I'll make you proud."

Olivia quickly replied. "You've already made me so very happy and very proud, Serena."

92

That night the cafe became full. All around Tantico the word had spread of Serena's extraordinary dance at the Fiesta. She sat quietly in a back room as Alicia prepared her hair.

"What are you thinking of?" Alicia asked her friend; a little concerned she might be nervous.

"I'm going over something Mother instructed me about this morning. In my mind, I'm dancing and doing exactly as she told me to do. When I do this over and over in my mind, I can then do the same thing when I dance."

"Oh," Alicia replied. "I thought you might be nervous because of all the people that have come to see you dance."

Serena smiled. "I'm not nervous. The audience has no power over me and they never will have."

In the cafe there soon became room to stand only. All the waitresses were busy, and the kitchen was quickly overwhelmed. Cooks began to do smaller orders outside in a small fenced off area to help alleviate the extra load.

Olivia and Elisa sat in the back, astounded by the sudden boom in business.

"I can't believe this!" Elisa said, almost shouting.

Olivia smiled coyly and replied. "You'll see something even more amazing if Serena is able to do what I believe she can."

Elisa seemed puzzled by the comment, so Olivia elaborated a bit more.

"My friend, I think tonight we'll witness the true emergence of a Flamenco star."

Elisa smiled, as if in anticipation and then nodded slightly.

When Serena stepped from the back door and then

gracefully onto the stage, everything became quiet. The guitarist began to play and in an almost surreal display of talent, Serena began to dance.

Eyes grew wide as the pace of the dance quickened. She twirled about and appeared to be moving everything at once, and yet, she moved as if there was no effort involved.

Her feet tapped out fantastic rhythms and at the same time she moved in elegant and exotic motions that blurred into one fantastic and alluring show of feminine splendor.

Then, after a heightened crescendo of this beautiful and exciting display, the dance ended.

Serena stood just as her mother told her to, with her side facing the audience. And just as Olivia told her, time seemed to stop in that brief instant after the dance had ended.

Everyone appeared to be in a frozen anticipation of her next move. She slowly and seductively turned her head. Her eyes scanned the room and connected with every transfixed soul in the audience.

Then, with a sudden and brilliant movement, her head returned to the forward position; slightly turned up, she walked briskly off the stage, almost as a lover might do after an argument.

The crowd erupted in a volcanic explosion of applause and cheers that could be heard blocks away.

"It's your signature move Olivia! I've seen many dancers try to execute it, but none have ever mastered it! Now your daughter has!"

Olivia smiled and then put her hand to her mouth as several

tears of joy rolled down her cheeks. She could only nod in affirmation to confirm her friend's assessment.

Serena had indeed mastered the move flawlessly. Olivia now knew her daughter could go as far as she wanted.

Business at the Cafe Flamenco had never been better. Serena's fame spread, and she soon occupied the stage for almost hours at a time as the audience demanded to see this amazing new Flamenco dancer.

Her days as a waitress officially ended when her mother removed the waitress clothes from her wardrobe and forbid her to ever handle a dishrag again.

Serena became even more immersed in the dance with this move. She ate, slept, and breathed the dance as she prepared for her next challenge; the annual Music and Dance Festival.

"You're sure to win at the festival this year. The cafe is packed every night that you dance."

Alicia prepared Serena's hair and strategically placed a large flower at the side.

"I hope so. I want so much to make Mother proud."

Alicia made a funny face as she maneuvered Serena's head into a different position.

"For heavens sake Gi...I mean, Serena… I'm sorry."

Serena gave her friend a quick disdainful glance.

"How could you ever think your mother would not be proud of you? You're a sensation all over Tantico. Even beyond Tantico. I heard a man say he rode his burro almost ten miles just to see you dance."

Serena smiled a little when her friend told her this.

"Yes, but I promised her I would win at the festival. Until I win, I can't relax. She's done so much for me and I love her so much. I want to win for her this year. If I don't win this year, I don't know how I'll live with myself for another year."

Alicia now jerked her friend's head around a bit as she worked on her hair.

"Hey, what's that about?"

"It's about you, being silly, Serena. You're the best dancer in Mexico if you ask me. You should relax, do you hear me?"

Serena thought about this a few seconds as she watched her friend in the mirror. Then she said something that popped into her mind at that instant.

"I hear you. But I'll tell you this my friend, if I should ever leave Tantico, I'm taking you with me. Do you hear me?"

Alicia smiled now and became gentler with Serena's hair. She now glanced back at Serena in the mirror.

"Yes, I hear you... I hope you'll take me to your home in 'Italy'"

They both laughed out loud as only she and a few others actually knew where Serena was really from.

As the festival approached, Serena practiced tirelessly. She worked with an almost unnatural resolve now that she had moved into her mother's home. Olivia would find her still practicing moves in her room by candlelight, long after dark.

She would suggest that Serena go to bed but considering her newly adopted daughter was almost twenty years old now, Olivia didn't press the issue much.

Serena reacted as if she might lose everything should she

not master the Flamenco and win at the Festival for her new mother.

Olivia worried that her daughter may push herself too hard. Early in the morning she might be awakened by the sound of castanets or a tambourine resonating from Serena's room.

At the cafe, people would come throughout the day as they'd become aware of the fact that even when she wasn't on stage, Serena would be beside it, practicing bare footed while other students danced.

With Serena's increasing fame and tireless efforts to improve, a great excitement began to grow in the area around the Cafe Flamenco.

In anticipation of her debut at the festival more and more people began to wish Serena well. She had become the area sweetheart and now everyone felt vested in her potential success at the festival.

Serena remained completely focused on the challenge ahead however. With this effort, she didn't notice the amazing things happening all around her. She was quickly becoming a celebrity and was adored by all the people in the area.

The harder she worked, the more popular she became. Olivia stood in the shadows and watched with pride as her fans came and went, all talking about how she was sure to succeed at the festival.

One day, late in the afternoon, Serena sat at a table, rubbing her sore feet. Olivia and Elisa were out on cafe business. A break between dancers created a lull and the cafe had fewer customers at that moment.

As the guitar player strummed a light and vibrant tune in the corner, a small man approached Serena.

"Excuse me, Miss Frisco."

The man wore faded and worn clothes. His hair had grayed long ago, and the top of his head had few of the gray hairs left. He stood behind Serena holding his ragged hat with both hands.

"Oh, hello, can I help you, Sir?" She turned around in her chair to face the old gentleman.

"Well, um, I just wanted to wish you luck next week at the festival; and to give you something, if you'll have them."

Serena now turned the chair around to better talk with the man.

"Please have a seat, Mr...?"

"Garcia," the man replied meekly.

"Here, please sit here Mr. Garcia. Thank you so much for the kind wishes."

The old gentleman gazed around the cafe, as if he'd not been in a place such as this very often.

He appeared to be a farmer or of some occupation that paid little. After assuring himself no one would object to his sitting in the cafe, he gently sat down.

"Miss Frisco, I saw you dance at the fiesta your mother gave when she adopted you some months back. I was, in the distance, not close. But I've never seen such a beautiful thing in my life."

Serena now heard nothing but this poor, elderly man as he spoke in a quiet gentle voice. The guitar and all the noises from the kitchen faded out as she listened to him.

"I have something I wish for you to have."

He pulled from his pocket a small rag. He gently opened the worn cloth to reveal two shining brass finger cymbals.

"I've cleaned them as much as I could. I hope you can use them somehow."

Serena had been in Mexico long enough to realize this man could sell these and possibly eat for several days from the money.

"I can't take those, Mr. Garcia. They're much too nice. You should give those to your children. Or sell them to buy something for yourself."

The man expressed sadness when Serena said this.

"I have no children, Miss Frisco. I could sell them, but they were given to me by my grandmother. I have no one to pass them on to and I wish for them to be used in some way as they were intended."

The man gazed lovingly down at the cymbals, as if recalling his grandmother.

"They've sat quietly for years, waiting for someone such as you to play them. My grandmother told me they're a fine quality and were made in Istanbul. It would make me very happy for you to have them; even more so if you could find some way to use them in your dance. I know my grandmother would love for someone like you to have them."

Serena felt a tear roll down her check. She wiped it quickly.

"Alright, I'll accept them as a wonderful gift. And in honor of your grandmother, I'll find a way to use them."

The man smiled graciously and handed the small cymbals to Serena.

"Thank you, Miss Frisco. Thank you." He bowed a little as he stood up and then backed towards the door of the cafe, smiling and raising his worn hat up and down in a gesture to say good bye.

"Wait; let me have the kitchen prepare you something to eat."

The man gazed around the cafe as if he were not comfortable in such a nice place.

"No, no I am not so hungry. Thank you though, Miss Frisco. Good-bye, Miss Frisco and good luck," he then disappeared out the door.

Serena gazed down at the tiny cymbals. She put them on her fingers and tapped them lightly together. A beautiful bright sound resulted, causing her to instantly smile.

"I'm sure I can find some way to use you two little gems," with a gleam in her eyes, she spoke as if they were her new pets.

The following week Olivia's small group once again moved towards the Music and Dance festival.

Nina and Serena were chosen to represent the Cafe Flamenco in the Flamenco dance competition. Alicia came as the assistant this year.

Serena stared blankly out into space as the wagon swayed back and forth on the rugged roads. In her mind she went over dance routines and moves she wanted to practice.

Nina sat on the other side of her in the back of the wagon; sewing a small ornament onto her dance dress.

"The competition will be brutal this year."

Nina spoke casually as she sewed another stitch and tried not to poke her finger while the wagon jostled about.

Serena now retracted from her self-induced trance to give Nina her attention.

After she considered what Nina said she replied.

"I've no doubt about that, because we'll be there."

Nina stopped sewing. Still staring down at her dress, she suddenly realized she'd spoken in an effort to make Serena nervous.

She still thought of Serena as her competition. Yet Serena now offered her friendship and the desire to be her teammate.

Nina tried to think of anything Serena had done to her. Maybe if Serena had done something bad to her she could justify the remark. But there was nothing.

She realized now that over the last few years, Serena had worked harder than her or any other dancer. She had mopped the floors of the cafe and only stopped long enough to dance. She would then immediately return to her mop and bucket without complaint.

As she stared down at her needle and thread she wanted to cry, but her pride wouldn't let her. And this was why Serena was the stronger person. She would have wept if she'd done something to hurt Nina. She would have wept and asked her to please forgive her.

Nina now relinquished in her heart to Serena what she had earned through her endless effort and resolve to be a better dancer and person. Nina no longer felt the urge to fight and compete with the young woman sitting in the small wagon across from her.

She slowly turned a gaze of guilt up to Serena, who gently smiled back to her. Nina smiled also.

"Yes, you're right, Serena. We'll be there, so the competition will be very tough."

Serena laughed and then Nina laughed as well. From this time on, Nina was a loyal friend to Serena. Regardless of the situation, Serena would find Nina by her side ready to defend her if needed.

Upon arriving at the festival grounds, the Cafe Flamenco group searched for a place to camp. The mass of people created an atmosphere of excitement.

As they set up their campsite, the smell of meats and spices drifted in the air from the multitude of festival attendees. The sounds of guitars floated on the breeze and laughter mingled with tambourines, lifting everyone's spirits.

Once the campsite was up, Alicia, Serena and Nina all strolled around the massive festival grounds.

Serena felt her heart swell inside her as she absorbed the wonderful smells and sounds. She felt as if this was where she had always belonged.

Young men would follow and flirt with the three beautiful young ladies.

They, in turn, would giggle and react as if they were not interested. Then Nina might turn back to see if they were still following.

The evening began to move in when the three came upon a crowd of people.

"What is this all about?" Serena asked as they tried to get closer.

Slowly the three women moved into the crowd far enough to observe a beautiful Flamenco dancer practicing atop of wooden sheets placed on the ground.

"That's Miranda Santos. She won first place in Flamenco dance last year."

Nina said this in a manner indicating she had faced this dancer in the previous year's competition.

Then Serena recalled watching Nina dance against this young woman. When she watched Miranda dance the year before, she had admired her style and skill. Now these same things she had admired appeared as threats to her goal.

She watched Miranda closely and for the first time realized the many hours of hard work would not be in vain. This would be a very tough competition. She would need to summon a tremendous effort if she hoped to win.

"Come on, let's go back to camp. We should practice and then get some rest for tomorrow."

Alicia and Nina agreed with her and they moved out of the crowd and back towards their campsite.

The first day of the dance competition both Serena and Nina moved up step by step, dancing as often as two or three times an hour.

The second day they danced less as other dancers were eliminated from the competition.

When they did dance however, the competition became much more intense and both girls knew it would be tough from here on.

By 3:00pm the second day, Nina fell from the competition.

Serena now stood alone representing the Cafe Flamenco.

Nina became an extra assistant for Serena and even let her use a dress for one dance.

Serena could now feel the effects of two intense days of dancing. Everything began to hurt.

She sat alone as the sun began to wane before the final elimination. Only she and Miranda Santos remained in the competition. She knew Miranda must have started dancing at a very young age.

Serena placed her face in her hands and tried to find some way to regain her strength and motivation. She felt weak and her entire body ached.

She knew Miranda had surely been in many of these competitions and also knew tricks that Serena didn't.

With her eyes closed and everything dark, she suddenly found herself back in the sea, floating alone and scared for a very brief second. She opened her eyes quickly, as if to get away from that place.

She stood up and felt stronger than a few moments earlier. As she walked towards the stage to prepare for her dance, Nina came to her.

"I'm sorry you've had to face the last challenges alone. I hoped to make it further in the competition."

Serena stared at Nina for a few seconds, with an expression of gratitude.

"It's alright my friend. This is not the first time I've been alone."

Serena then put her arm inside Nina's and they walked arm in arm to the stage.

A small entourage gathered around Miranda Santos as she prepared for the final elimination. As the reigning champion, Miranda had chosen to dance first.

When Serena and Nina walked up to the stage area they were both talking and laughing about something.

Miranda immediately glanced at Serena with anger in her eyes. She knew for certain what Miranda thought. She could see in Miranda's eyes that she felt Serena should be serious and stoic at this point in the competition. The fact that Serena would laugh at this point was almost an insult to Miranda.

The smile slowly fell from Serena's face as Miranda returned to her preparations with a stern and focused expression.

Nina noticed the change in Serena's demeanor. "What are you thinking?"

Without much thought, Serena replied. "I'm thinking, Miranda is not very happy right now."

Nina expressed some puzzlement at this answer but didn't ask what prompted Serena to say this.

The two young women found Elisa and sat down. Soon Alicia and Olivia arrived.

Olivia sat down beside Serena.

"In the final dance, the judges will be watching for something special."

She put her arm around Serena and hugged her daughter.

"If you've saved anything special, this will be the time to use it."

Serena smiled to her mother in an effort of reassuring her she would be alright.

105

Then, as she considered what her mother told her, she did remember something special.

"I'll be right back, Mother."

She jumped up and lifting her dancing dress from her feet, darted back towards their campsite. A few moments later she returned just in time for the ending of Miranda's performance.

"What's wrong?" Olivia expressed concern with her daughter's sudden urgency.

"Nothing, Mother, I just remembered something special for my dance."

Olivia smiled; a little puzzled, as Serena moved towards the stage.

She maneuvered her elaborate dancing dress through the people as she passed Miranda and the entourage that crowded around her.

A woman that looked to be her mother fanned her and another woman held a drink for her. As Serena passed by the group, Miranda sneered at Serena, as if she had no right to be stepping onto the same stage Miranda had just stepped off.

The crowd became silent and as the music began to play and Serena danced, her heart filled with joy. This was her safe place, and she loved to be here. She was completely alone and yet able to connect with the thousands of people in the audience, all at the same time.

Her moves were precise and yet delicate. She swished her beautiful dancing dress as a swan gracefully flaps its wings. Her feet tapped rapid and crisp rhythms that seemed almost impossible.

The performance was a marvelous display that none could turn away from and it all flowed together in a masterpiece of Flamenco.

Still, Olivia didn't see the 'special' thing her daughter spoke of.

As the dance ended, Serena made what had now become her signature move. She ended with her side to the audience.

Everyone appeared to be in a slight trance from the fantastic display. She turned her head, seductively scanning over the audience.

After she held them briefly like this, and as they all anticipated her quick departure from the stage, something different happened.

A crisp, brilliant chime of the finger cymbals given to her by the elderly man sounded out.

As if she too had been released from the dance by this clear chime; Serena quickly turned her head straight and walked briskly to the back of the stage, then down the steps.

The audience went crazy with a tremendous applause that endured long after Serena had departed.

Olivia laughed from joy as she clapped. "I didn't teach her that! Where did she learn that?" She had to shout for Elisa to hear her.

Elisa simply laughed and shrugged her arms indicating she didn't know either.

The small cymbals were exactly the 'special something' the judges wanted to see.

Serena won first place at the festival and as they struggled to leave the area, many people approached Olivia in the hope of securing Serena as a dancer for their cantina or entertainment establishment.

Serena noticed her mother turning them all down and this caused her even more joy. She had a home and a loving mother.

The celebration lasted a week once they arrived back at the Cafe Flamenco and the year following her triumph at the festival would be one of the happiest of her life.

She became a local celebrity and her admirers were many.

Business at the Cafe Flamenco increased so much that the building had to be renovated and an addition added on.

CHAPTER FIVE:

A Past that Waits

Alicia felt very happy for her friend as the young Flamenco dancer finally seemed to relax some.

After winning at the festival she slowly settled into the masterful dancer she had become. She now practiced because she loved the dance and it had become a part of her.

The younger dancers around the cafe often followed her around and she spent much time showing them techniques and assisting her mother as a teacher.

These young admirers would bring her something to drink or eat from the kitchen in the hope of being able to linger around the table for a while and listen to Serena, Nina and other senior dancers talk.

As the festival again came closer though, Serena became more and more focused on the challenge ahead. She knew well the hard work necessary to win and she felt the victory also belonged to her mother.

The unthinkable notion of losing at the festival motivated Serena to slowly move back into the focused and tireless dancer Alicia remembered before the previous festival.

"You've been dancing since six this morning, Serena. The

other dancers get no attention from the audience because you're practicing beside the stage and the audience watches you instead of them."

Serena had just finished another dance and sat down at the small table as Alicia said this. She appeared to not hear her friend at all. She gazed out to someplace over the crowded cafe. Alicia stared at her friend for a few seconds.

The brilliant and beautiful dancer pulled a shoe off and began to massage her foot. She then stared back to the spot over the tables and many customers.

Serena seemed to be dancing through a routine in her mind. Alicia continued to watch the odd expression on her face and could almost see the intricate moves taking place inside the dancer's thoughts.

"Did you hear anything I just said?"

Now Serena turned to Alicia.

"I'm sorry, what did you say?"

Then she reached down and placed her shoe back on and pulled the shoe from her other foot and began to massage it.

Alicia laughed. "Nothing, it wouldn't make a difference anyway."

Serena gave her friend a puzzled look and continued to massage her sore foot.

She became more and more detached from anyone or anything other than the dance. She practiced and worked once again as if she would lose everything should she not win at the festival. All the things she had obtained over the recent years seemed to be attached to the dance. In her mind, the Flamenco had given her value, and this is what brought the things she'd wanted so dearly. To fail in the dance now, perhaps meant losing all that she loved. She refused to risk this.

The day came to load up and again travel the rugged roads to the Music and Dance Festival.

"You're twice as good as last year, no, three times as good! I know I'd have thought that to be impossible last year, but no one has a chance against you this year, Serena. Really, it's going to be over before it gets started."

Alicia had long become Serena's best friend and self-appointed cheerleader. Serena smiled as they wobbled along in the small wooden wagon.

"You're going to have me overconfident. If Miranda Santos competes again this year it may not be so easy. I'm sure she will have worked hard all year as well."

Alicia made a face and waved her hand in a dismissive manner.

"Miranda, is that the girl that thought she could beat you last year? You're going to show all the judges what a real Flamenco dancer is."

Olivia sat at the front of the wagon, enjoying the entertaining conversation behind her.

Then she thought about the festival. The smile fell from her face as she considered the next few days.

Again, the group found a place to camp. This time however, other groups quickly scampered for the areas surrounding the reigning Flamenco champion.

After their camp was set up, many younger dancers would hover around to watch Serena practice.

Time went by and a steady stream of people floated around the campsite, if only to get a better look at Serena. She seemed to notice none of this as she was focused completely on the challenge ahead.

As the festival progressed, Alicia's vision turned out to be prophetic. The best dancers struggled fiercely to put up some type of competition.

The contrast would always become clear as soon as Serena began to dance. She commanded the stage with a grace and style none of the other dancers could come close to.

In obvious desperation, a few of the dancers resorted to imitating Serena's signature move, in a vain effort to stay in the competition. Nothing they tried could get them close to her level.

For the most part, the other dancers stayed and gathered around close to the stage, so they could watch and learn as much as possible from the natural. And she did move now as if born with the ability to dance.

At the end of the first day, few doubts remained as to who would win first place.

By the middle of the second day there were no doubts in anyone's mind that Serena would be the winner again.

During the two-day competition many cantina and entertainment people expressed interest in Serena dancing full time at their establishments. Olivia fended off these offers until after the competition.

However, as she knew would happen this year, once the competition ended, the offers became almost overwhelming.

Serena became quite surprised now to find her mother arranging appointments for the following day to speak with these people.

Olivia carefully took names and told the people what time to come to their campsite and talk business.

Serena ate silently by the campfire that night. Olivia worked through the notes but glanced over at her withdrawn daughter.

She thought of going over and talking with her, but she knew Serena must decide if she would trust her mother or not.

The next day as groups were departing the festival grounds, Serena found a quiet place and watched at a distance while her mother talked to the strangers. Even Alicia couldn't get the despondent dancer to talk about her concerns.

Serena couldn't understand why her mother would do such a thing. She did decide to trust her mother but continued to sulk as the festival grounds slowly became vacant. Olivia meanwhile talked with the various business people by their campfire until long after dark.

Serena walked up to the camp site after the last of these people left. She sat down across the fire and her mother. She gazed into her face with a confused and hurt expression.

Her mother understood immediately what she felt. She stood up and went to Serena's side and sat down beside her.

"Do you want me to leave, Mother?" She could barely hold back her tears.

"Of course, I don't want you to leave my child." Olivia put her arm around her.

"Then why are you talking to those people? I don't want to dance for them. I dance for you, and the Cafe Flamenco. They want me to leave you."

Now Serena began to cry.

Olivia could no longer hold back a few tears either and escaping her eyes they rolled down her cheeks. She reached over and pulled her daughter closer to her.

She took a deep breath to regain her composure and began.

"You must know, Serena, this is the most difficult decision I've ever made. I want so much for you to stay with me and never go anywhere that I can't have you close by. The thought of not having you with me is almost unbearable. But, I know in my heart I must do the right thing. I've made the mistake of not doing what I know in my heart I must do, and the consequences have been severe and painful."

She paused briefly and looked out over the fire to gather her thoughts.

"Years ago, when I began to teach the Flamenco, I prepared two talks for students that achieved the level of dance you have. I soon realized how difficult to find such a person as that would be. After years of teaching I became almost hopeless in finding a student such as you."

Now Serena dried her eyes and sat back some to see her mother's face; sensing she was again telling her something of importance.

Olivia in turn also maneuvered to where she could gaze into Serena's eyes as she spoke, to be sure her daughter understood her.

114

She wiped the remainder of a tear from Serena's cheek with her thumb and caressed the side of her face with the palm of her hand. Serena took her mother's hand and kissed the palm as she often did when Olivia caressed her cheek this way.

"I almost forgot the two talks I'd prepared. I could never have imagined that I'd someday give these talks to my daughter. Then you came into my life; a frightened girl from 'Italy,' which turned out to be America."

Serena laughed a little and Olivia joined in with a laugh as well.

"I knew you were special when I saw you dancing in that tiny backroom by candlelight."

Serena seemed a little surprised by this. "I didn't know you saw that."

Olivia smiled coyly.

"Yes, I saw that, and I saw something no other student had up to that point; a special ingredient that can't be taught or trained into a student. You have that special something, Serena."

Olivia turned and gazed again into the fire for several seconds before continuing.

"I gave you the first talk after you danced so brilliantly at the fiesta. Now the time has come for the second talk."

Serena smiled slightly and listened very closely.

"Years ago, I had successfully found a way to detach myself from the audience after such an intimate and intense dance. Later, I won first place here at the festival.

"You followed my instructions perfectly and now you'll not

become tangled in a love affair with the audience. And though they'll love you; don't ever forget they love you for the dance, not for the person you are. If you begin to give yourself to the audience, the audience will begin to manipulate you and they have no ability to master the dance, it's you that must do that."

Olivia now stood up and walked over to the wagon. She searched in a bag and pulled something out. Then she came back to Serena and sat back down holding the item secure in her hands.

"I knew you would win first place again this year. I've felt so proud knowing this and yet I've also dreaded this time, because I knew there would be an even higher demand for your talent.

"I went through a similar situation years ago. From my heartaches and heartbreak, I've learned one very important thing, and now I'll tell that thing to you, my daughter."

She moved closer to her and put her hand on Serena's arm.

"Every dance has a purpose and every dancer has a destiny."

She paused briefly as if to allow Serena to take the vital message in. Then she continued.

"You must allow the dance and destiny to flow through you as one. You master the dance, but the art demands a price in return."

Serena seemed to not completely understand this last statement.

"Do you mean, I have to pay something?"

Olivia thought about her daughter's question for a second.

"Yes, perhaps that you must pay for the dance to flow through you as it does. You're like a flower in bloom right now. If you stay at the Cafe Flamenco, you'll wither and lose your opportunity to bloom completely as is your destiny. To go out in the world and express your beautiful talent is part of the price you must pay."

Serena took her mother's free hand and held it. She began to understand her mother truly desired the best for her. She began to understand why her mother spoke with the people and why she must trust her mother in this matter.

Alicia walked around the wagon and noticing Serena and Olivia in a mother and daughter talk, put a few pieces of wood on the fire and then went back to her sleeping spot beside the wagon.

Olivia continued.

"I failed to pay my debt years ago."

When she said this, her head lowered as if she felt ashamed.

Serena turned her head down a little also to still gaze into her mother's face.

Olivia raised her head up slightly and a tear rolled down her cheek. She wiped it quickly with the back of the hand holding the object and tried to recover.

Serena squeezed her mother's hand to support her. But without control a few tears also escaped due to her mother's apparent pain.

"Tell me why you're sad, Mother." she asked gently.

"I knew how to handle the audience, but I failed at controlling my own heart. I didn't stay true to myself."

When she said this, Serena sat back just a little bit. Her mother quickly wiped another tear and continued.

"I fell in love. I knew in my heart I should stay true to the dance, but I wanted more. I left the path I should have remained on and began to follow an attractive man. His name was Paco Rivera."

Olivia slowly pulled a rag from around the object in her hand and turned the slightly faded, but nicely framed photograph where Serena could see it.

"I don't tell any of my students about this, but I brought this because I knew I would need to have this talk with you."

Serena studied the picture in the light of the campfire. The man in the picture appeared attractive and confident; well-dressed and well groomed. She could see he must have been about twenty-six or twenty-seven when the picture was taken.

Olivia then looked at the picture in a reminiscent way and sat it down in her lap.

"He knew all the right things to say. He was a wolf and I didn't see that because I was a lamb.

"Men such as Paco hunger for the chase, but when they've caught their prey and have it lying before them, crippled and helpless, they have no real desire for it any longer."

She paused briefly and glanced down at the picture again, as if she still had a longing in her heart for the man that had given her so much grief.

"You must not fall in love until your destiny has been achieved, Serena. I learned this the hard way and suffered because of it. I ran after love and abandoned myself and my true destiny in the process."

Now Serena expressed a little fright. Her face became pale as she considered what her mother had just said. She looked away as if something in the darkness had caught her attention. After several seconds, she spoke to Olivia with a nervous tone.

"Can you… really abandon yourself in such a way?"

Olivia studied Serena's face. Her daughter now appeared deep in thought. She wondered about this and tried to think of an appropriate answer.

"Well, to be true to those whom we love, we must first be true to ourselves. I made a mistake. I knew in my heart what I should do and not do, but I still followed a foolish desire. This changed my destiny. I've struggled for years to correct that mistake."

Serena lowered her head now. Olivia noticed a tear fall to her lap. She reached up and wiped her daughter's cheek, but Serena didn't look up.

"I want you to reach your destiny, Serena. If you stay at the Cafe Flamenco, you'll not reach the potential you have inside. You must achieve the destiny inside your soul if you wish to have a complete and full life."

Serena raised her face now and the firelight exposed tears in her eyes.

Olivia's heart sank a bit as she thought her daughter must be very sensitive about leaving her and the Cafe Flamenco.

"How can I know when my destiny has been reached, Mother?"

Olivia thought briefly before replying.

"I believe a resolution will be met when you achieve your

destiny. When I saw you dancing in that tiny room, I began to see a resolution.

"When I fell in love with Paco, my dancing began to fail. I was torn between two loves.

"He promised to take me to Europe and make me a star there. Yet as my dancing began to suffer, I realized too late that Paco had fallen in love with the dancer not with me. He left me in Mexico, heart broken."

Several more tears trickled down Serena's face as her heart also broke with this new revelation. Olivia gently wiped one of the tears from her daughter's face and continued.

"I lost almost everything when Paco discarded me, as if I were of no real value. I couldn't dance because my heart was broken. I realized then what I'd been given and what I'd tossed away for a man unworthy of it.

"I should have danced the beautiful Flamenco for so many people. But I could no longer express the beautiful art as before. That debt has burdened my heart for so long."

Olivia paused briefly to comfort Serena who now gently moved over to lay her head in Olivia's lap. Another tear escaped as Olivia gently pulled her dark hair from her daughter's dampened face. Then she continued.

"In an attempt to pay this debt, I began to teach. I still had a reputation in Tantico from winning the festival and dancing at many places afterwards. Yet, year after year I found no student that could dance at a level needed to erase the debt. I'd almost given up when you came into my life.

"Since you've entered my life, Serena, I've begun to realize that a resolution to that debt may flow through you. I'm afraid the task now falls upon you, my daughter, to pay a debt I failed to pay so long ago. I truly believe you will be the dancer I should have been."

Serena now sat back up and faced her mother. In the flickering light of the fire she studied her face. She felt closer to her now than ever before. She'd almost lost all track of a life before Olivia adopted her. In her heart she thought that Olivia must have somehow always been her mother.

Olivia also sensed what she felt, just as any mother would.

"You've filled a vacant place in my heart, Serena. I only hope that I've done the same for you. Somehow, I'm sure you were sent to me and our destinies have been woven together."

Serena smiled as she knew for certain this truly was her mother now. Even though Olivia had not given birth to her, their relationship was as close as any mother and daughter could be.

"I believe that too. I'll pay the debt for both of us, I promise you, and I'll never let you down. I love you so much. You're my mother and it's my destiny now, because I'm your daughter, and nothing can change that can it?"

Olivia hugged Serena tightly.

"Nothing will ever change that my child, no matter what."

After a few moments in this heartfelt embrace, Olivia continued to do what she could to help prepare Serena for the events to come.

"Men will pursue you without relent. They will fight for a simple glance from you. You must brush these men off as you will the pedals of the flowers tossed onto you by an adoring audience."

Serena listened intently as Olivia laid out the foundation of her future before her by the light of the fire.

"There will be a time to fall in love; a time to get married and have children. That time must come after you've reached your full potential. If you leave the road for any reason, there will be no return. A dancer can only stay at the level you're at by remaining focused on the dance. You must follow the path of the Flamenco."

Serena had a puzzled expression now.

"How will I know where the path leads?"

As she'd come to do in things concerning the welfare of her students, Olivia thought before answering.

"When you have a safe way to express the dance to those who wouldn't see it otherwise, you should take the dance to them. It's like a beautiful painting that should be seen by many.

"Don't put yourself into danger, Serena, but always remember, this is an art that you carry within you; this art should be shared by all those who'll appreciate it. When you've expressed this art to the best of your ability, you'll know it in your heart. Then you can dance with peace in your soul. You can fall in love and have children and still dance with joy.

"If you don't share the beauty of this dance that's within you to the fullest extent possible, you'll feel as I have felt for so long. I want you, my daughter, to bloom in the sunshine and to feel the joy of sharing the gift you have with a world that is dark and cold. When you do this, you'll be bringing that sunshine into the hearts of so many people who need it desperately."

After these and many other words, along with the tears and laughter, the two finally went to bed. Serena slept as one who had climbed a mountain.

In the morning the warm sun shined on her. Alicia turned from her efforts of preparing the morning meal and smiled at Serena as her friend opened her eyes.

The smell of breakfast cooked over an open fire was comforting to Serena and she now felt much more prepared to meet the unseen destiny that lay ahead.

As she stretched and rose from the blankets laid on the ground, she knew her life would soon change. This frightened her some, but now with this new day and fresh perspective, she also felt excited about what lay ahead.

She then watched Alicia move about the campsite.

"*If I'm leaving Tantico, I'm taking you with me,*" she thought to herself. "*I told you once I would, and I will.*"

Alicia looked at Serena and smiled again, as if she knew Serena had been thinking about something involving her. Serena smiled back to her.

"*Our lives are going to change my friend,*" she again thought to herself. "*We must get ready for that.*"

All day long people came and spoke with Olivia. As she did so Serena and Alicia watched from a distance.

"You're going with me, you know that don't you?"

Alicia studied Serena's face as if waiting for her to laugh. After she didn't, Alicia realized her friend was serious.

"I want that more than anything, but I don't know if my parents will let me."

"You're old enough to do as you wish."

Alicia gave her a frown.

"That may be the way things are done in... Italy." They both smiled at this.

"But here we don't just run off as we please."

Serena didn't know what to say now. After a few seconds she simply said, "I know."

"Where're you going?" Alicia asked.

"I don't know yet. Mother said she thinks it'll be Vista Cruz, but that man there is really trying hard to have me dance for him at his cantina."

They gazed over at the man haggling with Olivia, as if he were buying a horse or donkey.

"When I talked with her an hour ago, she said this man just doesn't want to give up. This is the third time he's returned to make a deal for me. He knows he must be offering twice the money of anyone else, but Mother said she doesn't trust him and his cantina may be more of a brothel than anything else."

Alicia made a shivering sound and appeared to shudder at the thought of going to such a place.

Finally, after an outward expression of frustration, the man appeared to give up and left.

After briefly reviewing her paperwork and making some notes, Olivia strolled out to Serena and Alicia.

"Alright, it's pretty much settled. Mr. and Mrs. Perez own a cantina in Vista Cruz named 'The Red Gate'. They have Fandango dancers and a variety of other entertainment, but they need a star attraction. They heard about your dance at the festival last year, just as most of the others did, and came in hopes of recruiting you for the Red Gate's line up."

When Olivia got to this point Serena suddenly blurted out, "I'm not going without Alicia!"

Olivia stared at her daughter, as if in a bit of shock; her hands still frozen in the position of trying to explain the plan. She then turned to Alicia.

"Do you want to go with her?"

"More than anything in the world!" she replied without hesitation. "I just don't know if my parents will let me."

Olivia straightened up and thought about the situation a few seconds.

"Well, I'll talk with your parents. It's just a good thing you're not an only child. With five brothers and three sisters I think you have a chance."

Now Alicia and Serena both smiled and allowed Olivia to finish explaining the plan.

The following morning, they left Hernan with the wagon and gear. They went to a hotel to speak with the Perezes. In the taxi along the way, Olivia explained again that this couple had a good reputation as cantina owners and from all the prospects, she felt they would treat Serena the best.

Once they reached the hotel, Serena met the couple and could see why her mother decided they were a good option.

"I'm sure we weren't able to offer the most money, Serena but as we told your mother, you'll have a room at the cantina where you'll be safe. You can also eat at the cantina.

"Vista Cruz is a port city and you'll need to become familiar with it before venturing far, but we'll help you with that as well."

After telling Serena this, Mrs. Perez smiled. Serena liked her smile. She appeared sincere and truthful.

"I want Alicia to come with me. She's my assistant."

Alicia gazed over at the Perezes and smiled a little, then waved at them as if to identify herself as Serena's assistant. The Perezes both turned to Olivia now in a puzzled manner.

Olivia simply smiled, saying nothing.

"Well, we didn't really have the money set aside to pay an assistant." Mr. Perez seemed less comfortable talking business than his wife.

"I'll pay her from my salary if necessary," Serena replied rather loudly and in an insistent tone of voice.

"I guess the room is large enough for the two of you, if that's alright," Mrs. Perez replied and looked to her husband who nodded in agreement.

"That'll be fine, but I'll not go if she's not with me, I'll tell you that now."

Olivia put her hand on Serena's leg as if to calm her down, and then said to the Perezes.

"She really has become quite dependent on Alicia's assistance. I'm sure you'll be very pleased when you see how well they work together."

This appeared to put them back at ease.

Eventually, the contract reached put Serena under the employment of Mr. and Mrs. Perez for one year with an agreed upon salary. After one year the Perezes could negotiate with Serena for additional employment if they wished.

Olivia wisely had the agreement include the provision of Alicia being able to accompany Serena and Serena made a mental note of this.

When the two young ladies were ready to make the move to Vista Cruz, Olivia would send a telegram to the Perezes and in turn they would send their car and driver to bring them to their new home.

"There is one more thing, Serena."

Olivia now had the tone of voice Serena recognized as indicating she had something important to say. Serena, thinking everything had been settled, turned and sat back down next to Olivia.

"The Perezes mentioned something yesterday that I believe is a good idea. At first, I was against it, but after some thought I feel you should do it."

Serena stared at her mother in obvious wonder.

"We feel you should use another last name, Serena." Mrs. Perez said.

Serena appeared shocked. "I don't want to use another last name! Why should I use another name? I want to use Frisco. Why can't I use Frisco?"

She became animated and looked at Olivia with a frightened gaze. Again, Olivia placed her hand on Serena's leg to calm her down.

Mrs. Perez also tried to intercede, to help calm her.

"It will just be a stage name, Serena. A lot of artists and performers do this now. It's what people call a working name in the entertainment business."

This seemed to do little to calm her down though and Serena continued to object.

"I don't want a stage name. Mother, why can't I use Frisco?"

Olivia appeared touched by her daughter's desire to use Frisco as her working name.

She nodded slightly and again tried to calm Serena down and reason with her.

"Serena, listen to me. At first I felt the same way as I did when you wanted to change your name to Serena."

When Olivia said this, it put her daughter in a position to listen to her. She had, after all, found a reason to change her name once. Now her mother called her attention to this and continued.

"When the Perezes suggested you use a different last name I had reservations. But they made several good points about the matter and after some thought I tend to agree with them.

"First you must understand that people around Vista Cruz still remember me dancing in that area. There will likely be awkward questions, and this could be difficult for you, as well as distracting."

Olivia paused a few seconds as if attempting to see what affect this had on her daughter. But Serena appeared unimpressed with this thought, so Olivia continued.

"Above this reason however, is that you should reach your full potential without a constant comparison to my career. You're a brilliant dancer Serena and I'm concerned that people will tend to judge you in relation to my days of professional dancing and this wouldn't be fair to the skills you've worked so hard developing.

"You should dance your own Flamenco path, and I suspect you'll far outshine my career if you have the freedom to do that. I want you to perform brilliantly, without feeling you're somehow in my shadow. With a stage name you can be who you are, not the daughter of Olivia Frisco, which also happens to dance. I want people to appreciate you for who you are and the dancer you are. Do you understand?"

Serena now appeared a little deflated. She thought about what Olivia said and realized her mother once again had her best interest in mind. With a softened voice she finally replied.

"I understand Mother. I'll do it. But I want you to pick the name."

Olivia smiled and caressed Serena's cheek, which caused her to smile as well.

"Alright, I'll pick one for you."

Olivia gave this a long thought and then suggested the name 'De La Rosa'.

"Serena De La Rosa, I like that. It really seems to dance over the tongue," Mrs. Perez said, seeming eager to encourage the young dancer.

Then everyone said it over and over several times as if also testing the new name.

Serena sat silently, watching the others as if they were speaking a foreign language.

Eventually everyone turned to her. She looked at them and realized they expected a response concerning the name.

She slowly and softly said. "Serena De La Rosa."

"Well, what do you think?" Olivia asked with excitement.

"I like it, I guess."

Everyone appeared to exhale with a breath of relief.

"Fantastic." Mrs. Perez said.

"We have several other performers who've done this, so we know the process to have everything put in legal and proper order. We'll have everything ready for you to sign when you get to Vista Cruz." She then turned to Serena's mother. "Don't worry Olivia; we'll take very good care of her."

Olivia smiled, and Serena smiled as well. She then turned to Alicia who gave her a quick nod of confirmation, indicating she liked the deal, as well as the Perezes. This made Serena feel better.

Olivia knew she would need to talk with Alicia's parents first. Even though Alicia was twenty years old, daughters didn't move out without parental consent in Mexico. With the reasonable salary Serena would receive, she could pay Alicia and still live well. Olivia felt she could present this as a good job opportunity for Alicia.

After almost a week, the group wearily arrived back at the Cafe Flamenco.

A celebration soon got underway for Serena winning first place at the festival two years in a row.

Olivia spoke with Alicia's parents. They also felt this would be an opportunity for their daughter and everyone knew she would be upset and miserable without Serena around.

After the celebration and things returned to normal, Olivia began to let the people in the area know that Serena would be leaving. This brought a flood of admirers in through the doors of the Cafe Flamenco. They all wished her well but also expressed sadness that she would be absent from their lives.

In her total commitment to master the Flamenco Serena hadn't realized the full effect she was having on those around her. Now she finally saw how much difference a simple dancer could make in the lives of people. She wept as the admirers expressed their fondness for her. She would never forget this special time with her new family and friends.

CHAPTER SIX:

Life in Vista

Two weeks after the agreement with the Perezes had been made, their car and driver pulled up to the Cafe Flamenco.

Almost everyone cried as the good-byes were said again and again.

Olivia took her daughter's arm. She had something in her other hand that was wrapped in a nice piece of cloth.

"Walk with me."

The two slowly moved arm in arm up the street and for a few moments nothing was said between them. Then, when they were a fair distance from the others, Olivia spoke.

"This is one of the proudest and most agonizing moments of my life, Serena. The only way I can let you go is by knowing in my heart you'll return someday and never leave me again. You'll reach your destiny. I know in my heart you will. You are so much stronger than anyone is aware of."

Serena looked at her mother and wanted to say something, but she found nothing adequate to express her feelings. Olivia also glanced at her daughter and smiled, as if she understood. Then she continued.

"My love will always be with you. No matter where you go.

No matter what obstacles you may face. I will go with you in your heart. And every day I'll think of you and love you in my heart as well, no matter what."

Olivia then stopped and turned to Serena.

"If you ever feel down or discouraged; if you ever face anything difficult and need strength, I want you to look at this and know in your heart that I send my love and my strength to you, my daughter. I love you more than anything, Serena and I believe you'll return to me when you have peace in your heart."

She handed her the item in her hand. Serena pulled it from the cloth and found the picture of Olivia that she had shown her the first night in the tiny back room of the Cafe.

Serena held it to her heart as a few tears rolled down her cheek.

"I know you want the best for me, Mother. I know this is the right thing to do because I know in my heart you love me, and you wouldn't let me go unless it was the right thing for me. I'll miss you so much and I promise you I'll come back. I promise you I'll do as you've asked me to do and I'll not waver from the path I must travel as a dancer. When I have peace in my heart as you said, I'll return, and we'll never be apart again. Isn't that right?"

Olivia took Serena in her arms and embraced her as several tears fell onto Serena's hair. She ran her hand along the back of Serena's head lovingly.

"That's right, my daughter, I promise you that's right."

With Serena cradling her mother's picture in her arms, the two walked back to the others.

Then, the twenty-one-year-old, Serena, and the twenty-year-old, Alicia, loaded into the car and watched the Cafe Flamenco slowly disappear.

They looked at each other and the realization took hold that they were approaching a new chapter of their lives. Both sat silently for some time with their thoughts.

As the Cafe Flamenco became more distant, they began to talk again and soon became excited about the future they now moved quickly towards.

Vista Cruz was a port city as Tantico, but much larger. Tantico sat more inland and handled domestic shipping. Vista Cruz however sat directly on the coast and handled international ships and shipping.

Cafe Flamenco sat on the outer part of Tantico and most of the customers were regulars and often known by name.

The Red Gate Cantina on the other hand, would be a major change for the girls. It would be much larger, much more active and the customers, according to the Perezes were often foreign sailors that spoke little or no Spanish.

After a long drive on an often very rough road, the city of Vista Cruz began to close in around the travelers.

The streets were busy, and traffic was a mix of automobiles, trolleys and horse and wagon. Serena and Alicia sat watching out the windows as the sights of their new home city passed by.

Serena would grab Alicia by the arm as they moved passed something interesting. Then Alicia would grab Serena when she saw something, and Serena would slide over to view the sight.

Finally, they arrived at The Red Gate. The cantina was huge in comparison to the Cafe Flamenco. From the hillside it sat on, the coast could be seen in the distance. They could also see the tops of ships in the port below.

The driver dropped them off at the front and after picking up their modest baggage the girls walked into the busy cantina.

"I can't believe how big this place is!" Alicia grabbed Serena's arm as if she might be swallowed up if not for holding onto something.

Dancers moved about on a stage that appeared to be as large as the Cafe Flamenco. Musicians played in an area in front of the stage that would likely swallow up the stage at the Cafe Flamenco.

"What do we do?" Alicia was obviously nervous as the two attempted to take everything in while still standing directly inside the door.

"I guess we need to find Mr. or Mrs. Perez," Serena said after a few seconds.

Just then, an intoxicated man walked in through the doors and almost ran over Serena.

"Excuse me." He blurted out in Spanish but with an unusual accent.

He stopped and turned back around, looking the two girls over as a shopper might examine something in the market.

"You two beauties should let me buy you a drink. Come-on, I'll buy you a drink." The man seemed to have trouble standing.

"No thank you." Serena now took Alicia by the arm so that they had each other's arm in a locked position.

"What, you think you're too good for me to buy you a drink?" The man appeared to be angry now and as he spoke, saliva spewed from his mouth.

"Hi, would one of you happen to be Serena De La Rosa?" A very pretty woman in a beautiful dance outfit approached the girls.

Initially Serena didn't acknowledge the name. Then, Alicia pulled her arm and Serena suddenly realized the woman meant her.

"Yes, I'm Serena De La Rosa."

The woman then glanced at the intoxicated man.

"Go on now. These girls aren't interested in you."

"Ahh, stahhpp." The man blurted out odd sounds and then waved a hand as if he were not interested either. He then staggered on into the building.

"Hi, Serena, I'm Lavina Manzano. Please come with me, we've been expecting you."

Lavina motioned for them to follow her just as several rowdy sailors from some country other than Mexico stumbled past, making what most likely amounted to vulgar statements and gestures towards the women.

The two young women picked up their bags again and moved quickly in behind Lavina.

"You're going to have to get a little rough with some of these men or they'll never leave you alone."

Lavina almost shouted back to Serena and Alicia as they

followed her through a mass of people, eating, drinking and basically creating a lot of noise to coincide with the band playing.

"Mrs. Perez saw you and sent me to get you." Lavina pointed to a corner of the building and the two girls could see Mrs. Perez in a sectioned off area.

Serena thought she appeared to be like a military officer giving orders in the middle of a battle. People would come up to her and she would tell them something and away they would go. Then she would look back down to paperwork in her hands as if it were a map.

As the three came closer, Mrs. Perez turned and noticed them approaching. She smiled and waved at them. Serena felt so glad that her mother had spent the time to find someone such as the Perezes. She wondered briefly how walking into an environment such as this would be if someone with a kind heart were not there to meet them.

"Hello Serena! I'm glad you finally made it. How was the drive down?" The three girls walked through a wooden gate that swung open and closed behind as they passed through.

"Fine, Mrs. Perez, thank you."

"I'll have to chat later as we're quite busy now. We'll talk after closing time."

"What time is closing time?" Alicia asked.

"Around 11:30 tonight, but it will take a little longer to get everyone out. There's always a few that would stay all night if we let them."

Mrs. Perez then turned to Lavina, "Would you show them to

the room you helped me prepare last week?"

Lavina nodded and again the three were dodging waitresses and waiters along with customers moving to and fro, past the band and around the stage.

Serena gazed up at the dancers as they passed. She noticed these women danced more of a Fandango type dance. She'd seen this and other folk dances before at the festival, which had presented many different types of dances to her.

Then, on into the back they went, through some large wooden doors. Beyond the doors the music and mayhem became muted, though still vibrating through the walls.

"This'll be your room." Lavina opened the door and the two weary girls walked in and immediately sat their bags down.

The room would easily hold four of the rooms Serena stayed in at the Cafe Flamenco. But it was only slightly larger than the bedroom at her mother's house.

A bed and a large trunk sat against one wall. On the other wall a bed and an old chest of drawers sat.

The girls noticed in a corner of the room there stood a small table with an old vase. The table appeared to be homemade.

On one wall a faded poster of a Flamenco dancer hung with a faceless group of people in the background seeming to watch her dance.

"We tried to make the room comfortable. I hope your bed is alright." Lavina said looking at Alicia.

"It'll be fine I'm sure, thank you." She replied politely.

"Mrs. Perez found that trunk for you to use for your things."

Alicia opened the large lid of the trunk and peered in.

"Yes, this'll be good." Alicia said. "There's more room than I need. Do you need to put some things in the trunk Serena?"

"I have plenty of room in these drawers." The dancer replied, as she opened and closed one of the large drawers.

"Just let me know if I can help you with anything. I've got to go. My number is coming up."

The two girls thanked Lavina as she left. They sat down on their beds and gazed around the room. Then they looked at each other and both laughed nervously for no reason.

They unpacked and cleaned up in a restroom a few doors down. Later, Lavina brought them something to eat.

"You'll get used to the cantina. I wasn't sure about dancing here when I first arrived, but I love it now." She said this as Serena and Alicia ate.

They finished their food and intended to stay awake and talk with Mrs. Perez, but both lay back on their bed and were soon sleeping soundly.

The next morning, they changed and went into the cantina feeling a bit embarrassed.

Though it must have only been around 8:30 in the morning, the establishment already had a few customers eating and drinking coffee.

The front doors were wide open, allowing the morning sunshine to stream in and expose the places unseen in the dim lights of the night before.

Mrs. Perez sat at a desk in the cordoned corner of the building. As the two girls crept past the stage and into the large open area of the cantina, Mr. Perez strolled in from what appeared to be the kitchen area.

"Well, here are the two new girls now." He said.

Alicia giggled.

"Good morning Mr. Perez," Serena replied.

Mrs. Perez came out of her office area, "good morning you two."

"Good morning, Mrs. Perez," Alicia and Serena replied almost in unison.

"You'll be staying up later and getting up earlier around here. You should learn to drink coffee if you don't already. Stay away from wine and other drinks with alcohol if possible.

Mrs. Perez paused for a few seconds as she looked the two over, and then continued.

"I realize Serena is responsible for your pay Alicia, but if you'll do a few chores around the cantina I'll include your meals with the room. I can't pay you, but that'll allow you to eat and live here with Serena."

Alicia looked at Serena and Serena quickly replied, "Thank you Mrs. Perez. I believe that will work well for us."

Mrs. Perez began to walk around the building. She continued to speak, as the girls followed her.

"We have several men, as well as Mr. Perez that watch out for you and the other girls, but you'll need to keep a firm hand with the male customers. Don't give them any reason to think they can touch you or anything else for that matter. If any customer tries to touch either of you, hit them with anything handy.

"If you're on stage Serena and any of the men try to touch you, kick them as hard as you can.

"We have men from all over the world that come in on merchant ships. Many think they can misbehave while they're here, so don't hesitate to set them straight. Do you understand?"

Mrs. Perez turned and gave both a very serious stare.

"Yes, Mrs. Perez," again both women spoke almost in unison.

Mrs. Perez then instructed them to get something to eat and she would get back with them later in the morning.

Later, Serena took a bite of her breakfast.

"Do you think you'll be able to kick somebody like Mrs. Perez said?" Alicia expressed concern and then took a sip of coffee. Serena smiled when her friend winced at the taste. She then swallowed her bite and thought about the question for a second.

"I don't know. I guess if I have to I will. I'm not going to let one of them get their hands on me, I know that for certain."

Serena then took a drink of coffee and almost spit it out. Alicia laughed a little seeing Serena make a face.

The two finished breakfast and Lavina found them standing by the stage.

"Come on you two. I'll introduce you to Estelle."

They followed Lavina through the halls and back ways of the cantina until arriving at a room about three times the size of Serena and Alicia's room.

Inside were some large mirrors on the wall. Several guitars sat in various locations. Tables with tambourines and other hand herald instruments; racks of dresses and costumes, along with several large changing blinds were all strategically placed throughout the room.

A few dancers were moving about and adjusting their outfits in the mirrors. A single guitar player sat in a corner playing a song and then stopping to write in a notebook. Then he would again play a little and stop, go over the same thing and stop again to write in the notebook.

Beside a wall, a beautiful woman in a very nice dress stood leaning against a podium, studying a book. Lavina took the two girls to where this woman stood.

"Estelle, this is Serena De La Rosa and her assistant Alicia Banes."

Estelle turned to the three young women.

"Serena De La Rosa, I've heard a lot about you. Mrs. Perez feels you'll be one of our best attractions."

Serena smiled and gently shook Estelle's hand.

"I'm pleased to meet you as well, Alicia."

Alicia shook her hand also.

Lavina continued.

"Estelle is the assistant manager to Mrs. Perez. She also coordinates all the dances. So, she'll be your boss."

"Come over and have a cup of coffee with me," Estelle said and walked over to a small table; then she pulled several cups from hangers on the wall beside the table.

She poured a cup for her, but as she poured Serena a cup, she held her hand up and stopped Estelle about half-way full.

"I've already had some coffee this morning," she said.

Alicia also stopped Estelle from pouring a full cup. They all sat down and began sipping their coffee as the guitarist continued to play pieces of songs.

"I'm glad Mrs. Perez hired you Serena. We've been needing some fresh talent around here."

"Thank you, I'm glad to be here as well."

Estelle stared at her a few seconds as if studying the new dancer.

"I realize you must be very talented to win first place at the Tantico Music and Dance Festival two years in a row. But you're in an entirely new environment here at The Red Gate." Estelle took another drink of coffee and sat her cup down.

"Whatever you've learned about strict discipline to the traditional Flamenco dance can be thrown out the window of your mind right now. Do you understand?"

Serena seemed a bit surprised by this and her face expressed it.

"Don't get me wrong, Serena. Keeping the traditional foundation of the dance is fine. But those strict traditionalists, who teach you to never vary from those traditions, are the people who dance a few times a year and don't rely on the art for a living. They're people who also don't seem to realize that all those traditions they hold dear, were developed over the years in cafes and cantinas such as this one."

She picked her cup up, took another sip, sat it back down and continued.

"In fact, the Flamenco and other traditional Spanish and Mexican dances have all changed over the years and change is a part of art."

Serena tried to think of something to say about this.

"So, what am I to do? I believe I've learned everything somewhat according to the traditional methods."

Estelle smiled.

"Yes, but you've learned the Spanish Gypsy style Flamenco and from a great teacher. Your teacher, Olivia Frisco is still well known in the entertainment industry. And the Spanish Gypsy style of Flamenco is perhaps a little more flexible."

She picked her coffee up but rather than taking a drink, she seemed to consider what she wanted to tell Serena and while still holding her cup, continued.

"What I want to do is to put you on an aggressive training routine that will help you incorporate choreography techniques into your dance. You'll soon be changing your routines to keep things fresh, and eventually you'll oversee choreographing your back-up dancers. I'll take care of that for a while, but as a central dancer you must learn to organize the actions of those dancers who will be dancing to support your routines."

Serena again appeared surprised.

"I've never danced with other dancers."

Estelle finally took the drink of coffee and after sitting the cup down responded to Serena.

"As I said Serena, you should throw those strict ideas out the window. There are those who might say we in the entertainment business are making a shamble of traditions. But I should remind you, and I would also remind our critics, that without our efforts in the entertainment business the dance would die out eventually."

She paused and seemed to allow Serena to take this in. Then she continued.

"We keep the dance alive and vibrant. The way we do this is by meeting the customer's demands. And we do that by creating fresh routines and new dances. You'll be learning many new things here and you'll see in time that the dance is an art, but without funding, art cannot survive. We finance our art by being creative for our paying customers and that's how art works."

Estelle gazed across the table at Serena as if awaiting her response.

"So, when will I be able to dance?" Serena finally asked.

Seeming delighted that Serena was concerned about this, Estelle continued.

"You'll start dancing right away. Mrs. Perez runs a tight ship around here and we'll be using your talents as specials mixed into the regular program. This will immediately give our current line up a fresh face. Then, as I see what routines you have and as you learn the way our program works here, there will be new routines developed by myself. Eventually you'll develop routines for yourself and your back-up dancers."

Serena thought of this a few seconds as she made another effort to drink the coffee.

"I'm just glad I can start dancing right away."

Estelle smiled again.

"I believe Mrs. Perez made a wise decision hiring you Serena."

True to her word, Estelle had Serena dance early that afternoon. This appeared to be the best time for her to become accustomed to the new environment. The cantina was only around half-full, and the customers were not as rowdy as the evening crowd.

Serena continued to dance during this time for a while but also began to train with the other dancers. To help her learn all aspects of her new entertainment-oriented surroundings, Estelle had her learn to dance as a back-up for Fandango and various other folk dancers. This immediately began to broadened Serena's knowledge and skill level.

However, it was on an occasion that she danced as a back-up for one of the Fandango dancers that a drunken sailor rushed up to the side of the stage and latched onto Serena's leg. He then attempted to lick her leg. Shocked, she pulled to get away from him.

Suddenly and quite effectively, Lavina moved up and kicked the sailor square in the face.

The sailor let go of Serena's leg and fell back to the floor with blood running from his nose. Several men from the cantina retrieved him and carried him out.

The crowd laughed at this as Serena stood for a second, still in shock from the incident. Lavina pulled her by the arm and back into the dance that had never missed a beat otherwise.

From this time on, Serena decided she would not hesitate to insert her dance shoe into the face of an overzealous customer.

The thought of a strange drunken man licking her leg created the necessary motivation to be watchful of this happening, and either moving back and out of reach, or if need be kicking a man before he got hold of her.

Within a month of this incident it became necessary for her to kick a drunken and rowdy man. This time Serena didn't waver in kicking the man swiftly and accurately in the face.

From this point forward, the regular patrons knew Serena could, and would deal a vengeful foot to their face if they got out of line. Only the foreign sailors were careless enough to occasionally test her.

As the days, weeks and months began to pass by; the two young women immersed themselves in the new and exciting world of the cantina. Alicia immediately began to assist with waitress duties around the establishment, when not working with Serena, and as with the Cafe Flamenco, she quickly became an asset to The Red Gate.

Just as Lavina had told them when they arrived, they fell in love with the festive atmosphere.

Estelle pushed her dancers to new creative levels and Serena thrived in this aspect of the cantina.

Eventually the two young women from Tantico began to venture out and explore their new home city. Though Lavina lived with her family, she began taking them around Vista Cruz, showing the two interesting places or stores to shop for the newest fashions.

Serena and Alicia developed a fondness for the theater and shopping. Also, they would often go to a small beach area. Serena would relax and read a book while Alicia played in the surf or got some sun.

Close to a year after arriving, Serena began choreographing the routines for her own program. Her and Alicia would stay up until two or three o'clock in the morning laughing and sharpening the routines.

Then, around eight o'clock they would be drinking coffee, eating breakfast and going over notes or discussing ideas with other dancers.

As Serena's popularity increased, her photograph appeared on advertisements and posters that were put up around Vista Cruz. She would write her mother often and send some of these items home.

Olivia always delighted in her daughter's success and would mount the items carefully on the wall of the Cafe Flamenco. This always excited and inspired her students.

On a regular basis Olivia would also write to Serena and tell her of happenings around the cafe. Alicia would become quite amused as Serena would read the letters aloud to her and become very excited about something as simple as the curtains being replaced.

Serena's confidence grew strong during this time and she had no reservations of being on the path she should be. She knew in her heart that she must dance and couldn't imagine a life without the ability to express those many complex emotions inside her.

Alicia also thrived at Vista Cruz, but she always hovered under Serena's wings. Serena in turn protected and watched over Alicia as if she were a younger sister.

Though they were close to the same age, the fame and popularity Serena attained from the dance caused her to seem "larger than life" to Alicia. She enjoyed the attention and excitement that came with being near the star dancer but preferred to reside at the edge and in the shadows.

At times Alicia would clean the large stage and admire her friend's ability to dance with hundreds of eyes watching her. She thought Serena must surely be fearless and felt safe by her side.

Several years after their arrival at the Red Gate, Serena, Alicia and Lavina sat at a table together in the afternoon.

"He's looking at you again." Alicia observed the young man across the room with interest.

"I don't care, so stop telling me." Serena turned back to Lavina and continued with her conversation.

"He is nice looking though," Alicia continued. "Oh, he's getting up. I think he's coming over here, Serena!"

Alicia turned quickly to her drink and acted as if she wasn't watching him.

The young man approached the three girls with an obvious air of nervousness.

"Excuse me, Miss De La Rosa."

The young man peered down at Serena. She turned to him with a look of being disturbed.

"Can I help you?"

The well-dressed man exhibited an appearance of being from a wealthy Vista Cruz family. There was no mistaking his current and costly apparel. He carried himself well and as Alicia noticed, would have turned most young ladies' heads in Vista Cruz.

"I wondered if I could sit and maybe have a drink with you."

Serena knew these men were important to the cantina. She knew well it wouldn't be wise to treat an influential man of the city rudely.

"If you wish," she replied.

"My name is Enrique Verano." He pulled a chair out and sat down. "I must say Miss De La Rosa, you dance so beautifully. I'm sure you've been told that many times."

Serena studied the man that appeared to be three years older than her, maybe around twenty-six or twenty-seven. He ordered a drink and requested the waitress bring another round of bottled soda for the three young ladies.

"Are you related to Juan Verano?" Lavina asked the young man.

"Yes, he's my father." Enrique said this with a tone of satisfaction that Lavina knew of his family.

"Juan Verano owns much of Vista Cruz, as well as some ships." Lavina said this to Serena as if she might be interested in the young man who was seemingly attracted to her.

"Well, actually they're not real ships so much as coastal craft for moving goods up and down the coast." He replied.

The dapper young man then proceeded to talk about himself and his father for five more minutes.

Serena examined this man as he spoke, and Alicia watched her friend watching Enrique.

She had personally witnessed Serena brush off possibly hundreds of eligible young men. Many were quite good looking. Some were well off financially. None however matched the prospects of this young man.

Alicia solemnly considered if the adventure away from home would soon end. No eligible young woman of Tantico could turn down such a bright future as this man offered.

She also had no doubts that her friend possessed the charm and class to win Enrique. If ever a woman had the ability to gain a man's heart, Serena had it.

Surely, Alicia thought to herself, Serena would relinquish her dance career to become involved with this highly desirable bachelor. This would mean she would be going home to Tantico and her adventure would come to an end.

After a lengthy description of his managerial duties with his father's company, Enrique turned to Serena.

"So, do you plan on going into acting, Serena?"

Alicia now watched her friend do something amazing and realized immediately there was much more to Serena than even she was aware of.

Once Enrique had asked her this, Serena looked at him with a smile and never blinking an eye replied.

"Well, as soon as I find a rich man to marry, I'm going to Europe where I hear the casinos are the tops."

After saying this, she batted her eyes at him in an obviously flirtatious manner.

Alicia was taking a drink when Serena said this and though she contained herself while she spoke to Enrique, the eye batting caused her to come completely apart. She inhaled some of her drink as she tried to stifle a laugh.

Then she had to turn and put her head down to cough at the floor rather than all over everyone.

Enrique lightly patted her back to assist her.

Alicia glanced up at Serena and noticed she never moved out of character. She simply watched on as if having no idea why her friend was choking.

"Are you alright, child?" she now asked.

This again forced Alicia to stifle another laughing episode.

To remain in control, she had to get up and try to excuse herself, then darted towards the back rooms.

Lavina had also turned to hide her smile and laugh.

Enrique, now completely shaken, stated he should check on Alicia and left the table.

He quickly moved in a new direction around the back of Serena and Lavina to avoid them seeing him exit the cantina. Once he had left the building, Lavina laughed out loud and raised her glass to Serena.

"That was a fine piece of work, Serena."

She raised her glass and toasted Lavina, then smiled with a bit of satisfaction.

When Serena entered their room to check on Alicia, she was met at the door.

"Are you alright… child?" Alicia said with a quirky voice and laughed.

"What's that all about?"

Serena giggled. "Oh, I just didn't want him to get his hopes up."

"You're crazy," Alicia took hold of Serena's arm, as if needing something to hold herself up due to the laughing.

"You may be sorry you chased him off. He seemed like a nice guy, and rich!"

Serena smiled. "There'll be time to fall in love and get married later. Right now, I must dance."

Alicia now regained her composure and sat down on the bed. She studied her friend briefly.

"What if something happened and you couldn't dance anymore?"

Serena gazed down at her and slowly replied in a serious tone of voice.

"Every dance has a purpose… and every dancer has a destiny. I'll dance until I complete my destiny. If I don't, I'll always regret it."

She then slowly walked over to the old poster of the Flamenco dancer on the wall and ran her fingers across the faded and faceless crowd in the background. In almost a whisper she said.

"And, I have a debt to pay."

Alicia didn't understand what she meant by having a debt to pay and she was afraid to ask her friend, so she said nothing.

She did however begin to see her friend in a new way. As she watched Serena lean against the wall and stare at the old poster, she began to realize there was something much larger going on deep inside Serena.

Somehow, she felt that Serena had become part of something bigger than herself.

Alicia had a brief sensation that her friend would need her in some way during this journey.

She decided right then, as she watched the dancer stare at

the faceless crowd of that old, faded poster, she would try her best to never let Serena face the unknown future alone.

CHAPTER SEVEN:

A Lonely Cry

Serena studied Alicia from across the table. The breeze brushed the three women's hair into their faces as they sat on the outdoor patio of a local cafe.

She then reached up and gently pulled a few strands of hair from their entanglement with her newly purchased, tinted sunglasses. These were another indication of Serena's success as few people could buy such a luxury.

Their location on the patio overlooked the port and far below, ships could be seen being unloaded and loaded.

The sun felt good on her skin and Serena smiled as Alicia opened her present.

They had changed so much since first arriving in Vista Cruz. She was twenty-four years old now and Alicia turned twenty-three today.

Serena and her friend, who was also dressed in the most current fashions, were both confident, cosmopolitan women; far from the frightened young girls that stood in the door of the cantina three years earlier.

"I love it." Alicia held the necklace up to her neck to show Serena and Lavina how it looked.

"It looks great on you," Serena replied as Alicia peered down to see for herself.

Serena had become one of the most successful dancers in Vista Cruz. She now choreographed all her routines and Serena's salary had tripled since they came to Vista Cruz. She gazed out over the port and once again pulled some of her dark brown hair from her face.

As she gazed out over the ocean she felt loneliness inside that disturbed her.

"What are you thinking about?" Alicia asked as Lavina also now noticed Serena.

She didn't reply right away, but after a few seconds of thought said softly.

"The ocean smells so strong today. I wonder why."

When she said this Alicia and Lavina looked at each other with a confused expression. Serena noticed this.

"Don't you smell it?"

The other two women shook their heads, indicating they didn't. Then Lavina said. "Maybe you can smell better than we can, Serena."

"Yes, maybe that's it. Oh well, it's nothing to worry about."

The other two smiled and returned to the small celebration.

"Here you go, happy birthday Alicia!"

Alicia smiled as Lavina handed her a present.

Serena took a deep breath and tried to focus on the happy occasion. She attempted another carefree smile as Alicia worked to open the present.

She then gazed back out over the port as her two friends

laughed about Alicia's difficulty in getting the wrapping paper off the small box.

"Excuse me, Ms. De La Rosa?"

Serena turned to see a man and a woman. Then she noticed a young girl of about eight standing behind them. The girl appeared to be a bit shy, but she smiled at Serena when she noticed her.

"Yes." Serena replied.

"I told you it was her." The woman softly nudged the man as she said this.

"I hope we're not bothering you."

"No, it's okay. Can I help you?"

Alicia and Lavina now turned their attention to the small family as well.

"Well, my husband and I saw you dance a few months ago. You dance so beautifully. I just can't believe anyone can dance like that."

Serena smiled modestly as the woman said this.

"Thank you."

The woman then reached back and pulled the girl from behind her and to the front of her and her husband.

"Our daughter Lore wants to be a dancer. We told her about you and we got her one of your photographs. She has it on her wall at home. She would really like to meet you if you have time."

Serena now took her tinted sunglasses off and gazed down at the young girl.

"Yes, I have time."

She then studied the girl for a few seconds.

"Hmm, yes, you have the look of a dancer alright."

Serena turned her head slightly when she said this, as if she had discovered some unseen trait in the girl's face. This immediately brought a very big smile from Lore.

"Really?" the young girl asked gleefully. "I hope I can be as good as you some day, Ms. De La Rosa."

Serena smiled lovingly and then put her hand to the girl's cheek.

"I believe you can be a great dancer, Lore."

Now Lore beamed with obvious pride and her eyes sparkled with delight.

"Thank you so much Ms. De La Rosa. Thank you. Come on Lore, I'm sure Ms. De La Rosa is very busy. Thank you again Ms. De La Rosa."

The couple ushered Lore away and Serena waved bye to the young girl as she left with her parents.

"Well, you've become quite famous, Serena." Lavina said with a smile and then took a drink.

Serena said nothing but smiled back slightly as she put her tinted sunglasses back on. She then gazed back out to the ocean.

The lonely feeling came back immediately. Maybe it was the smell of the ocean. It made her feel as if, something was missing inside her. She tried to dismiss the feeling.

She turned back to her friends and once again attempted to become involved in the conversation.

That evening Serena stared at the faceless crowd of the old

poster on the wall in their room.

Alicia sat on her bed and silently watched her friend. She seemed to be trying to solve a math problem, or maybe locate the missing piece of a puzzle.

Serena would become increasingly distant as the days went by. Alicia dismissed this as an effect of her becoming a star.

Certainly, Serena was modest enough considering her fame. The quiet and detached woman she was slowly becoming must be from having so many admirers every day Alicia thought.

A month after the birthday gathering, Serena danced on stage at the Cantina.

As had become usual, The Red Gate was packed and couldn't hold any more people. The waitresses fought to get through the crowd.

Towards the end of the dance Serena noticed an older, but distinguished gentleman sitting in the corner office area with Mr. and Mrs. Perez.

She wondered about this a little as Mrs. Perez seldom sat and watched the entertainment.

The next morning Serena, Alicia and Lavina, drank coffee and worked on notes in her book.

"What if we add another dancer on this end and when I move to the left side of the stage, they move to the front and do that side-step thing we want to do?"

She pointed to the notebook and Lavina nodded as if she understood and was considering it.

"Serena, girls, good morning," Mrs. Perez came walking up

to the table with the man Serena had noticed sitting next to her the night before.

"May we sit down?"

"Yes, please do. We're just talking about the new routine for this Saturday."

They sat down at the table and Mrs. Perez asked one of the waitresses to bring some coffee for them.

"This is a good friend of ours, Torre Cantelli."

"Hello Serena, ladies, I'm so pleased to meet you. I'll apologize in advance for my poor Spanish."

Serena shook his hand.

"I'm happy to meet you, Mr. Cantelli. I noticed you sitting with Mrs. Perez last night. Did you enjoy the show?"

Mr. Cantelli smiled. "I did enjoy it. In fact, I'm from Italy, where I have a traveling variety show of my own."

He took a cup of coffee being handed to him by the waitress and continued.

"I've traveled here on a number of vacations, oh let's see, four times now."

He looked at Mrs. Perez as if expecting affirmation.

"Well, I never came during the war, but I believe I first came in 1909 wasn't it, Marguerite?

Mrs. Perez thought for a moment.

"Yes, I believe it was 1909 the first time we met, my how the time goes by."

"Indeed." He replied with another smile and then turned back to Serena.

"I really enjoyed your dances, Serena. Marguerite tells me

you've been choreographing your own routines for several years now."

"Yes, I'm very grateful for the opportunity the Perezes have given me. They've been great to Alicia and me over the last three years."

Mrs. Perez smiled as she took a sip of her coffee. She then sat her cup down and pulled herself closer to the table as if she were about to negotiate a deal.

"Serena, I told Torre he could speak with you this morning. He presented something to me last night and I feel you may wish to hear his proposal."

Serena turned her head a little, indicating she was curious as to what the proposal could be.

"I'll listen to what you have to say Mr. Cantelli." She replied with an interested tone.

Now Mr. Cantelli sat up in his chair as if he were about to negotiate a business deal.

"Ms. De La Rosa, as I said, I have a variety show back in Italy. We have dancers as well as a comedian. I recently acquired the services of a pretty good magician also. We travel throughout Europe and have been quite successful. People want a variety now, not just one show with one type of entertainment. I would like to add your talent to my show."

Serena looked at Mrs. Perez with a surprised expression.

"I don't want to lose you, Serena. However, you've exceeded the capacity of our little cantina here. I'm paying you as much as I can, but you're worth more. This cantina can hold no more customers. We're always full and this is in large part due to the program you've help establish here."

Mrs. Perez paused briefly.

"You're welcome to stay here as long as you want. I felt that you should hear Mr. Cantelli's offer though. He has a much larger venue to showcase talent such as yours. And he can pay you closer to what you're worth. As much as I love you and want you to stay, the right thing to do is to allow you the capacity to grow if you desire to do that."

She then smiled, and Serena again knew her mother had chosen wisely when she chose the Perezes three years earlier.

"Well, I, um, I should think about it I suppose," Serena replied as they all seemed focused on her.

"Yes, that'll be fine; I'll be here for three more weeks. I would like to know as soon as possible though so we can discuss the details if you decide to join our company. Also, I would rather secure the services of a good Flamenco guitarist and other musicians here in Mexico, if needed."

He then stood up from the table.

"Marguerite, it's been a pleasure as always. You know my hotel; please send word as soon as possible."

"I'll do that Torre, thank you."

He then made his way out of the cantina with a splash of sunlight as he passed through the door.

"Italy, Europe, I can't believe it!!" Lavina pushed Serena lightly on the arm as she made a fuss over the offer.

Serena smiled, but only to please Lavina. Inside, her thoughts raced.

Alicia appeared concerned. Serena had known her long enough to feel certain she was worried. Certainly, she must be concerned whether she would be able to go should Serena choose to accept the offer.

She then turned to Mrs. Perez and realized she had also been studying the dancer.

"What do you think, Mrs. Perez?" Serena asked.

The waitress brought a coffee pot around and Mrs. Perez held her cup out for a refill.

"I think you must make your own decision. But I'll tell you this. I've known Mr. Cantelli for many years. I believe he's a good man and treats his people fairly. As far as opportunities go, I feel this is a good one for a dancer such as you. You've outgrown this cantina. I would love for you to stay. But, if you do stay, there will be many people in Europe that'll miss the chance to see how beautiful the Flamenco can be."

When Mrs. Perez said the last part, concerning people missing a chance to see the Flamenco dance, Serena felt a pull in the pit of her stomach. Though she still wanted to think about her decision, she somehow knew this offer involved the path she must follow.

"Thank you, Mrs. Perez. I think that will help me a lot in making a decision."

Serena sat back in her chair with an expression of bewilderment and then held out her coffee cup for a refill.

The waitress had already walked away from the table, but when she noticed Serena she moved quickly across the room to refill the star dancer's cup.

Lavina and Alicia simply sat and gazed at their friend who seemed to be far away in thought.

Later that evening, Alicia sat on the bed when Serena walked in after her final dance. Alicia still appeared worried.

"So, what do you think of Mr. Cantelli's offer?" She asked, as Alicia began helping her out of her dress.

"I guess the decision is yours to make not mine."

Once Alicia had undone the fastenings, Serena appeared to breathe a sigh of relief and struggled to free herself from the elaborate Spanish-style dancing dress.

"Well, the decision is not all mine, if you don't want to go, I'm not going without you; you should know that by now."

Serena had her back to Alicia, but she caught a glimpse of her in a small mirror sitting on the chest of drawers.

Alicia smiled as a young girl might when Serena said this, and her face appeared to light up. Serena turned a little, to be sure her friend didn't catch her smiling in the same mirror.

"I'll think about it tonight," she said as Serena turned back around.

"Alright, but just keep in mind that we're a team. If we go, we go as a team and if we stay we stay as a team."

Alicia smiled again at this and nodded her head in agreement.

The next morning Serena found Alicia sitting alone in the cantina.

She poured herself a cup of coffee and went to the table to sit with her.

"So, have you decided?" Serena then took a sip of her coffee but watched Alicia from over the rim of the cup.

Alicia glanced down at her fingers and rubbed her finger

nails, as if a little nervous. She then spoke softly.

"I've decided that I don't know what I would do if I wasn't with you. My life would be boring. I can't imagine anything other than assisting you and being with you."

Serena sat her cup down. She wanted to smile at this comment but remained serious.

"It's a long way from home, and a long way from your family. Does that worry you?"

Alicia turned to Serena.

"You're my family now. The only thing that worries me is if for some reason I couldn't be with you. I don't think I could handle that. As long as I'm with you I'm not afraid."

Serena glanced down at her coffee when Alicia said this. She hadn't considered the possibility of Alicia not being able to stay with her. She couldn't bear the thought of not having Alicia with her.

She looked back up to Alicia. At this instant she decided something in her heart. She then told that decision to Alicia.

"I promise you, we'll stay together on this journey. No matter what may come, we will stay together and help protect each other."

Alicia smiled when Serena said this.

"Then I'll go, as long as I can stay with you."

Serena smiled and picked up her coffee. Then Alicia also picked up her coffee to take a drink.

Lavina now came to the table that Serena and Alicia sat at.

"So, have you decided yet?" she asked as she sat down.

"Yes," Serena replied.

"Well, don't keep me in suspense. Are you going or not?!"

"Alicia just said she would go. So, if she goes with me, I'll go."

Lavina seemed content after Serena said this. She looked at the table as if a little envious.

"I wish I could go somewhere like Europe, but it's just too far. I can't imagine not being able to see my family every night."

She held her cup out for the waitress who came from the kitchen with a coffee pot. Serena held hers out for a refill also.

"I believe I made my decision yesterday when Mrs. Perez said a lot of people would get to see the Flamenco that wouldn't otherwise. I wanted Alicia to make her decision though. I wouldn't go without her."

Once Serena told the Perezes her decision, Mrs. Perez contacted Mr. Cantelli and he soon arrived to negotiate the terms of Serena's employment.

"We can decide on the terms of the contract Serena and I'll have the official papers drawn up for us to sign in a few days."

She turned to Mrs. Perez whom she'd asked to be present with her at the negotiations.

"Serena, you should be clear with Mr. Cantelli about what you want. These things will be put in the contract if you both agree. Now is the time to establish the terms of your employment with Mr. Cantelli."

She thought about what Mrs. Perez said for a few seconds and then quickly replied.

"Alicia must have a contract as my assistant. If she is

mistreated or dismissed from employment for any reason, I'll not dance for you anymore. We're a team and if you want me you'll have to take her as well."

Mrs. Perez laughed a little as she recalled Serena's demands three years earlier. "I'm afraid she'll not budge on that stipulation Torre."

Mr. Cantelli appeared a bit surprised.

"Well, I ah, suppose we could, maybe work something out. But you must understand Serena; I have two partners who hold ownership in this company as well."

He then paused as if remembering something.

"At one time I owned the entire company and there would have been no problem putting that into Alicia's contract. But during the war there was little demand for entertainment and I almost went bankrupt. The only way to hold on was to sell part of the company. After the war everything picked back up and we are in high demand again."

Serena considered this for a moment.

"I understand your position, Mr. Cantelli. But that is the first and most important item on my list."

She gazed over to the stage area where Alicia and Lavina stood talking.

"I'll not take any chances on Alicia being in a position to come home alone or not be with me. She's always assisted me; she's my best friend as well. You'll have to find a way, or you'll return to Italy without me."

Mr. Cantelli thought about the situation as he sipped his coffee. After a few moments he appeared to arrive at a decision.

"There's no problem giving Alicia a contract as your assistant. An entertainer of your talent will generally have an assistant or even two. The problem is putting the type of guarantee you speak of into her contract. Her contract as an assistant will be a simple one-page agreement. I'm sure my partners would notice such a thing and object."

He took another sip of coffee and continued.

"However, as the artist, your contract will be much more extensive. Perhaps we could put a simple stipulation on the third or fourth page. Something short but clear that, should for any reason Alicia be dismissed or removed from employment you will have the option to cancel your obligations to the agreement. It's unusual, but I doubt anyone would notice it. If they did however, I would have much better grounds to stand on since as the entertainer you're in a position to ask for such a thing."

Serena appeared thoughtful after Mr. Cantelli said this. Then after a moment she replied in a deliberate tone.

"That'll be sufficient Mr. Cantelli, as long as Alicia's security is covered in either her contract or mine. I'm sorry if this puts you in a difficult position. But the fact that there are others involved in the company's management make it that much more important for me to make such demands."

"I understand, Serena. And I do own the majority of share in the company, so I do have a little room to maneuver. I own forty percent and the other partners own thirty percent each, so if they don't get together on this for some reason, I still have the weight to make such an agreement in the manner I suggested. I just don't want to create a problem with my partners as they depend on me to make good business decisions. In the method I proposed though I suspect we'll be fine."

After negotiating the additional terms, he left with his notes and assured Serena he would return in a few days with contracts for her and Alicia to sign.

"I suppose you and Alicia should start getting ready for the trip," Mrs. Perez said as she stood up. Serena stood up and immediately hugged her.

She laughed a little and embraced Serena as well.

When Alicia saw this and realized the negotiations were over she came and hugged Mrs. Perez as well.

"You're going to knock those Europeans off their feet, Serena."

The three women shared a few special moments together before the cantina became too busy for such a thing.

"You've been so good to us Mrs. Perez. We'll miss you so much."

Serena then took Mrs. Perez' hand in a subtle show of affection for the woman that had been their friend and employer for over three years.

As it turned out, this would be the last few peaceful moments before a flurry of frantic activity needed to obtain passage on the ship as well as pack, purchase necessities and close loose ends before leaving.

The Vista Cruz newspapers wrote several articles about Serena's approaching departure to Europe and many fans came by to see her dance again and wish her well.

Flowers began arriving daily at The Red Gate and once again Serena realized how important her dancing had become to the people of Vista Cruz. She felt a responsibility to the Flamenco and vowed never to abuse this gift she'd been given.

She also considered her mother during this time and knew she must have been heartbroken when she could no longer dance and express this beautiful art as she once had.

Her resolve increased to show her mother she'd been successful through lovingly teaching her daughter the beautiful Flamenco dance.

The day of departure finally came. When the group arrived at the port to board the ship Serena again had the recollection of the lonely feeling.

Now, the smell of the sea became so strong that she slowed as they moved closer to the ship. Her heart beat rapidly and a mild panic began to stir inside her.

Serena stopped. The others all stopped and looked back at her. She took a deep breath.

"Are you alright?" Alicia came back to her.

"Yes, I'm alright. I just remembered something."

"What is it, is there something I forgot to bring?" Alicia expressed concern.

"No, it's just, I..." She looked back towards Vista Cruz nervously as the others watched her. She wanted to run from the sea. Everything inside her was telling her to run away.

Then she thought of her mother. This was her path, she mustn't waver. She turned back towards the ship in front of her and paying no attention to the others, who watched her curiously, she began to walk forward as if laboring against a strong breeze.

"Are you alright?" Mr. Cantelli asked as she passed him.

"Yes." Serena replied, completely focused on moving towards the huge ship.

Now the others glanced at each other with a bit of confusion as they filed in behind her.

While they boarded the large ship, Alicia noticed Serena glancing out over the ocean. Then she turned her attention back to the boarding bridge.

Once on board, Serena appeared to relax some. The two women located Mr. Cantelli and they all went to eat lunch as the ship slowly left the dock.

"You girls will love Europe. You'll need to learn Italian as soon as possible though since most all the performers speak it. There's a young woman whose father is a Spaniard and she speaks Spanish as well as Italian. I'll assign her to assist the two of you until you can communicate in Italian."

Serena gave no reply but sipped a glass of wine, still appearing nervous.

That night after the ship was far out to sea; Alicia awoke and wanted a drink of water.

She got a drink and went to lie back down but realized Serena's bed was empty.

Quickly getting dressed, she began cautiously searching for her friend through the dimly lit halls of the ship.

After walking around the large ship long enough to become

very concerned, she finally spotted Serena on the deck, alone and gazing out over the dark ocean.

For a few moments Alicia stood at a distance curiously watching her.

Serena appeared to be hypnotized by the water and never moved during the time Alicia watched her.

Slowly, she approached her friend, hoping she wouldn't startle her.

"I woke up and noticed your bed empty, I got a little worried."

Serena looked at Alicia and smiled slightly but said nothing as she turned her attention back to the dark sea.

"How long have you been here?"

Serena seemed hesitant to say anything, but after a pause replied.

"Several hours, I think." Then a long silence went by.

Alicia gazed out into the night to see what Serena had found so interesting.

Then Serena said something that she didn't understand.

"I'm beginning to realize, it may be lost forever."

Alicia thought about what she said for a few seconds before asking about the odd statement.

"What's lost forever?"

Without turning, Serena replied in a sad tone, "the part of me I left out there, alone in the sea."

Suddenly and unexpectedly, the reasons for Serena's behavior, as well as her unique characteristics, fell into place in Alicia's mind.

She understood Serena had fallen from a boat, and that she'd washed up on a beach, but she never actually thought much about it. Serena spoke very little about the matter and somehow the event always seemed like a simple thing to Alicia.

Now with the black and lonely ocean spread out before her, she realized what the ordeal her friend endured really meant.

This abrupt realization caused a flood of emotions inside her. Tears welled up in her eyes. Alicia turned her head away, so Serena wouldn't see as several rolled down her checks.

She wanted to be strong for the friend that was like a sister, but she barely held herself together as the emotions surged inside her heart. She wanted to cry on Serena's shoulder and tell her she had never realized the pain she must have endured. But Alicia knew this wasn't what her friend needed now.

With a great effort Alicia gazed out into the ocean and grasped the rail tightly to keep Serena from seeing her tremble.

When her friend began to speak again Alicia felt relieved. Even though Serena's words caused another surge of emotions, she knew if she had to say anything, her voice would betray her.

"I've realized that I left Gina out there that night. I abandoned her. I was so mad that she would take such a chance. I didn't want to be the foolish girl who got herself into that situation.

"I knew there would be no one to miss her when she drowned alone in the sea. No one would look for her. When her body washed up on a shore somewhere, no one would come to claim her.

"I pushed her away from me and I abandoned her, just as my real mother had left me. I decided I would die anonymous and I rejected her. I left her out there, alone and scared in the dark ocean."

Serena stopped speaking for a few seconds. Alicia wanted to say something, but she could think of nothing adequate for this situation. She remained silent as another tear fell and landed on her hand.

She remained quiet, hoping not to betray the torrent of emotions inside her. If she kept her head turned, maybe Serena wouldn't know how broken she really was at this moment.

Alicia then gently put her arm around Serena's waist. It was the only thing she was able to do. But it seemed to help her friend and after a short break Serena began to speak again.

"For so long it didn't matter to me. I gladly became Serena Frisco. I tried to forget Gina from the time I woke up on the beach. I intentionally ignored any thoughts of her. But as time has passed, I've begun to realize she simply made a mistake and I didn't stay true to myself as I should have."

Serena took a deep breath of the moist air. Then, she continued with a voice of weariness.

"We all make mistakes, she just made a mistake. I've begun to feel ashamed of myself for leaving her out there. I want so badly to apologize to her. I want to bring her back and tell her I'm sorry. Gina didn't deserve to be abandoned and forgotten that way. She had a life and dreams of her own. But she's too far away now. I've tried to bring her back, but I can't find her. I don't even remember her face anymore. There's only Serena now."

She paused.

"Now my heart breaks for her, because I feel that she's somewhere, lost, alone, crying for help. I want so badly to help her, but I've pushed her so far away that I can't find her."

After this, they stood for a while and said nothing. Then Alicia pulled on Serena and managed to say, "Let's go back to the room."

Once she got Serena to the room and back in bed, Alicia laid back down. She held her hand gently to her mouth as several tears dropped to her pillow. She felt incapable of helping Serena and this frightened her more than anything.

But Alicia knew at this moment she would never leave her friend alone. She would stay by her side always. Somehow, or someday she would find a way to help her. With this thought in mind she slowly drifted back to sleep.

Several days later, a crewman unlocked a door and after opening it, Serena, Alicia and the guitar player that Mr. Cantelli had hired in Mexico all walked into the musty room.

"Yes, this will work." Serena said, after examining the large room.

A few wooden chairs sat about in disarray. A small stage stood against the wall opposite the door.

From what the crewman had told them, this was a rehearsal room at one time. But as the entertainment changed, the room became used less and less.

"It smells a little stuffy in here." Alicia noted. "Can we leave the door open?"

"Yes, let's leave the door open. Otherwise it'll be hot in here."

Serena then stepped up on the small stage in a testing manner.

After a brief inspection she stepped back down and began talking with the guitar player.

As she and the guitarist discussed the music to play, Alicia attempted to straighten the room a bit.

Then, the guitarist began to play a song Alicia was very familiar with. She pulled a chair in front of the stage and sat down as Serena began to dance.

Her heart began to beat faster as she realized the person on stage was not the same person she'd seen dance thousands of times before.

This woman was still her best friend, but since Serena had told her about the night alone in the violent sea, Alicia now saw her as never before.

Her hands began to sweat as the music became faster and Serena twirled about and tapped her feet in rapid staccato.

She became a little dizzy as something inside her attempted to identify the exact reason Serena danced as she does.

Alicia didn't know precisely what it was, but she now knew it had something to do with what was going on deep inside the dancer.

There were many complex emotions that seemed to be flowing out of her as she danced. She moved with an almost violent force. Yet, with these movements came a release of energy. Alicia finally realized that Serena danced to live. If she didn't dance, she would somehow come apart.

As her mind grappled with these things, someone walked

up beside her, she turned to see a passenger had come in to watch Serena.

The next day Serena again stepped up on the small stage to rehearse.

While the guitarist strummed out the tune, Alicia played the tambourine lightly and watched Serena.

Again, she noticed tiny details of Serena's dance that she'd not noticed before, facial expressions; as if Serena were against a strong wind and slow movements that expressed beauty and strife almost at the same time.

When the music stopped, Serena made her signature move, as if she had an audience.

Then when she turned her head back and quickly stepped off the stage, Alicia became surprised by a sudden applause. She turned around and realized the small room had become half-full of passengers, all watching Serena with delight.

As the days passed, the rehearsal room became packed and Alicia often had to struggle to assist her friend. This would be the situation for the remainder of the trip. When Serena danced, the audience appeared.

Several nights later, Alicia awoke to find Serena's bed empty again. She sat and stared at the bed for a few seconds, wondering if she should go look for her.

Then lightning erupted from outside and lit up their small cabin. Alicia's heart felt as if it might stop as she became aware of the storm.

Thoughts began to race through her mind. What if Serena was out on the deck with the storm raging? What if she'd become washed overboard?

Tears again welled up in her eyes as she quickly put on her robe and darted out the door. She ran to the place she'd found Serena before.

When she came to the door leading out to the deck, she could see the rain whipping in furiously. She crept slowly up to the doorway and gazed out into the storm.

There sat Serena on the edge of a deck chair, motionless in the harsh storm; drenched from the violent rain.

Her hair lay flat against her body. Her head turned upwards, as if she wanted the rain to land on her bare face. Her eyes were closed, and she appeared to be somewhere else in thought.

A cry slipped from Alicia's mouth and she put her hand up quickly to muffle it. She turned from the heartbreaking sight and slid away, with her back against the wall.

She began to cry. She couldn't stop herself as her heart ached for Serena.

When she was a safe distance from the door she sat against the wall and grieved for her. She could no longer cry silently; she knew she was far enough from the door that Serena couldn't hear her. She wept eagerly to release the sadness inside, only moving over from time to time to glance out the door.

Her greatest fear was of Serena walking through the door to find her friend in an emotional break down. What would she think of such a thing, Serena De La Rosa; the woman who had weathered so much heartbreak and still managed to triumph as a magnificent Flamenco dancer.

Alicia then felt ashamed of herself and this made her cry even more. How could she help her friend when she could only wait on the wet floor with tears in her eyes?

Finally, exhausted and feeling stronger from the release of emotions, she regained her composure.

She moved back up to the doorway and carefully peeked around again as she cleared the last few tears from her eyes. Serena still sat silently in the wind and rain.

Alicia carefully positioned herself in the corner of the door, so she could watch over her troubled friend. She sat there trying not to move as the storm blew its fury onto the decks and invaded the small corner of the door she sat in.

She became soaked, but she didn't care. She wouldn't leave Serena. Sleep beckoned her, and she began to doze off, her head lowering and then jerking suddenly up time to time.

Still, Serena sat motionless in the storm; with the same unnatural strength she displayed on stage. She seemed to have merged with it, as if she wanted to somehow be a part of it.

What felt to be an hour passed, and just as Alicia had dozed off and awoke again, she saw Serena stand up.

Alicia quickly moved away from the door and ran back to the room. Again, tears came as she became frightened Serena would discover she'd watched over her.

In their cabin, she pulled her wet clothes off and desperately put a long nightgown on.

Just as she climbed into bed and covered up, Serena came in.

Alicia lay motionless with her back to Serena. She heard her wet dress dripping onto the floor. Then, the dancer moved quietly into the small bathroom to change. Finally, she lay down.

Trembling, to remain motionless, Alicia lay awake under her covers. While lying in the bed, she realized in her heart that she'd grown up out on the rain-drenched deck of the ship. She'd been a carefree young girl until now.

As she attempted to breathe quietly, she recalled the days at the Cafe Flamenco and The Red Gate. She'd always basked in the light of Serena's triumph on stage. She'd loved the life of adventure that her friend's dancing had brought to her.

Only now, did she realize Serena's magnificent skills and talent had roots that connected to a dark and lonely place deep inside her.

She felt certain no one else knew of this, and Alicia resolved to protect her friend, no matter what may come. She wouldn't be the careless and carefree friend anymore. She would be the friend Serena needed from this point on. With this thought, Alicia finally fell asleep.

The rest of the trip went smoothly, even though Serena remained distant and preoccupied by the open sea.

Alicia sensed a burden lift from her heart when they finally floated into the Italian port of Naples. She wanted her friend back. She now understood that the ocean held some form of control over Serena and Alicia was glad when they could get away from it.

CHAPTER EIGHT:

Flower of My Heart

Once they were on land, Serena slowly returned to the person Alicia knew and loved. Yet this person was not the same one she knew when they left Vista Cruz.

She had no doubt returning to the sea had changed Serena in some way, but she also knew it was herself that had changed more than Serena.

Alicia had learned something about her friend that she somehow never saw until that night on the deck of the ship. Perhaps she was the only one that knew this about the dancer and she was glad Serena had told her the things she did. Other than Olivia, she knew Serena wouldn't have told anyone else these things; and this became a bond between them.

In Naples, a dainty little dancer floated into the office of Mr. Cantelli's entertainment company. She appeared to be around eighteen-years-old, maybe nineteen.

She was dressed in what Serena and Alicia immediately recognized to be the current fashion. Her dark brown hair was cut short as was also the current trend.

"Mimi, this is Serena De La Rosa, a famous Flamenco dancer from Mexico. She's joined our company. And this is Alicia, her assistant. I want you to help them as they don't speak Italian."

The young woman waved shyly as if she wasn't sure how to greet them. Mr. Cantelli continued.

"Mimi is one of our line dancers. She dances in our Cancan program and as I mentioned on the ship, her father is Spanish, and her mother is Italian. She speaks both languages fluently and can help you learn Italian."

Serena walked over to Mimi and shook her hand. "I'm pleased to meet you Mimi."

"I'm pleased to meet you too, Ms. De La Rosa."

Serena immediately felt a fondness for this young woman, though she wasn't initially sure of the reason.

"How long have you been with this company?" Serena asked.

"I've been with the company around three years, Ms. De La Rosa."

"Please, call me Serena."

"Yes Ms., I mean Serena."

She continued her interest in Mimi. "How old are you?"

Mimi replied meekly, "Nineteen."

"So, you came to work here when you were sixteen?"

Mimi appeared reserved and hesitant to answer the question. Then she replied, "Yes, I was sixteen."

Noticing Mimi was uncomfortable with the questions, Serena didn't ask anything else.

They walked into the large company building. When they found a place to sit down, all three sat and watched the activity around the building.

Mimi now relaxed a little and after a few moments she began to talk as she stared out into the activity of the open area.

"My mother danced for this company. I learned to dance from her. My father left us for another dancer and I've not seen him since I was twelve-years-old."

She glanced at Serena, as if to see whether this shocked her or not. When she showed no expression, Mimi continued.

"My mother and I did alright until she was hurt in an automobile accident. She couldn't dance anymore, so Mr. Cantelli let me take her place. He was so kind to do that. I wasn't a very good dancer at first."

She laughed a little, as if recalling her initial dancing skills.

"We have an apartment about twelve blocks from here."

Serena and Alicia said nothing. After Mimi had told them this she turned to them again. They both smiled compassionately, and she smiled back in understanding.

An even stronger connection grew in Serena's heart for this young woman.

She and Alicia began working with Mimi during the several weeks they waited as other performers arrived and began to prepare for the next tour.

Most all the performers had gone home or on an extended vacation after their previous tour of Europe. Now they began to return by ones and twos, to get ready for the next tour.

The company's facilities in Naples consisted of offices and a storage area that housed the equipment and items needed for the entertainment company.

Also, a large open area of the main building could be used

for rehearsals and practicing. The three women often strolled around the open area and talked together.

They watched as a few performers sorted costumes and a magician with his assistant worked on some equipment.

"Mimi, I want you to teach us Italian as quickly as possible." Serena told the young woman.

"Alicia, we should learn as soon as we can. I don't want to be at a disadvantage any longer than necessary. We should always try to speak in Italian if we know any of the words."

Alicia nodded in agreement

"We can start doing that right away if you wish. There are some similarities in Spanish and Italian." Mimi responded with enthusiasm.

"Yes, please, we'll begin right away Mimi. Let us try to speak Italian first and then you can help us if needed."

While they worked on their Italian, and as the upcoming tour came closer, Mimi expressed concerns to Serena and Alicia.

Several days later she spoke with a tone of caution. "You should be careful around Tonia and Carla."

The other performers had begun to arrive in earnest. The building had become more and more active as the women spoke together.

"What do you mean?" Serena asked slowly as she struggled for the words.

Mimi smiled and helped her several times in choosing the correct ones. Then she replied slowly in Italian.

"They order all of the dancers around. They boss me around all the time. I don't like it, but what can I do?"

Alicia asked her to repeat what she'd said. Mimi repeated it and then said a few words in Spanish.

After Alicia tried to reply in Italian she became frustrated and blurted out in Spanish.

"Are they the boss or just trying to be the boss?"

Serena frowned at Alicia, but then tried to catch Mimi's reply in Italian, and then in Spanish as both women seemed to only catch a few of the words.

"I don't think they've been made a boss of any kind, but the stage manager doesn't want to organize the dancers and he doesn't know how to choreograph dances. Tonia is the only one that knows how to put the dances together. So, they just, sort of boss everyone around."

Serena considered this new development as she rehearsed for the coming tour.

The very next day Tonia arrived. Just as Mimi implied, there would be no mistaking her for anyone else.

Serena and Alicia viewed the ill-tempered woman from across the room. She wasted no time in making her presence known to the other dancers directly upon arrival.

"I don't know all of what she's saying, but none of it sounds very nice," Alicia commented.

Serena simply studied the loud woman as she appeared to be upset with several dancers.

Soon Carla arrived and took to following Tonia around. From what Serena could observe, Carla appeared to be bossed around almost as much as everyone else. Yet, she was inexplicably tethered by Tonia's side, whether she wanted to be or not.

Eventually, Tonia made her way around to Serena and Alicia. She tried to tell them what to do but Serena simply stood and stared at her.

Alicia also stood firm by Serena's side. She had personally witnessed Serena fight off many sailors and rough men from the stage, and though she'd never seen her use her hands to fight, she felt sure Serena wouldn't allow herself to be bossed by this woman.

Serena and Tonia both appeared to be around the same age and size. Tonia was a pretty woman and had long dark hair as Serena did. Yet Alicia felt that Tonia's poor personality made her much less attractive than Serena.

After neither woman gave a response or made any move to accommodate Tonia, she eventually gave up and said something seemingly degrading to them as she walked away, smugly laughing.

"What do you think?" Alicia asked her friend. After a few seconds of thought Serena replied with confidence.

"I think that woman will cross the line with me sooner or later. I also believe she'll regret that day."

Alicia smiled slightly, but made no comment, she simply nodded. She also felt Tonia would regret the day she crossed the line with Serena.

The two moved over to an area they'd been using for rehearsals. The large building now bustled with activity and a wide range of noises as the various acts brushed up their routines. The entire company would move into launch mode soon.

Once they set out on tour, the group would continue to move from location to location until the tour ended nine months later. They would start in Italy and finish in England.

This would be a learning experience for both Serena and Alicia. Mimi worked hard to help the two get oriented with the new environment and language.

Finally, the launch day arrived, and the entire company loaded equipment into trucks and the entertainers then went to the train station to begin the busy touring season.

For the most part, the entertainers would travel by train, though on occasions they would travel in buses, trucks and even boats.

Serena ignored Tonia and a relationship of neither speaking with each other developed. But she severely disliked the way Tonia treated the other dancers.

While on the train, Serena knocked on Mr. Cantelli's compartment. Once inside she sat and spoke with him about the way Tonia treated the dancers.

"I don't like the way Tonia treats the dancers either, Serena. But she's the only one, other than you, that has adequate choreography skills to lead the dancers.

"When you're ready to take those responsibilities over, just let me know and I'll move Tonia out of that position. I never gave her the lead dancer position to begin with, but since I have no one else right now I can't do much about it."

Serena nodded in agreement and made her way back to the small compartment on the train.

The trains weren't very comfortable and although Serena

eventually learned to sleep on them, she didn't sleep very soundly.

Soon the days turned into weeks and the weeks into months.

A routine developed, and the two women became more proficient in their new language and positions in the traveling show.

Early one morning, Alicia watched as Serena gazed out the train window while the German countryside passed by.

They'd now been on the tour for five months and with a little more than half the tour over Serena and Alicia had become accustomed to trains, boats, bus and truck travel.

Alicia watched her friend for several moments before finally asking her.

"What are you thinking about?"

She turned to Alicia, who sat across from her on a bench seat, still holding a blanket, attempting to get some rest.

"Mother," was all Serena said.

She then turned back to the window and appeared to be searching for Olivia somewhere in the countryside.

Alicia had witnessed her friend gaze out over the audience, and on her face, she seemed to see all of them at the same time.

Now, she appeared to be gazing out over an invisible audience rolling by; searching for her mother's face amongst the crowd.

Traveling constantly meant the letters from Olivia were slow to catch up to the company. Every month or so some of the crew would return from Naples and bring the mail. Serena expressed a need for the letters from Olivia, just as a flower needed sunshine.

She would almost tremble when the letters finally arrived. Alicia would wait to open her own mail as Serena would smile and read the letters from Olivia with joy. She would show the tiny piece of cloth to Alicia and explain it was from a dress her mother was making.

Finally, after going through all her mother's letters, as a small child might, Serena would ask Alicia about her mail. Alicia would then react as if she had almost forgotten she had letters and begin reading hers. Serena would sit down beside her and examine them closely as Alicia read aloud.

This was in fact the only time Serena showed the unusual innocent side of her nature. Alicia marveled at this in her mind and again realized this to be a part of Serena only she or Olivia would ever see. Somehow these letters from her mother magically brought the little girl out of this magnificent Flamenco dancer. Alicia began to understand that Serena had not been able to complete her childhood with her real mother and perhaps this was happening now with her adoptive mother.

Alicia thought of these things and then hoped they would get some mail soon. She wanted to see Serena laugh and smile brightly as she always would after receiving letters from her mother. She pulled the blanket back up over her and drifted off to sleep again as the train clicked out its rhythmic sounds and vibrations.

The company performed few shows in Germany as the economy still hadn't recovered from the war. Everyone cheered up when they rolled into Belgium. The atmosphere continued to improve as they moved from show to show.

Tonia however continued to boss all the dancers except Serena and Alicia. Serena's performance had nothing to do with the other dancers and this kept Tonia out of her hair for the most part.

Serena requested Mimi to assist her regularly and Mr. Cantelli agreed, much to the chagrin of Tonia.

Mimi tried very hard to stay away from Tonia, but since Mimi danced in the Cancan routines this was almost impossible.

As time went by, Tonia expressed an effort to boss Mimi around more and became extra critical of her simply because Serena made efforts to protect the petite little dancer.

While the tour came closer to the end, everyone became aware of an impending showdown between Serena and Tonia, with Mimi unfortunately being caught in the middle.

Serena told Mimi to hold herself together and be strong. "That woman will regret it if she ever harms you in any way." Serena became more and more agitated as the days passed. When the actual event took place, it happened so fast that everyone except Serena became completely shocked.

Tonia by this time had become increasingly brazen with her rants against the line dancers.

Alicia stood beside Serena in an Amsterdam theater. The company had arrived the night before and now as the equipment moved in on dollies through the back doors the dancers attempted to rehearse in a small area backstage.

Possibly because Serena hadn't intervened on Mimi's behalf so far, Tonia felt she had a free reign over the dancers. She may have felt Serena was afraid of her and wouldn't do anything to assist Mimi or the other dancers. If this was what she thought, then she was very wrong, and correction came that day as a bolt of lightening from the sky.

"No, no, no, you're all a bunch of stupid, uncoordinated, idiots!"

Tonia paced angrily back and forth in front of the dancers.

Serena watched as Mimi grimaced from this verbal abuse.

Then, Tonia suddenly grabbed Mimi's dress and pulled her out of the line, slinging her to the floor.

"You're the most stupid and uncoordinated of the bunch!" she yelled out as Mimi fell violently to the floor.

Alicia saw only a flash from the corner of her eye as Serena moved with the ferocity of a lion towards its prey.

Just as Tonia turned, Serena flew into her with both arms out. The full momentum of the Flamenco dancer landed on Tonia's chest and upper body.

Tonia flew into the air and backwards, smashing against Carla. Both then fell with a tremendous crash into a rack of costumes.

The entire event unfolded with the intensity of an automobile crash, with the two women landing hard onto the floor with costumes falling on top of them.

Alicia stood watching this but not actually comprehending what had just happen until after Tonia and Carla had already hit the floor.

None of the dancers seemed to understand what had happened until Serena stood over the two women staring down at them.

Tonia and Carla were both in shock as well. They began to pull themselves out of the clothing. Their expressions were of two women that had just been violently hit by a costume truck.

Once Alicia realized what had occurred, she quickly moved to Serena's side. As she came up to her, she heard Serena say in a clear voice but slightly broken Italian.

"If you ever touch her again, I'll break your legs."

She continued to stare down at both women. By this time, they'd pulled enough of the clothing away to understand what hit them.

Both expressed fright as they gazed up at Serena.

Then, something unusual took place. Alicia didn't quite understand why Serena did this until considering it later.

She stood over the two for what seemed to be a long time. The actual amount of time may have only been a few seconds. However, as she stood there, Alicia began to wonder why Serena remained standing and staring down at the two women she'd just put on the floor.

They in turn stared up at her with a startled expression on their face. Serena didn't budge from this stance as the silence in the building became almost unbearable.

And, during this time, something amazing started to happen. All the other dancers began to slowly move up to and around Serena.

She never turned from Tonia and Carla though as the other

dancers now came to their senses and showed their support for her.

Within a few short moments, all the dancers stood around Serena and Alicia, staring down at the woman that had bossed them and mistreated them for years.

Alicia realized Serena had given them enough time to decide they should stand with her while they had the chance and to end the tyrannical rule of Tonia.

Considering the situation later, she also felt sure this was likely something of a bonus rather than Serena's actual plan. She felt Serena must have been holding the two in place, just as she holds the audience at the end of a dance.

She established then and there who was in control. Tonia and Carla wisely made no move against her and as Serena confirmed her dominance, the dancers wisely gave her their vote of support.

In a matter of three minutes, Serena effectively tore down the Tonia and Carla dictatorship.

During the commotion, no one saw exactly what had happened to Mimi. Alicia thought she might have moved out of harms way once Serena acted.

Regardless of where she went, she would forever remember and show gratitude for what Serena did for her.

The very next morning Serena became a bit surprised to find a single rose in a beautiful small vase sitting on her dressing table.

Eventually it was confirmed that Mimi was the one putting the flowers in Serena's dressing room.

And, as Serena came to realize that Mimi would often stand outside the door, peeking in to see her reaction to the flower, the dancer began to intentionally pick the flower up and regardless of what the type of flower it was, she would smell it with delight.

This in turn would cause Mimi to smile happily on the occasions she witnessed the dancer do this.

Serena now began leading the dancers and Tonia became very uncooperative in doing anything other than dancing her regular routines.

Carla obviously tried to stay away from Tonia, but now Tonia clung to her since she was the only dancer that would associate with her.

When the company wearily returned to Naples after nine long months of touring Europe, Tonia requested a release from her contract and Mr. Cantelli obliged her. He then officially asked Serena to be the lead dancer and to take over the choreography duties.

Tonia wanted Carla to go with her, but Carla refused. Instead she went to Serena in private and told her she never really liked the way Tonia treated the dancers. She also felt frightened of Tonia and if Serena would allow her to, she would like to stay with the company. Serena agreed and even asked if she might be willing to help in the future with choreography duties.

This proved to be a wise decision on Serena's part as Carla became very proficient after being freed from the hard-hand of Tonia.

As a cool winter closed in on Italy, Serena and Alicia found an apartment and tried to make the most of their time off.

Serena sent letters and photos to Olivia and as Alicia had noticed would always react as a child when receiving letters from her adoptive mother.

In the same manner Lavina had done years before in Vista Cruz, Mimi now took the two women around Naples and the three enjoyed each other's company as if they were sisters.

They went to the theaters and shopping. Once they even traveled to Rome and the two women from Mexico marveled at the ancient city.

With Serena in a lead position now, she and Alicia would often go to the entertainment company's building to rehearse and plan the dance routines of the upcoming tour.

"I would like for you to put together a Flamenco program to complement our Cancan numbers." Mr. Cantelli poured her a glass of wine and passed it over the desk.

"Do you think you can have something ready before the next tour?"

Serena pulled her coat a little tighter and then took a drink of the wine before answering.

"I can have one number worked up and ready for the start of the tour. This won't be a difficult routine, but we should be able to have all the girls ready before we leave Naples. I can have two more ready by the first month of the tour. How many numbers do you need?"

Mr. Cantelli thought for a second and then replied.

"Three will be enough. However, I want at least one of those to be a special number with you as the main dancer. Can you do that?"

Serena answered quickly.

"Yes, I can do that. I have a number I can organize quickly. It's one I performed in Vista Cruz. I'll start putting it together right away. As soon as the other girls begin returning I'll have Carla start rehearsing with them."

Mr. Cantelli sat back in his chair, which made a screeching sound as he rocked a little and gazed out the window of his office.

"I think this will be a great year," he said and then took another drink of his wine.

Later Serena went over the plan with Carla and Alicia.

"Are you sure you want me to work with the dancers?" Carla appeared surprised that Serena would ask her to work with the dancers in this manner.

"I'll work with you on and off until everything runs smoothly. I never saw you get abusive with the dancers. The fact that you were something of an assistant to Tonia is both good and bad. The bad part is you must overcome that stigma with the dancers. I suggest you begin by telling them something like you told me at the end of last year's tour. Apologize, sincerely, and then ask them one by one if they mind you assisting me in new programs."

Serena paused briefly and then continued.

"The good thing is that you know all the routines and much of the choreography side of the dances. If we can use the knowledge you gained while assisting Tonia and put things on the right track, then I believe we'll have a great program."

Carla smiled a little, seeming to understand why she'd asked her to do this.

"Thanks for giving me another chance, Serena. Whether this works or not I want you to know I appreciate the opportunity to make things right."

Serena smiled and knew Carla meant what she had said.

As the launch date drew closer, Serena found herself much busier than the year before. Even though Tonia never held real authority, she did keep the dancers on track.

As they prepared for the tour, the morale of the dancers could be seen quickly and dramatically improving from the previous year.

Serena also enjoyed the opportunity to have a dance routine with the other dancers. Though aware that some people back home in Mexico might consider it sacrilege, she recalled what Estelle had told her and knew that the audience was the proving ground for the art. If it sold tickets, and if people loved it, then the art was successful in its purpose. No form of art advanced while closed behind doors and restricted to a few spectators who claim to be protecting it.

Serena choreographed several special dances with the other dancers and they soon delighted in receiving their new Spanish-style dance costumes.

As the tour launched and moved through Europe the company began to come together as if one large family. With the friction caused by Tonia gone, everyone became more pleasant and for a few months Serena felt Mr. Cantelli's prediction of a great year would be true.

Each show became tighter and the audience enjoyed this as the new 'family type' atmosphere reflected in the performers.

Confidence entrenched itself in the company as the days passed and this would be the stabilizing force in the turbulent days to come.

A very dark day began when no one noticed the rough dressed man sneaking in the back door of the theater. Yet, they would all try to recall the fateful event afterwards.

None in the company was aware that a few months earlier a dancer had been raped and killed in the very same city.

The show had ended and as the audience left from the front, the performers began to also thin out backstage; leaving for their hotels one or two at a time.

Serena and Alicia moved about preparing for the following day's performances. Carla also worked on the other side of the stage, preparing costumes for the next show.

As had become commonplace, Serena relied heavily on Alicia's ability to take notes while they moved about. She spoke, and Alicia followed with notebook in hand, somehow getting all the information down.

"Also, I need to remind Ines to stop moving her leg to the left during the introduction of the second routine. I told her about that, but she's still doing it."

Alicia wrote the notes as the two moved around backstage.

"And the flowers on these outfits must be moved a little. I swear it appears as though the flower has been placed squarely on Mimi's breast."

She pulled Mimi's costume from the others hanging on the rack.

"You see this? I'll not have Mimi dancing any longer with this flower bouncing up and down on the front of her breast. We've got to fix this. The poor girl, why would they put the flower there anyway?"

Serena tugged at the flower and tried to see what held it on the costume.

"It's only a small stitch holding it on."

"I have thread and a needle in the dressing room. If you want, I can move the flower right now," Alicia replied.

Serena studied the costume for a second.

"Yes, let's move this one now. It's the worst one. If we can move this up a little, then the others will be alright until we get to Brussels. We can have that nice seamstress we employed last year do the other modifications."

Alicia nodded and strolled off towards the dressing rooms. Serena continued to examine the other costumes while she waited for Alicia.

While moving towards the dressing rooms, Alicia spotted Ines and another dancer making their way to the back door. They were some of the last dancers leaving for the night. Alicia, remembering her note stopped to speak with her.

"Ines, Serena needs to speak with you tomorrow about one of the routines. Can you talk with her before the performance tomorrow?"

The pretty little Italian dancer appeared distraught.

"Oh, I'll bet it's about the introduction of the second routine, isn't it? She talked to me before about that and I've been trying not to move that way. I don't know why I keep doing that."

Alicia simply stood with the notebook in her arms, expressing a smile and understanding.

"It's about the second routine isn't it?" Ines asked.

"I think so," Alicia replied softly.

"I knew it. Alright, I'll talk with her tomorrow."

"Thanks," Alicia then marked something in the notebook.

Ines moved with her friend towards the door and Alicia could hear her saying, "I don't know why I keep doing that, you know that part at the introduction of the second routine?"

Then they were both out the back door. Alicia smiled again at the thought of Ines having trouble with the move. She then continued towards the dressing rooms.

She passed by a janitor's closet and didn't notice that the door was slightly open.

Alicia had no awareness of the stranger peeking out of the cracked door and waiting with evil intentions.

Suddenly, after she moved passed the door, something came over her head. Something pulled around her neck tightly.

She dropped her notebook and pulled the thing around her neck. She was being pulled backwards into the large closet. She couldn't breathe.

Alicia struggled fiercely and managed to grasp a short breath of air. Then she was thrown onto a pile of clothes or maybe some old curtains, she wasn't for certain.

A man hovered over her. He held the rope or whatever it was around her neck. She struggled, and he tightened the item around her throat. Her lungs screamed in her chest. She stopped moving and he let her get a small gasp of air.

The man then grabbed the top of her dress and tore it. He grabbed Alicia's breast and began fondling it. She struggled and again he tightened the rope. She began to panic and could feel her body again aching for air.

Alicia stopped struggling and the man again let her have another small gasp of air. She realized now what was happening and thought for certain she would die after he'd finished with her.

He began to pull her dress up. She looked at the man. He appeared as a demon to her. For some reason he had the face of death and though she couldn't see him well, she could see he was unkempt and likely from a ghetto area.

The man struggled to get through her undergarments and kicked something in the closet with his leg. Maybe someone would hear Alicia thought. But it would likely be too late as she could feel her last gasp of air begin to lose its power in her lungs.

Serena began to wonder where Alicia could be. She never dallied while working. She began to walk towards the dressing rooms.

There was almost no one else in the theater now and most of the lights had been turned down. Serena could see Carla at the corner of the stage doing something.

She continued towards the dressing rooms. She looked down the stairs towards the dressing area. Then, she heard something to her right. It came from what appeared to be a cleaning or janitors' closet.

Serena noticed Alicia's notebook lying on the floor and a

few feet in front of the door. She moved over to the closet wondering what Alicia could be doing.

She opened the door and there on the floor laid Alicia with a man on top of her. Alicia's eyes screamed out in terror to her friend. Serena's mind went blank. Her heart began to pound rapidly inside her chest. It felt as if the air around her had become thick and difficult to pull inside her lungs.

Quickly, she turned and looked around to find someone to help her as panic attempted to overtake her mind. There was no one.

At this instant she had to act immediately, no matter what. She ran around looking for anything.

The man didn't seem to notice her open the door as he was busy trying to pull Alicia's clothes off.

Serena found some pipes on a rack. They were used as anchors for the curtain ropes. She pulled one out of the rack and just as she did, Carla walked up to her.

"Help me," was all Serena could say before darting back towards the closet.

She opened the door and moved inside with the pipe held up high.

The man now began to realize someone stood behind him. Possibly he saw Alicia looking up at Serena.

It didn't matter though. Just as he began to turn his head to look back, Serena swung the pipe down as hard as she could.

The metal pipe struck the man on the side of his skull with a cracking sound. He then fell dead on top of Alicia.

Alicia tried to raise her hand to pull the rope away but had no strength left.

Serena dropped to her knees and pushed the man off. She then desperately pulled the rope from Alicia's neck.

Alicia took a breath and immediately tears rushed from her eyes. Serena pulled her from under the dead man and held her in her arms. Alicia fell completely apart, trembling and weeping without restraint.

Carla, who had seen everything from the doorway said. "I'll get help," and left towards the back door.

Later, as the local police detective finished his questions; Alicia still lay in Serena's arms as a child. Mr. Cantelli stood behind them with a sad and concerned expression.

"We're almost certain this man is responsible for killing a dancer on the other side of town a few months ago. Everything seems to match. No one saw him enter the building then either. The girl was found strangled in a spare room."

Serena held Alicia close as she listened to the policeman and watched the dead man being carried out of the building on a stretcher.

"Are you sure your friend is alright? Do you want to see a doctor, Miss?" He asked with concern.

She shook her head no from under the blanket and hugged Serena a little tighter as she would a mother.

"I'll take care of her," Serena replied.

"Alright, we've got all we need, so we'll leave you to care for her. Thanks again, this man would have killed your friend if you hadn't stopped him." The officer then turned and left.

Serena took Alicia to their hotel room. Once she had her cleaned up and into bed she ran her hand along Alicia's cheek.

She sat on Alicia's bed until her friend drifted off to sleep from sheer exhaustion.

Serena walked out of Alicia's room and quietly closed the door. As she turned, her entire body began to tremble without control. Tears erupted from her eyes and streamed down her cheeks. She took several steps, and slowly fell to her knees and onto her hands, as a giant tree might fall in the forest. On her hands and knees now, she put one hand to her mouth and held it tightly, to restrain her cries. She coughed behind her hand as the anguish tried again and again to escape. She felt sick and weak. She struggled but couldn't find the strength to stand back up. Her tears dropped to the floor as she attempted to control her quivering body.

The thought of the man's skull cracking under the metal pipe made her feel ill and nauseous, but the thought of almost losing Alicia became completely overwhelming.

She gave into the flood of emotions and lay down on the floor in a fetal position, holding her hand over her mouth, crying as quietly as possible for over an hour.

Finally, exhausted and unable to weep any longer, Serena took hold of a chair and pulled herself to her feet. With her eyes still damp from tears, she peeked into Alicia's room to make sure she still lay asleep.

She wearily moved back to the chair and sat down. After a few moments she fell into a deep sleep, not arousing until morning.

The Flamenco star didn't dance for weeks after the event. At first, she thought she might never dance again. She desperately clung to her friend and both women drifted deeper into depression.

Serena sat at the edge of Alicia's bed, holding her hand as her friend stared blankly at the ceiling. When Alicia spoke, it would only be one or two words at a time.

The dancer seldom left her friend alone, and though she tried to open the curtains to allow some sun in, neither of them felt comfortable in the light.

Only a small amount of sunshine was able to filter through the closed curtains. The darkened room had a secure feeling; a feeling of being hid from the evils of a dangerous world outside.

When it came time to move, Serena held Alicia in the dimly lit compartment of the train.

Initially no one knew what to do for the two women that had brought so much warmth to the company.

Mimi came and went to their room for a while but struggled not to become depressed herself. Her heart moaned when seeing the tragic state of the two troubled women that had become as sisters to her.

After several weeks, a meeting was held by the entire company to find some way to help Alicia and Serena.

They all realized how much these two women meant to the company. At this meeting all the performers united as a family and eventually decided to do everything they could in order to help lift the two from the darkness.

The first step would be to send in the young woman they all knew was the closest to them. They instructed Mimi to use her positive and beaming nature around Serena and Alicia, and then the rest would support her in every way possible.

With this new sense of hope and direction in mind, Mimi became a dynamo and shifted into a constant effort of bringing Serena and Alicia back to a functioning state.

She brought flowers every day. Then, she would bring the comedian by, as if they just happen to be in the area. The comedian would talk casually at first but eventually ended up telling jokes that sooner or later got the two women to laugh a little.

The next day she might show up with the magician or a line dancer. Together they would be cheerful and tell the two of something funny that happened during the show.

She brought meals and smiled and laughed every chance she could.

Mimi began to open the curtains wide every morning and then check back time and time again to make sure they remained open, and the sunshine was allowed in.

Serena soon became delighted by the Herculean effort her young friend put forth to get them well.

The young Italian dancer, as well as entire company's efforts, began to pay off as Alicia and Serena both became infected by this young woman's positive energy and the supporting cast of all the other performers and crew.

After five weeks and much improvement from both women, all three sat in Alicia's room talking. Alicia told Serena and Mimi the man didn't completely rape her but groped her and if Serena had not arrived when she did he would have either killed her or successfully raped her in a matter of minutes.

The personal discussion brought some closure to the event and they all three cried for a while. Eventually, Mimi did something to make them laugh, as she often would, and this turned out to be the tonic Serena and Alicia needed. They began to work again the following day.

Finally, the company returned to its close-knit atmosphere and for a while Serena again enjoyed the stage and the people around her that felt to be her family.

CHAPTER NINE:

Autumn Arrives

Four months after the near-fatal incident, Serena danced on stage. She had no idea that a certain man sat in the audience during this dance, and as he watched her dance, this man decided something.

Following the show that night, Serena strolled across the stage. As she did so, she heard someone call her name. She gazed down into the seats and saw Mr. Cantelli sitting with another man. The man sitting with him called her name again.

"Serena," he then motioned with his hand for her to come down.

She went to the corner of the stage and walked down some steps, then moved over to where Mr. Cantelli and the stranger sat.

As she came closer to the men, her heart began to beat stronger. She immediately wanted to run away as a panic crept up from her stomach and into her chest. She slowed down but continued to move towards the men until standing directly in front of them.

The man smiled at her and she knew immediately who he was. He had some gray hairs mixed in with the black, but there was no doubt in her mind as to who this man was.

She didn't smile back but rather stood frozen, staring at the well-dressed man. He appeared to be in his mid-forties.

"Well Mr. Cantelli, can you introduce us please, now that I've managed to get this remarkable woman down from the stage?"

She cringed inside when he spoke. She turned her gaze to Mr. Cantelli who appeared very uncomfortable and she could see frustration in his eyes as he spoke.

"Serena De La Rosa, this is Mr. Paco Rivera."

Paco held his hand out for her to shake.

"Ms. De La Rosa, I must say you dance magnificently. You remind me of someone in fact but I'm not sure whom. Maybe it's the way you dance. I'm certain whoever it is, she's nothing compared to you."

Serena made no move as she stared at the man that broke her mother's heart and left her with nothing.

Though older than in the picture Olivia showed her, he was still distinguished and well groomed.

She knew what lay behind the dapper appearance though and she wanted to slap him or hit him with something. She wanted her eyes to burn holes into him. But she couldn't do anything. She seemed frozen and helpless, staring at him without any sign of emotion.

Paco lowered his hand after realizing she wouldn't shake it. Serena mustered all her strength, turned and promptly walked away.

Mr. Cantelli and Paco Rivera stared as she went back up the stage steps and then behind the curtains.

"I'm sorry, Paco, she's..."

Before Mr. Cantelli could think of the right word Paco replied, "She's magnificent."

Mr. Cantelli thought of this for a second.

"Well, yes, that too." He replied with a dry tone.

Still staring at the corner of the stage where Serena disappeared, Paco continued.

"Why would such a woman need to say anything? She's the most beautiful dancer I've ever seen. Her talent is far beyond exceptional."

Mr. Cantelli said nothing.

Serena went to her dressing room and sat down. She felt weak and almost ill. She pulled the picture of her mother from the drawer. Olivia stood in her magnificent dancing dress and staring out to Serena. She was young and beautiful as she appeared to be frozen in the middle of a dance.

She fondly looked at her mother's picture and suddenly felt alone. She wanted to hug her, to cry on her shoulder. A single teardrop splashed onto her mother's picture and Serena quickly wiped it off with her dress.

Having been around many different men over the years, she knew the look in Paco's eyes. There was little doubt in her mind of Paco's intentions.

Another tear landed on the glass; again, she quickly wiped it with her dress.

"Are you alright?" Alicia came into the room and stood behind Serena.

Sitting with her mother's picture in hand and a tear in her eye, Serena nodded that she was fine.

"I just… miss her so much right now."

Alicia hugged her friend and replied softly.

"I know, I miss her too, I miss all of my family as well. It seems like it's been forever instead of five years."

Serena put her hand on top of her friend's hand.

"Alright, what do you say we go to the hotel and try to get some rest?" Alicia then helped her up.

The following day Serena located Mr. Cantelli, who was sitting in the theater seats going over paperwork. As soon as he saw her approaching he began to apologize.

"I'm so sorry, Serena. That was Mr. Rivera's idea. I suggested we have coffee or something and he could meet you that way, but he couldn't wait."

She sat down and stared at Mr. Cantelli for a few seconds.

"Why did he want to meet me?"

Mr. Cantelli breathed out a deep breath, as if he were getting ready to do something undesirable. Then he began to speak slowly, choosing his words carefully.

"He heard about your skills as a dancer while in Amsterdam. He said he's been trying to catch up with the company, so he could see you dance and meet you."

Mr. Cantelli then took another deep breath and continued as if begrudgingly.

"Paco isn't a friend, he used to be a partner of mine years ago; as time has passed and I've learned the true nature of Mr. Rivera, I've become somewhat embarrassed by that partnership."

Mr. Cantelli noticed Serena begin to relax some. He realized he was doing the right thing to tell her everything, so he also sat back and continued.

"Paco Rivera actually got me into the entertainment business. I owned a business that was failing, and I barely got out of with some capital left in hand. I met Mr. Rivera and even then, he was a shrewd businessman.

"I invested in a Cancan show he was putting together at that time. Everything went well for a while. We traveled about and made a decent return. After a year in the partnership Mr. Rivera came up with the idea of finding other types of routines for our show.

"It was Paco that originated the idea of traveling to Mexico in search of fresh talent. He speaks Spanish, as well as several other languages. So, we traveled to Mexico one year during the off-season in the hopes of securing an affordable act we could add to the show."

Serena began to tense up as Mr. Cantelli revealed this tale to her.

"After arriving in Mexico, we began searching for a fresh act of some type. Paco however, left me in Vista Cruz as my Spanish was so poor. I stayed around The Red Gate Cantina and became good friends with the Perezes. He traveled around searching on his own.

"After a month with no sign of Paco, I realized I needed to leave Mexico to arrive back in time to prepare for our next tour. So, I came back to Naples, not knowing what had become of him.

"I got the show ready and we began the tour. Several

months into the tour Paco turned back up. I was of course upset at him and when he began to brag about affairs he had with several dancers in Mexico I could barely contain myself. But I remained silent.

"He had it seems, traveled about Mexico courting numerous dancers and doing little more than enjoying himself. I held my tongue as I now knew this man was not of a good character."

Serena almost began to cry, but she held her tears back and tried to focus on the matter at hand rather than her feelings.

"He became much worse after returning from Mexico. He began having affairs with our dancers and basically doing little other than womanizing.

"I began to save everything I could at this point and a year later I talked Mr. Rivera into selling me his half of the show. We parted ways on good terms, though I was quite glad to be away from him."

Mr. Cantelli paused for a few seconds to gather his thoughts. He then continued.

"I don't believe Paco ever realized my real opinion of him when we parted ways. I did fine on my own with the show until the war. No one wanted much to do with entertainment while there was a war on. I almost went out of business. I lost all my entertainers and almost lost all of the equipment due to storage fees. I had to find investors just to keep a foundation.

"Then when the war ended, there was an almost instant boom in entertainment. Suddenly everyone wanted to be entertained. Paco had ridden the war out without much trouble as he'd already gained considerable wealth."

Mr. Cantelli stopped and glanced at Serena. She appeared far away in thought. When she didn't make any response, he went on.

"He's increasingly become a ruthless and arrogant Jackass. I've tried to stay away from him over the years, but our shows have crossed paths from time to time and he always has more money and fewer morals than the last time I saw him.

"He recently sold his part in another show and has been on the lookout for the next big thing. It seems he heard about you in Amsterdam and has since been making his way to our show just to watch you dance."

Serena's heart began to sink inside her as she weighed the implications of this new development.

"He has money and plenty of influence in the industry, though I don't think anyone actually likes him. He seems to always find a way to get what he wants though, and I'm afraid he now has an eye on you.

"He asked about buying your contract. I told him I wouldn't sell. That's when he saw you and called you over.

"You should know Serena, I'll do everything I can to protect you, but Paco has become indifferent to anyone's feelings other than his own. If he's as interested as he seems to be, he'll eventually bypass me and try to win you over directly. And, if he can't interest you with money, I suspect he'll try other ways to persuade you."

Mr. Cantelli stared at Serena with apparent sadness.

Serena felt ill when he said this. The thought of any contact with Paco Rivera was revolting. She tried not to hate anyone, but over the years this man had become something of a devil in her mind. The love for her mother was balanced by the contempt she felt for anyone that would do her adoptive mother wrong. Now this same man that had broken her mother's heart and left her with nothing was pursuing her.

She said nothing of this to Mr. Cantelli but simply sat back and stared into an empty space, deep in thought.

He watched her closely and wondered what she thought about this new development; yet waited patiently for her response.

Finally, after what seemed a long time, Serena replied softly.

"This man is thrilled by the pursuit of those things that seem rare or difficult to obtain. Yet when he does get what he pursues, he throws it aside in favor of another alluring prize. If the object of pursuit runs, he becomes even more excited and pursues it that much more... I know what this man is; Paco Rivera is a hunter."

Mr. Cantelli appeared surprised by her remarks.

"You're keenly aware of the true nature of men like Paco. But what will you do, Serena?"

She thought for a few seconds before replying. Then, with little emotion she said.

"There is only one thing I can do… dance."

She then stood up and walked backstage to prepare for the show.

That evening while Serena danced, she knew Paco watched her. She never saw him, but she felt his gaze on her.

Now that she was aware Paco was around, her senses were

heightened to his presence. She never changed her dance however. He wouldn't cause her to lower her level of performance.

After the show she again pulled her mother's picture from the drawer. She studied the photo for a while as if her mother might answer her questions. She then put the picture back into the drawer and slowly closed it.

The following day, Serena walked into the hotel room she shared with Alicia. She was surprised by an unfamiliar sight.

"What's this?"

She spotted the object inside Alicia's handbag. The bag lay on the counter and from its half-open state Serena could plainly see something frightful inside. She reached in and pulled out a pistol. Holding it up by two fingers she turned to Alicia with a puzzled look.

"It's a revolver, what else could it be?" Alicia took the gun as if it were a comb or some other utensil she might use daily. She put it back in her handbag and closed it quickly.

"I know it's a revolver. I meant why do you have such a thing?" Serena studied her friend as a big sister might study a younger sibling that had been caught doing something wrong.

"I feel safer with it." Alicia walked back to her room and Serena followed her.

"Safer? Do you even know how to shoot that thing?"

"Yes, I do. The place I bought it from told me about a firing range and I found a man to show me how to load and fire it."

She sat on her bed and appeared distraught that her friend didn't seem to understand.

Serena realized this woman had every right to feel insecure. She leaned against the doorway as she tried to think of the right thing to say.

"Well... I just want to be sure you know how to fire it, if you should ever need it."

Alicia looked up at her and smiled slightly. Serena smiled as well, then turned and went back to the larger sitting room; feeling a little sad that Alicia needed to carry a gun to feel safe.

The following week the company found itself in Zurich. As they settled into the hotel room Serena felt that maybe Paco hadn't followed the company. She began to believe this, and Alicia became a little surprised to see her smiling again.

"Well, I'm glad to see you're in a good mood. I thought the tour was beginning to wear you down or something."

Serena smiled at this comment from Alicia.

"Oh, I'm just glad to be back in Zurich. I kind of like it here."

Alicia wondered what the difference might be in Zurich, Frankfort or Brussels, but she thought Serena must like Zurich better and that was what mattered.

The following night Serena danced, and all her previous excitement came to a halt. As she came off the stage, Alicia knew something wasn't right.

"What's wrong?"

Serena stood in the corner of the backstage area. She appeared pale. Alicia asked again, "Are you alright?"

"He's here," she replied with a frightened gaze.

Alicia didn't understand.

"Who's here?"

Serena turned and tried to smile.

"Never mind, don't worry about it."

She went quickly to her room to prepare for the next number. There were no more doubts in her mind about how serious the situation had become.

A knock on the hotel room door alerted Serena the following day. She peered cautiously out of her bedroom door as Alicia moved from her room to answer it. After answering the door, she took something and turned towards Serena's room.

Seeing Serena standing in her bedroom doorway Alicia said, "It's two dozen roses, they're for you, Serena."

"Who are they from?"

"I don't know, another admirer I suppose. Does it matter?"

"Yes, it matters to me now," Serena replied sternly as she held her robe together.

Alicia turned to the person at the door. "Who are they from?" After the person pulled a small card from the flowers he said something to Alicia and she turned back to Serena.

"They're from a Mr. Rivera?"

Serena appeared startled; she tied her robe together and went quickly to the door. She took the large bunch of red roses from Alicia's hands and handed them back to the delivery boy.

"I want you to take these and put them in the trash can in the lobby. Make sure they stay there all day; do you understand? Here," she pulled a few bills from a pocket in her robe and handed the boy the money.

"Yes, Madam, I understand." He then took the flowers and after tipping his hat, he left.

Alicia stared at Serena with a confused expression. The dancer said nothing but went back to her room and closed the door.

A few seconds later Alicia knocked lightly on the door. "Serena."

She opened the door and could see the room was dark.

"What's wrong, Serena? You've never turned away flowers. Who is this Mr. Rivera person?"

The dancer sat on the edge of her bed appearing upset. She then stood up and walked out the door, past Alicia, and sat down in the area outside their rooms. Alicia came and sat across from her.

After fidgeting a few seconds and seeming reluctant to talk about it, Serena spoke with a soft voice.

"He's a wealthy man that's decided he wants me for a prize."

Alicia's face contorted slightly as if she had eaten something bitter. She thought for a few seconds.

"I've seen you make short work of men like that. What are you worried about?"

Serena didn't answer right away. She gazed out the window behind Alicia, trying to decide how much she wanted to tell her friend. After a few more seconds she continued.

"This man is different. He's older and much more skilled at the game he plays."

Now Alicia became concerned. If Serena felt worried about this man, Alicia knew he must be trouble.

After some additional thought Alicia replied.

"Tell Mr. Cantelli we need to leave. We can go somewhere

far away where he can't find you. There's only a few months left in the tour, surely he won't mind."

Serena made no expression but slowly stood up and moved to the window behind Alicia.

Alicia turned sideways to look up at her friend; who now stared out the window onto the busy streets below. She seemed reluctant to answer for a while.

Then in a subtle voice she said, "I can't run."

Alicia stood up and moved beside her friend.

"Why, why can't you run? This man is trouble; you shouldn't have anything to do with him."

Serena said nothing but put her hand to the glass as if she wished she could walk through it and into another world.

"Why can't we leave? Why can't you just walk away from this?"

Serena again replied softly, as she ran her fingers along the glass.

"Every dancer has a destiny."

Alicia took a few steps away from her. Her face felt flush with a surge of emotions. She wanted to yell at her. She felt angry and frightened at the same time. A tear trickled softly down her check. She turned and went quickly to her bedroom.

She sat on the bed and wondered why Serena insisted on facing this danger. Why must she do something like this?

Alicia stepped back out of her room a short time later. Serena still stood by the window.

She had her cheek and the palm of her hand pressed against the glass as if absorbing the coolness.

The brilliant dancer appeared to be gazing out of the window with interest at a far away object.

Alicia stood behind her in silence trying to think of what she wanted to say. Finally, she decided to simply say what she felt.

"I don't want you to get hurt. I love you as much as I love any of my sisters. I think I'm closer to you than my real sisters. But, there's just so much I don't understand about you. That frightens me."

Serena turned and gazed into her friend's eyes.

"I feel the same about you. I don't think that I could have a sister closer than you. There're things I can't explain right now; things larger than either one of us. I don't know what's going to happen. I just know what happened the last time I ran. And I know that must face this. I don't understand for certain why, but I know in my heart it's what I must do."

Alicia moved over to Serena and hugged her, placing her head on Serena's shoulder. She began to cry. Tears also ran down Serena's cheeks now. Alicia then mumbled in a barely audible voice.

"Tell me what I can do to help you."

Serena said nothing but ran her hand down Alicia's hair.

Downstairs in the lobby, Paco Rivera strolled into the hotel. He straightened his tie as he made his way to the counter.

"I need the number for Serena De La Rosa's room."

The man at the counter checked his book and then scanned over Mr. Rivera.

"And you are?"

Paco stared at the man with a bit of contempt. "She's a close friend."

The hotel clerk checked his book again and then replied, "Room 214."

Paco turned and made his way to the elevator. While waiting for the elevator, he noticed something in a trash can by the doors. Sticking out of the can he could clearly see a package of fresh roses.

He pulled the roses up enough to retrieve the card. Realizing the flowers were the ones he had sent earlier in the morning, he pushed them back into the waste can. His face grimaced in anger as the doors of the elevator opened.

"Going up, Sir?" The attendant asked. Paco stood for a second gazing down at the roses in the trash.

"No, not this time," he turned and left the hotel.

After performing the final show in Zurich, Mr. Cantelli sat down next to Serena.

The company was busily packing stage props and he observed the preparations to move for a few moments before speaking. Serena sat looking over a paper as if trying to determine some detail in a dance routine.

"I don't want to alarm you Serena, but Mr. Rivera approached me again last night about buying your contract."

She turned her attention to Mr. Cantelli.

"I think he's become somewhat obsessed with you. You must be very careful; he approaches his female interests in a manner as if he wishes to help them. In this way, if the women should reject him he feels justified in lashing out at them in anger. He has the power to destroy your dancing career, Serena. If all else fails, I wouldn't be surprised if he tried this angle to get what he wants from you."

Serena gazed back down to her notebook but continued to listen.

"I know of it happening to several dancers over the years. With a few telegrams you'll get no more work in Europe, regardless of how hard you try. I also wouldn't be able to book the company in a theater anywhere unless I dropped you."

She placed her hands together on her notebook and gazed out over the busy stage. She watched the activity moving about as she thought.

"Thank you for telling me," she finally said.

He patted her arm lightly as he stood back up. He smiled, as one might smile to someone who will soon endure a difficult journey, and then he slowly walked away.

Serena sat and quietly watched the activity on stage. For a long time, she stared at the stage as costume crates, various equipment and personnel moved back and forth.

The following day the company was on the move again. A picturesque European countryside drifted by as Serena stared out the window of the train.

Alicia and Mimi had left to get something to eat in the dinning car. She sat alone with her thoughts when the door to her compartment opened. Shock fell over her as she stared at Paco standing in the doorway.

"Hello, Ms. De La Rosa. Do you mind if I accompany you for a while?"

Serena thought for a second and then replied.

"Would it matter, one way or the other?"

He chuckled at this and came into the compartment, sitting

down across from her. He was well dressed and as Serena studied him she understood why women fell for him.

Even though he was old enough to be her father, she may have been compelled to be entertained by him if she didn't know his true nature.

He tried to look into her eyes, but she turned back to the window and the scenes of small cottages and sheep in the fields.

"I apologize for this intrusion, Serena, but I've found it quite difficult to simply have a few words with you."

She turned to Paco.

"Why do you feel the need to talk with me?"

Paco smiled.

"Why would any man feel the need to talk with you? You're a beautiful woman. I can't believe you could dance the way you do without a genuine understanding of the chemistry between a man and a woman. Surely you know the effects you can have on a man."

Serena made no expression but simply stared at him. The rhythm and sounds of the train filled the silence as she considered his comment. Then she replied dryly.

"I understand well the effects my dancing has on men. I dance to provoke many types of feelings. If I didn't understand them I wouldn't be here now. And yet, you're the first man to follow me onto a train, Mr. Rivera. Kicking a drunken sailor from the stage has become a simple thing for me. Your bold approach however leaves little opportunity for such a defense."

Paco smiled slyly, acknowledging her clever intellect.

"My hope is you'll allow me more time to make my case than you would give to a drunken sailor."

With that remark the door opened, and Alicia walked into the compartment followed by Mimi.

"Who's this?" Mimi asked.

Alicia quickly sat down next to Serena. This forced Mimi to sit next to Paco.

"Mr. Paco Rivera, this is Mimi."

"Hello," Mimi replied and put her hand out. Paco shook her hand.

"Hello Mimi, I'm pleased to meet you." He then pointed to Alicia. "And this lovely young woman is?"

"This is Alicia, my assistant."

Paco put his hand out for Alicia to shake but Alicia made no move to shake it.

"Well, I'm pleased to meet you too, Alicia," Paco said as he pulled his hand back to his lap.

She said nothing but continued to stare at Paco with contempt.

"Mr. Rivera was just leaving," Serena added.

"Oh, was I? I guess so." He stood up and, in a gesture, as if tipping an imaginary hat, he backed towards the door.

"Pleased to meet you ladies; and I'm glad to finally get a word with you, Ms. De La Rosa. I believe our little chat has helped me make a decision."

With those parting words he left the compartment.

"Don't be nice to him!" Alicia quickly barked at Mimi as soon as Paco had left.

"Why? He seems like a nice guy. What's wrong with him?"

"He's after Serena."

"Oh, I didn't know. You don't like him Serena? He looks rich."

Serena smiled a little at Mimi's naive comment.

"Paco Rivera purses his female interests as a sport, Mimi. He loves the hunt, but once he's captured the object of his pursuit, he throws it aside to seek something else that is a challenge for him."

After saying this she turned her attention back to the window.

"Oh," Mimi replied as she considered the new information.

"Well, I'm glad you told me. But if that's the case then won't he chase you even more if you don't like him?"

"That's the problem," Alicia said in a tone indicating she was still frustrated by the situation.

Mimi grimaced and sat back a little as if Alicia were a big sister getting on to her.

"Well, tell him you're engaged or something," Mimi said in a softer voice.

Serena continued to gaze out the window and seemed unconcerned with the conversation.

Alicia and Mimi however sat and stared at her in expectation of a reply.

Serena gathered her thoughts before saying anything because she knew they were expecting and answer.

Then, after she seemed to find a place to begin she spoke to them in a plain and deliberate tone. She spoke as if she were their mother telling them about the hazards of being a beautiful young woman.

"I'm afraid the situation is extremely complicated. I've given this much thought and to lie to Mr. Rivera would likely be what he expects or wants. At the very least, this would play right into his hands. He would have little trouble exposing such a thing and this would give him power over me.

"He knows I must dance, and this automatically gives him leverage to apply towards his final goal.

"What Mr. Rivera seeks is a prize to wear for a while, until something else comes along that excites him. He's very good at this game and has no intention of losing. So, if I run from him, he knows right away I'm in over my head. He'll simply trot alongside and wear me down.

"Not to run however means just as you stated Mimi. He becomes even more excited by the prospect of an exciting pursuit.

"He's already worked through the Cancan dancers and chorus girls long ago. I suspect these are only casual playthings for him to pass the time now. For a serious challenge he picks the quarry with care."

As Serena spoke to them, Alicia became aware of what her friend actually faced. She felt relieved that she didn't shout at her in the hotel.

Now she listened to her with the attention of a student listening to a teacher. She had peace in her heart knowing she'd done the right thing to simply stay by Serena's side no matter what.

"So, it sounds like he has all the cards and there's nothing you can do. That's not fair. Can't you just refuse to give him any attention at all," Mimi asked with a tone of concern.

"Yes, perhaps I could simply reject him or treat him so badly that he leaves me alone. However, Mr. Rivera approaches the women he desires in a manner implying he wants to help them. This is, perhaps another way to make sure he always wins.

"If he plays his usual game, Mr. Rivera will use his money and power to assist my dancing career. So, if I somehow embarrass him by a public rejection, he'll turn his money and power against me, or possibly even try to ruin my career. He seems to be evaluating the approach right now. Or, perhaps he simply wants to determine if the prize is worth an extensive effort on his part. I'm not sure of his plans yet, but he knows the odds are in his favor, no matter what.

"He's aware I have few, if any options. I can run but he'll follow until I relent. I can fight him, but he can then apply his power in the entertainment industry against my career. I can ignore him, but this simply allows him more opportunity to maneuver."

The two women appeared to be in a slight daze by this new insight of the circumstances. Serena turned her attention back to the passing countryside and the sounds of the train once again filled the silence. Finally, Mimi broke the uneasy calm.

"I can't believe this. How can someone do such a thing? It's not fair. He has money and power and he just plays games like this for a thrill."

Alicia stared at Mimi with a bit of disappointment. She understood the girl's anger, but Mimi seemed to be ranting now rather than helping.

"Surely there's something you can do, Serena. He can't have all the advantage, can he?"

Alicia sat back in her seat and let out a breath of frustration. She wanted to tell Mimi to be quiet, but she had nothing better to say herself, so she remained silent.

Mimi continued.

"Isn't there anything he forgot? Surely there's something he hasn't thought of?"

Alicia turned to Serena and they both stared at her now.

After another strained silence and without turning her gaze from the window, Serena replied in a soft voice.

"There is one thing I don't believe Mr. Rivera has thought of... I don't believe he's ever learned to dance."

Nothing else was said in the small compartment as the three women silently considered the situation.

The company set up their show in Luxemburg.

After two weeks with no sign of Paco, Serena eventually began to relax some.

"You know, when he left the train, he said something about making a decision. I'll bet he decided to leave you alone!"

Mimi smiled her usual contagious smile as she said this, and sure enough Serena smiled back.

Though not as optimistic as Mimi, she did feel more hopeful as the days passed.

Her and Mimi finished packing the costumes and pushed

the large crate on wheels out in the isle for the stage crew to secure and load.

"I hope you're right," Serena said softly as they moved on to another task.

"Sure, I'll bet the way Alicia stared at him, it scared him. Did you see the way she looked at him?"

Serena shook her head no and smiled again. Mimi had become the light of the company by now, always cheering everyone up and bouncing around with her natural friendliness and laughter.

"Oh, you should have seen it!"

Mimi began folding a costume and continued.

"If I were him, I wouldn't want to hang around either after a look such as that from Alicia."

Serena chuckled lightly as they busily prepared for the move to the next location.

CHAPTER TEN:

A Legendary Dance

"Amsterdam," Alicia seemed a bit irritated as she read the passing sign.

"You don't like Amsterdam?" Serena asked.

"Oh, I like it as well as any other city I suppose. It just has a smell, you know, a unique smell. I think it's the water and the canals, I'm not sure. Maybe that's what bothers me."

Serena laughed a little at this reply. She'd begun to laugh more lately. Having been over two and a half weeks since she last saw Paco on the train, she began to rest better at night and smile more. Now she even found herself laughing again.

Maybe Mimi got the situation right. Maybe Paco felt that Serena wouldn't give in easily and he decided to leave her alone. He did say he'd made a decision before leaving the compartment. Her hopes increased as the train came to a stop.

The dancers and entertainers found their respective hotels and settled in for the night.

The following day at the Cabaret, Serena and Alicia sat in front of the stage discussing preparations for the upcoming shows.

"Mr. Cantelli wants to see everyone right away." A dancer

told Serena and Alicia, then quickly moved towards the back of the stage.

Serena hadn't noticed performers making their way towards the back of the stage until this moment.

"I wonder what this is all about." Alicia appeared concerned as she sat her notebook in one of the seats beside her.

"I don't know. Something must be going on. We've never had a meeting like this while on tour."

The two women made their way backstage along with several other crew members that must have also heard the news late.

All the performers and crew were gathered in a large circle backstage. As the two women came closer, Serena could see Mr. Cantelli and someone standing beside him, but she couldn't make out who the person was due to the crowd in front of them.

As they moved in closer, her heart wavered. There, beside Mr. Cantelli stood Paco Rivera.

"Alright, do we have everyone?" Mr. Cantelli appeared pale and not at all well.

"Let me have your attention please, I'll try to explain the reason for this meeting quickly and as best I can. This is Mr. Paco Rivera. Mr. Rivera has recently acquired shares of this company from two other shareholders. The shares he purchased total sixty percent of this company. This means Mr. Rivera is now the major shareholder."

As Serena and Alicia came to the front of the crowd and Mr. Cantelli announced this, Paco looked directly at Serena and smiled subtly, as if he had just won an important victory.

Mr. Cantelli took a breath. He also glanced at her, but with obvious sadness in his eyes. She could tell this had been a surprise and shock for him as well.

He continued solemnly, as if announcing someone's death.

"As the major share holder, Mr. Rivera has decided to take over the general manager position. I'll be covering the stage manager position from now on. You'll report to Mr. Rivera for any matters concerning, pay, contracts, etc."

"All dancers will continue to report to Ms. De La Rosa for performance related issues. All other performers will report to me or Mr. Fedanza, who will move to an assistant stage manager position."

After a few additional comments Mr. Cantelli handed the meeting over to Paco.

Stepping to the center of the meeting, Paco again glanced at Serena, then proceeded.

"I want you to know I'm very excited about this opportunity to work with all of you. I've been in the entertainment business for many years and I plan to bring new opportunities to this company.

"We'll get along fine if you do as I ask and work with me. I want to help you, so let's cooperate and we can all enjoy success."

As Paco spoke Serena knew very well he spoke to her more than any other. He continued to look at her as he made key points about cooperation and comments pointing out that he was now in control of the company.

She felt trapped, but she knew Paco wanted her in a corner and would be pleased to see this in her eyes. He knew well this would be a surprise and he played the card masterfully.

Serena made no expression of any sort while he spoke. Although her heart raced, and her mind frantically searched for a counter move, she wouldn't let him have the satisfaction of knowing how she truly felt at this instant.

Later, after Paco left, Serena went to see Mr. Cantelli. She hoped for something, anything to help her get an edge.

"I'm so sorry, Serena. I had no idea Paco even knew about the other two shareholders. This is how he operates though, he'll not let up now."

As he spoke, Mr. Cantelli paced the floor to relieve the obvious stress he felt.

"I should have known. I should have seen this coming, Serena. I'm so sorry, I just never thought about that side of the equation. He's a shrewd operator. I should have thought about this."

He ran his fingers through his hair in apparent despair and continued to pace back and forth in front of her.

"It's alright, Mr. Cantelli, really. I know you did the best you could. I didn't consider that possibility either. I actually began to hope he'd moved on to other ventures."

Mr. Cantelli stopped and held his hand out.

"That's what I thought! He disappeared, and I thought he might be off somewhere with a chorus girl or something; far away from us at least. I should've known though. His reputation is as accurate as ever. Once he decides he wants something, there's nothing that will stand in his way."

He stopped and looked at Serena as if he had said a foul word.

"I'm sorry, Serena, I guess I'm not helping your situation any."

Serena gazed down at her hands and then rubbed them together a little.

"I can't pretend the situation is any better than what it is. You speak the truth and that's what I must be aware of."

He gazed down at her with sadness in his eyes.

"I'll do everything I can to help you Serena. But this man is of a completely different caliber regarding his way of doing business. I don't know how much I can do. I realize now he's far better at this type of maneuvering than I am."

She nodded and stood up.

"Thank you, Mr. Cantelli. I'll be alright, you shouldn't worry about me."

As she left the room, she felt as though she'd lied to him. She stared at the floor while making her way out and then to the hotel.

The next morning Serena came to the cabaret after breakfast and found Paco backstage.

"Good morning, Ms. De La Rosa." Paco made another imaginary hat tipping gesture as he greeted her.

"Mr. Rivera," was all Serena could muster.

As she continued to walk towards her dressing room he followed her. She walked through the door of the dressing room and looked back at Paco as he followed her in.

"You may own our contracts Mr. Rivera, but you don't own me," she said, rather sharply.

He chuckled and replied.

"Not yet, Ms. De La Rosa. But, we're both adults. I believe an intelligent woman as yourself understands the implications. I only want the best for you, Serena. I'm sure you'll come around in time. I can help you so much, if you'll just let me handle everything for you."

She walked over to the dressing table where Mimi had placed a single flower in the glass vase, just as she always did.

The flower was rather plain; it was nothing spectacular and appeared to be one Mimi had picked somewhere around the area.

Serena took the flower from the small vase and smelled it as if the fragrance might wash the presence of Paco from her room.

Paco watched her do this with a curious interest.

"You're an extraordinary woman, Serena De La Rosa. Perhaps that's one of the things I find so attractive about you."

She said nothing but continued to smell the small flower, and then held it against her chest as if it were a tiny treasure. Paco continued.

"You throw two dozen roses in the trash can, but you treat that pathetic little flower as if it were a precious gem."

When he said this Serena stared at him, her face tensed with anger. She turned away, as if protecting the small flower from him. After a few seconds she replied with a voice of contempt.

"I would choose this little flower over six dozen roses."

Paco laughed at this comment.

"That's good to know. It'll save me some money the next time I buy you flowers."

She turned quickly and replied with an aggressive tone.

"Save all of your money, Mr. Rivera. You cannot buy such a thing as this."

He laughed again with an arrogant tone, as if Serena's excited behavior aroused him. Then he slowly turned and left the room.

As the days went by Paco began to take the company in a different direction. In Brussels he purchased new outfits for the dancers. These outfits were more of the Burlesque nature than what the dancers were used to.

Serena cringed when she first saw little Mimi in one of the outfits that looked more like a negligee than a dance costume.

Paco also began to flirt with the dancers constantly, patting them on the rear as they came off stage.

A few of the dancers fell for his charms and became his playthings. Mimi however kept up a constant effort to remind the dancers of his actual nature.

Serena wondered why Paco hadn't gone to the trouble of putting her into an extremely revealing outfit. Then, they reached Paris and she walked into her dressing room to find a beautiful but extremely risqué outfit hanging where she wouldn't be able to miss it. She stared at the dress in a mild state of shock.

"You like it?" Paco entered her dressing room without knocking. She moved to extend the distance between them. After a brief silence she replied with a cold tone.

"That dress is dangerous."

He laughed, as if it pleased him that she knew the intention of the dress.

"Yes, and on you it will be extremely dangerous, Sweetheart. That's exactly what I want. I've managed to get us a single number booked at the Madam Rouge in two weeks. I had to pull a lot of strings to get this particular time slot."

Paco now moved closer to the dress and examined it as if he were imagining Serena in it. He continued.

"There'll be some very important people from the United States there on this particular night. You'll wear this dress and be very dangerous. This is for the big money Serena. I've been trying to get a deal with these people for a long time, so don't let me down."

Paco paused and then a strained look came over his face and he spoke in a very serious tone.

"I'll tell you this, Serena De La Rosa. You may play hard to get with me, but this is my business and I take it very seriously. If you're not beautiful, dangerous, and all the other stuff you need to be to get this deal through, you'll regret it. And all your little friends will regret it as well. Don't try anything cute, unless it's on the dance floor. From what I understand, Mimi needs this job. I believe she's the sole provider for her disabled mother. Don't mess this up, or she may not be working anywhere in Europe again. Do I make myself clear?"

Serena stared at Paco but made no expression. Then she replied softly.

"Yes."

He smiled and softened his tone. "I knew you'd come around with the right motivation. You just need to relax and let me run things, Serena. All you need to do is dance when and where I tell you to. Like I said, I can raise your dancing career to a new level."

Serena felt cold when he said this. He left the room and she quickly shut the door behind him.

She examined the dress a little closer. It was a beautiful dress. It was a crimson red satin with white lace and accents. What concerned her most however was the cut of the lower section. In the front, the dress had a high cut section to intentionally display her legs. The cut went above the knees and inside the bottom portion of the dress was lined with an orange, yellow and white pleated petticoat that fluffed out the skirt portion from underneath.

Altogether, the bottom part of the dress resembled a Calla Lilly turned upside down and her exposed legs would be accented by what appeared to be flame-colored pleats inside the dress.

She shuddered a little when the erotic implications became clear to her.

"This is a very dangerous dress," she said softly to herself.

Paco continued his relentless pursuit of Serena as they moved into the cabarets in and around Paris.

Although she wouldn't wear the dress until the show at the Madam Rouge, it continued to appear in her dressing room by the stage personnel; as instructed by Paco and where she would be forced to examine it daily, as if it were another victory in waiting for Paco.

"I can't believe he ordered you to wear that," Alicia said as she walked in, noticing Serena staring at it.

Serena smiled a little, in a sad way, and then softly replied.

"It seems Mr. Rivera has a strong desire to play with fire."

Alicia couldn't help but laugh out loud at her friend's ability to make light of the situation. This in turn caused Serena to laugh a bit. She was glad Alicia had come in when she did.

Several days before the show at the Madam Rouge, crates with new outfits for the back-up dancers arrived.

As the dancers pulled the outfits out and began trying them on Serena noticed these dresses were like the one she would wear and were also quite revealing.

Although the dancers had by now become somewhat accustomed to wearing less, they still seemed to feel a bit awkward in these outfits.

Mimi floated over to Serena in her outfit. Serena's heart went out to the young dancer as she approached.

"There's not much to these is there?"

Serena attempted to smile in a comforting way.

"No, there's not much to them. I think Mr. Rivera is more focused on the lightning than the thunder."

Mimi appeared puzzled by this but smiled and seemed content with Serena's comment.

Alicia moved up beside Serena as Mimi walked away.

"He'll try to have them dancing with nothing on before long."

Serena nodded in agreement.

"I don't believe Mr. Rivera has an actual appreciation of the art and beauty of dance. When he watches a dance, he becomes intoxicated by the erotic nuances rather than enjoying a display of beauty and skill."

She began to walk about the dancers as they adjusted their outfits.

"He wants us to use our sexuality to intoxicate some business people at the Madame Rouge show."

Alicia looked at her with a puzzled expression.

"What are you going to do?"

Serena thought for a second. "I don't know yet. He can easily destroy any of these girls' careers if we don't play his game. I'm afraid we may have to cooperate for now and hope something develops."

"I don't like that," Alicia replied quickly.

"I don't either. But, I know Mimi must have this job to care for her mother. The others I'm sure must also do as he says for the time being. I just hope something changes soon."

She gazed out over the scantily dressed dancers and added, "before the costumes get any smaller."

Serena struggled for an answer, as the important show grew closer. Nothing seemed to present itself to her. She found herself gazing at her mother's picture.

"I know every dance has a purpose, but is the purpose of this one really as it seems?"

A younger Olivia Frisco stared back at her. Then Serena added softly as if telling her mother. "This dance must be part of my destiny, I'll not waver now. I'll not let you down."

She carefully placed the picture back in the drawer of her dressing table and looked at herself in the mirror. How could she go through with this dance? How could she hand deliver another victory to Paco?

The show at the famous Madame Rouge arrived and Serena walked somberly to her tiny dressing room. She smiled a little when she spotted a red rose in the tiny glass vase on her makeup table.

She wondered how Mimi always managed to get a flower in her room before she arrived.

Gazing around, she thought the so-called 'dressing room' appeared more like a broom closet than an actual room.

But, she then considered her back-up dancers and felt fortunate. When they asked about a dressing area the stage manager informed them the hallway would have to suffice.

Setting her bag on the floor she pulled the new dress from the hook on the wall and examined it with reluctance. She still felt unwilling to dance in the manner Paco wanted her to.

Though she knew saving the other dancer's jobs should be enough, she wished there was some other motivation for such a flagrant exhibition of eroticism.

There was no doubt of her ability to perform in such a way. The problem remained who she was doing it for. To do such a dance for Paco Rivera made her furious.

She tried to focus on her fellow dancers as she began taking her dress off. She gazed down at the rose and thought of Mimi's mother who depended on the money her daughter sent home.

Alicia walked in as Serena had finished getting out of her dress. Without saying anything she began helping the dancer put the new dress on. Serena then sat at her dressing table.

Alicia began to apply Serena's make-up. Finally, she did her hair. As she worked on Serena's hair the dancer put Mimi's rose close to her nose and smelled it. She then carefully put it back into the vase.

Both women seemed to be contemplating what lay ahead. As she put the finishing touches on Serena's hair, Alicia finally spoke.

"You always say, 'every dance has a purpose.' What will the purpose of this dance be?"

Serena felt empty when Alicia asked her this. She stared at herself in the mirror and tried to think of what her mother would say.

Then she simply said what was in her heart.

"Whatever the purpose of this dance may be, I'm certain it's part of my destiny as a dancer."

Alicia stopped working on her hair and looked at her in the mirror. She put her hand up to her mouth to stifle a moan. A tear erupted from her eye and rolled down her cheek.

"I'm so sorry. I'm not helping you at all, am I?"

She then bent down and put her arms around Serena, holding her as several more tears dropped down onto the new dress.

Serena put her hand on Alicia's arm in a comforting manner.

"You're helping me more than you could ever know. I could never do this without you. I would have failed long ago without you."

Alicia buffered up now with these encouraging words. She rose up and tried to smile.

"Where's that ever-beaming smile of Mimi's when you need it?"

Serena picked up the rose from the small vase.

"She brought us this small bit of sunshine. It helps."

Alicia took the rose and smelled it. Then she handed it back to Serena with another tearful smile.

"Yes, it does help."

After Alicia finished, the two women moved down the hall past her back-up dancers as they made last minute adjustments and preparations.

Moving closer to the stage they could hear the music and feel the excitement in the air.

Then, Serena noticed something quite unusual. As she arrived at the back-stage area, she saw what appeared at first to be an almost completely nude black woman.

This woman was obviously very beautiful and when Serena was able to see her better she realized the woman wore a very tiny costume.

The bottom was the same color as her skin and looked more like underwear than a costume. Hanging around her tiny bottom piece were fake bananas strung together. The top she wore also barely covered anything and had a dark flesh color that gave the appearance of the top being less than it was.

Although her breasts were covered the design on the cloth consisted of two brown pieces right in front of where her nipples would be. From a distance it surely appeared the woman wore no top at all. Serena couldn't help but examine her with amazement and realized this woman must be a dancer of some type.

An assistant stood beside the woman and helped her put something on her skin. This lotion or oil made the woman's skin shimmer and shine.

The woman in the tiny costume had short hair that had been oiled as well. This caused her hair to stay in place but also lay flat on her head.

As the woman realized Serena stood watching her, she turned and spoke to her in perfect English.

"Try to warm them up for me, would you, Hon?"

Serena's mind went blank in a mild state of shock. It'd been so long since anyone spoke English directly to her, she almost didn't understand.

As she tried to think of a response in English, the beautiful black dancer said to her assistant, "I don't think she understands English."

Her assistant looked Serena over and quickly replied.

"It's just as well. Look at that outfit. All you can see is her legs and not enough of those are showing."

The dancer looked Serena over as she continued to put the lotion on.

"Yes, she won't do much for the audience dressed in that."

They both laughed a little as Serena and Alicia stood silent.

The dancer then made a little motion with her hand, as if shooing a fly away.

"Never mind, Hon, you go on and do your little dance. I'll take care of the audience."

Serena made no expression but slowly turned back towards the stage and began walking again.

Alicia, not understanding English asked Serena. "What did they say?"

Serena considered the question and then replied without emotion.

"They said the audience would like to see more of me than just my legs."

Alicia appeared puzzled by this and glanced back at the two women.

"They're probably right about that, but I don't think a Flamenco dancer should be dancing in bananas."

Serena smiled. "I agree."

As they approached the stage area, a small man holding a notebook and speaking with a definitive feminine voice walked up to the two women.

"Serena De La Rosa?"

"Yes, I'm Serena."

The man smiled and continued, "I'm Sorel Dufour, the stage manager. Please excuse my poor Italian, Ms. De La Rosa. I speak five languages, but Italian isn't one of my better ones."

"Do you speak Spanish?" Serena asked.

"Si, I do," he replied in Spanish. "And my Spanish is much better than my Italian, thank you."

He waved his hand as a woman might as he replied. Then he continued in Spanish.

"Alright, the band has the music and instructions from your stage manager Mr. Cantelli. Your guitarist is in position now.

Mr. Cantelli also spoke with the light crew earlier today. You'll be on next and you know your cue, so I think we're all set."

Sorel then checked a few items in his notebook and smiling he looked at the two women, as if expecting a remark.

Alicia busily made last minute adjustments on Serena's dress to make everything perfect.

When the women made no comment, Sorel continued as if he desired some conversation from Serena.

"So, I suppose you're excited to go onstage at the world famous 'Madam Rouge' aren't you?"

Serena held a part of her dress as Alicia adjusted it; she almost didn't catch what Sorel said. When she noticed he expected an answer she replied rather nonchalantly.

"You say this place is famous, Mr. Dufour?"

This obviously wasn't the answer Sorel expected. Seeming surprised, his eyebrows raised slightly.

"Well, um yes, it's, well at least here in France it's quite famous."

Serena smiled and nodded, still trying to help Alicia complete the finishing touches on her dress.

He paused at this point and appeared to take into consideration that Serena was busy when he'd asked her the first question. So, when Alicia finished working on her dress, he once again began to speak to her.

"I'm sure you must've never dreamed you'd be opening for the famous American Jazz dancer Jozephine Baxter. That must be very exciting for you?"

Serena appeared puzzled when the man asked her this.

"Who is this, Jozephine Baxter you speak of?"

When Serena asked him this, it appeared to bring a small pain to him. He stared at her for several seconds as if trying to decide whether she played a trick on him or not. Then, when he felt sure she didn't know who Jozephine Baxter was, Sorel continued.

"Jozephine Baxter, she's the tops right now. I thought I saw you talking with her earlier."

He pointed to the black woman Serena had passed on her way to the stage. She looked back to where Sorel pointed.

"Oh, you mean the banana lady?"

He now appeared to be quite confused by Serena's total lack of knowledge concerning Jozephine Baxter.

"Well, yes I suppose so. She's my favorite dancer of all time. She's one of the top dancers in the world right now."

As Sorel said this, Mimi and the other back-up dancers began to arrive.

He moved slightly but continued with what seemed an effort to defend Jozephine Baxter's integrity.

"In fact, do you see those people out there with the flowers?"

He pointed out to an area off the stage where Serena could see some of the audience holding flowers on their laps.

"Yes," she replied after moving to an angle that allowed her to see what he pointed at.

"Those flowers are all for Jozephine. After she finishes her dance, the audience sends them flying up on the stage. It's fantastic."

He became even more excited as he spoke.

"You'll see. In fact, you and your back-up dancers should watch her dance after you've finished your number. You'll learn something about dancing I'm sure."

When Sorel said this, Alicia noticed Serena's eyes lower to half open and her entire face appeared to drop slightly.

She stared at Sorel without any expression, but Alicia knew her well enough to know he'd just lit a fire in her.

Sorel never seemed to notice this and continued, never looking directly at Serena.

"But, I'm probably frightening you before your number. I don't mean to go on about Jozephine. It's just that she's so amazing. I'm sorry Ms. De La Rosa. You're not frightened, now are you?"

Serena stared coldly at him and had the expression of considering his question carefully.

Now Sorel noticed the pause after his question and turned from his notebook to look up at her.

She continued to examine him as he lowered his head and raised his eyebrows in a questioning manner.

Finally, she responded to his question in a deliberate voice.

"Is the sea frightened by the wind, Mr. Dufour?"

Sorel continued to examine her and now appeared completely confused. After a few seconds of this obvious confusion he replied with a slight tone of exasperation.

"I'm uh; sure, I don't know, Ms. De La Rosa."

Then after another quick expression as if Serena might be a little crazy he added.

"Alright then, well, good luck, I suppose." He then walked to another part of the backstage area.

As Mimi and the other dancers assembled in preparation for their number, Serena turned to Alicia.

"Bring me my finger cymbals and Mimi's rose. I now know the purpose of this dance."

Alicia smiled coyly as she knew something spectacular was about to happen. She took off briskly towards the dressing room.

Serena looked over the dancers as a teacher might examine her classroom.

Mimi, as always, watched Serena closely with her childlike eyes. The other dancers appeared nervous and disconnected.

Although they'd performed this dance hundreds of times, Serena realized the new outfits along with other irregularities had likely given them an unsettled feeling.

As the performance on stage ended, Alicia walked quickly up to Serena and handed her the small cymbals and Mimi's rose.

Serena handed Alicia one pair of her castanets and then broke the long stem from the rose making it a little shorter.

She put the cymbals on her fingers. Then looking at the dancers she realized they were all watching her in anxious expectation for some form of guidance. She quickly gazed into their eyes one by one as her cue grew closer.

The other performers left the other side of the stage and there was applause.

Serena raised the rose into the air and almost shouted to her dancers, in a confident and aggressive voice.

"Tonight.... We break hearts!"

The guitar began to play and with the precision of an army officer leading his soldiers into battle, Serena turned and floated onto the stage precisely on cue.

Mimi was the first to understand what Serena meant and a huge smile erupted onto her face.

Then, one by one the magic affected the other dancers and they all began to smile as the flash of excitement and confidence rushed through them.

Once on stage, Serena held the rose in her left-hand unseen by the audience as she also held the edge of her dress.

The introduction of the dance consisted of her alone at first with the guitarist. She began the dance slowly under the spotlight.

Meanwhile the other dancers moved into position almost unseen behind her in the darkness.

At a precise instant, when the guitar paused briefly, Serena froze in her trademark stance, yet this time during the brief pause she had her body towards the audience and her face turned towards the side of the stage, showing her profile to the audience.

She raised the rose up slowly and placed it between her teeth. Then the music began again with a sudden gusto and the band also lightly accompanied the guitar player.

As the excitement and music intensified, the lights opened on the backup dancers.

They began to move up behind Serena, slowly step by step with the rhythm of the music.

She moved with a beautiful intensity unseen before now and the audience couldn't turn away from her.

When the rush of her rhythmic tapping reached a peak she suddenly raised the excitement level with her castanets.

Now, from behind their backs the dancers brought out tambourines and this increased the energy even more.

Alicia watched from back stage and almost cried tears of joy as she realized Serena and the other dancers had effectively placed a spell on the audience.

She put her hands to her mouth as she scanned the mesmerized faces.

Jozephine and Sorel soon moved up beside her as they also realized something supernatural was taking place on stage.

They stared out in disbelief as Serena swished her skirt, tapped her feet and played the castanets in seemingly impossible rhythms to the music.

The other dancers moved in perfect unison. With the controlled lights from above the entire effect was something from another world; something from a magical place where beautiful women could move in such a splendid precision and grace that your heart overfilled with emotion from the sight alone.

When the music stopped with a sudden ferocity, Serena performed her signature move. She did so with mastery unseen before. The audience was completely hers. It was as if they were in a trance.

She froze with her right side to them and her left arm lifted into the air. She turned her head slowly and seductively, scanning over the entire audience.

The silence strained the very foundation of the cabaret.

As she finished gazing out over the audience and holding them in a frozen anticipation for more of her; she quickly raised her right hand, grasped the rose and tossed it out over the audience. At this very same instant she chimed the cymbals in her left hand.

Then, Serena quickly turned and walked to the right of the stage, as the other dancers went to the left of the stage.

As her rose floated over the audience, it triggered an immediate and spontaneous reaction.

Without restraint, cheers, applause and the flowers intended for Jozephine rained up onto the stage, creating a cascade of flowers raining down behind Serena as she moved off the stage.

She paid no attention to the eruption of applause or flowers flying onstage behind her. She was finished with her dance and never looked back.

From back stage Alicia applauded wildly but wondered why Serena had exited the stage on the right rather than the left with the other dancers.

When Serena reached the back-stage area where Jozephine and Sorel stood, still in disbelief, she stopped.

Looking straight at Jozephine, Serena spoke in English, but with a slight Spanish accent.

"Try to cool them down for me, would you, Hon?"

She then smiled slyly and moved on to the hall where her and the other dancers laughed and celebrated the phenomenal dance they'd just performed.

Sorel gazed out at the stage, now littered with flowers as the audience continued to raise a thunderous roar in the hope that Serena would dance again.

Turning to Jozephine who stood beside him, he said with obvious dismay.

"It seems we'll need to have the stage swept before you go on."

Jozephine turned and stared angrily at Sorel; then more or less yelled out.

"You think I'm going out there after that?" Then, she quickly stormed away to her dressing room.

After a brief celebration in the hall with Mimi and the other dancers Serena stepped into her tiny dressing room.

The roar from the audience could still be heard as she sat down at her make-up table and tried to catch her breath.

A few moments later Alicia knocked on Serena's dressing room door, just in case Serena had begun to undress.

"Serena," she peeked in the door.

"Mr. Dufour is outside and wishes to speak with you."

She stood up and looked behind Alicia to see Sorel. She nodded for her to let him in.

"Ms. De La Rosa, the audience wants another dance from you."

Serena gazed at the small man with a slight bit of irritation. After some obvious consideration on the matter she spoke.

"Mr. Dufour," she turned and pointed at the empty flower vase on her dressing table.

"Do you see that little vase?"

"Yes," he replied somewhat meekly.

Serena continued.

"Every day, when I enter my dressing room I find a very special flower in that little vase. Today it was a rose. At the end of my dance a few moments ago, I tossed my special rose out to the audience. I gave them my special flower, Mr. Dufour. Now, for me to perform another special dance, I'll need another special flower."

Sorel appeared perplexed by Serena's assertion. He replied.

"But, there are hundreds of roses from the stage, Ms. De La Rosa. Will one of those work?"

She gave him a sad face.

"I'm afraid, for another special dance I must have another special flower."

Alicia couldn't help but smile now and turned slightly so she wouldn't distract Serena from this bit of personal gratification, due to Mr. Dufour's earlier insult.

"You see Mr. Dufour, there are hundreds of dancers who could pick up one of those hundreds of ordinary roses from the stage floor and perform an ordinary dance for the audience. But what you seem to be telling me is the audience wants another 'special dance' from my dancers and me."

Now she paused for a second in thought.

"The problem is, when we do special dances, we require special things. Today the special thing was a rose and without another one, we'll not be able to do another special performance."

Sorel Dufour expressed a loss for words, but finally asked Serena.

"What should I do? The audience has become very agitated with a desire to see you dance again."

She peered off into space in an exaggerated expression of deep thought. Then, after a few seconds she reacted as if she'd suddenly thought of something.

"I know, perhaps you can ask Jozephine Baxter to dance. I believe she has some 'special bananas' hanging around somewhere."

When Serena said this Alicia burst into laughter and put her hand to her mouth as she backed out of the doorway and moved down the hall, continuing to laugh as she went.

Sorel, of course, now realized he deserved the treatment from Serena due to his excessive boasting on Jozephine's dancing skills.

He left Serena's dressing room and eventually talked Jozephine into dancing. This proved enough to appease the audience and avoid a riot from them.

As Serena and Alicia walked towards the back-stage door on their way to leave the Madam Rouge; a man in uniform called out.

"Serena De La Rosa?"

"Yes, I'm Serena De La Rosa."

The man opened the back door. "I'm here to take you to the hotel, Ms. De La Rosa."

Serena was suspicious, and Alicia took hold of her arm as if she also felt leery.

"Who instructed you to take us to the hotel?" Serena asked.

The driver pulled a small piece of paper from his coat pocket.

"It's… compliments of the Madam Rouge."

After some glances back and forth, the two women accepted this as being alright and stepped outside to find a large and very luxurious car waiting.

The driver opened the back door for the ladies. They giggled a bit to each other as they climbed into the car.

Once inside, they realized there were two leather seats facing each other.

Alicia opted to sit next to her friend rather than across from her. Serena pulled her cloak around her where it covered her completely as she settled back into the soft leather seat.

The car began to move, but then it stopped. Suddenly the door opened, and Paco Rivera climbed in.

It seemed he'd planned on sitting next to Serena, but as he entered and realized Alicia sat next to her it became necessary to change this plan and sit across from the women.

"Good evening, ladies."

Serena rolled her eyes and turned her head towards the window.

Alicia sneered at Paco and quickly replied.

"I thought you might be behind this, Paco."

He acted surprised. "What, can't I do something special for my girls once in a while?"

Again, Alicia quickly replied.

"We're not your girls, Paco."

The car moved slowly to the public road and stopped before turning.

In a flash, a man climbed onto the running board of the

vehicle and before anyone realized what was happening he had his head and shoulder inside the open window. He held something in his hand and appeared to be intoxicated.

In a loud voice the man said. "I love you, Serena, I love you. Please, I just want to talk to you for a minute. I love you."

Everyone was startled and jumped when the man appeared.

"Drive," Paco said loudly and began to push on the man. The car began to move again.

"Wait, wait… Serena, will you marry me? Please, wait, I love you Serena."

Then the man tossed what he had in his hand at the dancer.

Serena's arms were covered by her cloak. She turned her head and moved back as much as possible trying to avoid the item. It hit her chest area and then dropped to her lap.

The man fell from the car as it picked up speed and Paco pushed him.

All three sat stunned for several seconds. Paco then looked at the item the man threw and now lay in Serena's lap. Alicia also looked over at it.

Serena, still seeming a little startled, looked down in her lap to see the man had thrown half a dozen roses at her.

She examined them briefly and then she lifted her arms under her cloak and the roses fell to the floor of the car. Alicia and Paco watched silently. They both then turned to Serena with a bit of astonishment.

She stared at Paco for several seconds. Finally, after what felt to be a long moment, she said solemnly to him.

"I told you, that dress is dangerous."

Then, she sat back into her seat, turned back to the window and said nothing else.

Paco, now appearing a bit deflated, also sat quietly until they reached the hotel.

CHAPTER ELEVEN:

A Dark Stage

After the successful show at the Madame Rouge, the company performed at the last cabaret on their schedule for Paris.

They would now have various shortstops in France before wrapping up the long tour in London.

At one of these stops Paco again walked into Serena's dressing room without so much as a knock. She pulled her dress up to cover herself.

"Get out!"

She picked up a jar of cold cream from the dressing table and threw it at him. He dodged the flying object and laughed.

"You act as if I've never seen a disrobed woman before."

He sat on the edge of a table after saying this; indicating he had no plan to leave.

Serena retorted sharply.

"I'm sure many women have disrobed for you willingly, Mr. Rivera, but I'll never be one of those."

She moved behind a folding blind to finish putting her dress on.

Paco turned sideways as if attempting to not watch her. This was only an act however as he slyly watched her as much as possible.

"I just wanted to tell you the good news, Serena."

She finished dressing and moved from behind the blind to find Paco standing with his back to her, as if he'd not been watching.

"What good news?"

He turned around and acted glad she'd finished dressing.

"Oh, well, it concerns your performance at the Madam Rouge. The people from the United States I spoke of contacted me and we're in negotiations for a contract in America."

She stared at Paco coldly. He continued.

"Mr. Cantelli tells me you still have two years on your contract, so that shouldn't be a problem."

He smiled and patted her on the cheek. She moved away from his hand.

"You know Serena, this 'playing hard to get', it excites me. So, from now on, when you run from me, I'll consider it our special kind of foreplay."

She sneered at him.

"Oh yeah, just like that Sweetheart, you know what I like, don't you."

He laughed arrogantly and walked out.

True to his word Paco intensified his pursuit of Serena. She suspected him of having the locks on her dressing room disabled or taken off before she arrived, for him to stroll in as he pleased.

He also began to arrange for their hotel rooms to be next to each other.

As the company made its way through France, Paco became

ever more brazen in his efforts to subdue Serena. Alicia in turn became more protective of her friend. She began to stay by her every moment.

Mimi also realized the extent of the situation and between the two they managed to fend off much of Paco's advances simply by being at Serena's side all the time.

Paco in turn, was keenly aware they were getting in his way and made efforts to blunt their intrusions.

As the tour began its last leg, a knock on the hotel door brought Alicia to her feet. She'd been lying on a small couch taking a nap in the sitting area of her and Serena's room.

"Hello Alicia. I need you to run down to the cabaret and grab some costumes from backstage. They have repairs that are needed.

"They're hanging on a rack to the right of the back-stage door with papers pinned to them describing the repairs needed. Take them to this shop. I've let them know the costumes will be delivered soon."

Paco handed Alicia a piece of paper with the address to the seamstress shop on it. She gazed down at the paper and then back at Paco, appearing half awake and unsure about this generally unusual request.

"I'll need to ask Serena."

"Alicia, you know, Serena doesn't pay your salary; I do. You're Serena's assistant, but while we're off stage I may have errands for you. Do you understand?"

Alicia expressed irritation by this but replied.

"Yes."

He smiled, "Thanks," then turned and walked away.

"Who was that?" Serena asked as Alicia came to her room examining the paper Paco had given her.

"That was Paco. He wants me to take some costumes to be repaired."

Serena and Alicia both looked at each other as if hoping the other one might have an insight as to why he suddenly wanted Alicia to do extra duties.

"That's a bit odd," Serena finally said.

"That's what I thought. I'll have Mimi come up before I leave."

Serena nodded and began to pick her book up again, but then appeared to recall something.

"Mimi and Carla went to the beach today. I just remembered." She then picked the book up and sat down on the bed.

"I'll be fine, go ahead and have the costumes repaired."

Alicia gave her a look of concern. Serena at first made a face as if Alicia were being silly.

When Alicia didn't back down, Serena laid the book in her lap and appeared to consider the situation again. Neither one said anything; they looked at each other as if reading the other's thoughts.

Later, Alicia left the hotel room and strolled down the hall to the stairs. Then the sound of her footsteps echoed in the stairway to the lobby.

Unseen by Alicia, on the other side of her and Serena's room, Paco peeked out of his room once she'd disappeared down the stairs.

He then stepped out with what appeared to be a towel and possibly some shaving tools in his hand.

He moved down the hallway until he came to a room with the door open, then looked in and spotted the maid cleaning it.

"Excuse me. I believe my roommate has left and locked me out. Could you please open my door for me?"

The maid looked at Paco and knew she'd seen him around the hotel before.

"Yes Sir."

They walked down to Serena's room and she unlocked the door for him.

"Thank you," he said and slipped inside.

In Serena's room, Paco locked the door. He then went to the sitting room and glanced around the door to make sure Serena was not in sight.

He pulled the towel from his arm revealing a champagne bottle and two glasses. He poured both glasses full and sat the bottle on a small table. Taking both glasses, he headed for Serena's room.

As he stepped into the doorway, Serena still lay sitting up in bed reading her book.

"What are you doing here?"

She laid her book down on the bed beside her.

Holding the two glasses in his hands Paco smiled slyly as if he had done something clever to get into her room and find her lying in bed.

"I think its time you and I get better acquainted, Serena."

Realizing Paco would like to keep her in the bed; she stood

up quickly and moved to the edge of it just as he began to move inside her room. This blocked him from getting to the bed and sitting down by her, but it also put her closer to Paco.

As she stood almost face to face with him she replied in a stern voice.

"I didn't invite you here and I have no desire of becoming 'better acquainted' with you."

Paco replied without hesitation.

"Yes, I know you've not invited me to your room, Serena. You see that's the problem. I believe you've been playing hard to get for so long that it's all you know how to do. I feel what you really need is a capable man to come in and stoke those natural desires a little."

Serena moved a little to the side as if wanting to leave. Paco moved in front of her to block her escape.

"And, you've also decided that you're the man to stoke those desires?" She said after being blocked from the door.

"Precisely," he replied.

"Get out, Mr. Rivera," she now spoke with a tone of anger.

"Or what, Serena? What are you going to do if I don't get out?"

Serena looked past Paco's left side, at the doorway behind him. He thought she did this realizing he had her trapped.

"I'll do nothing," she said in a calm voice.

He smiled triumphantly and extended his right hand to give her the champagne glass.

Serena accepted the glass from his hand. She took a small drink and said, "However, Alicia will shoot you if you don't leave."

When Serena said this Paco heard the unmistakable sound of a pistol cocking behind him.

He immediately froze. He slowly turned around. Behind him Alicia stood in the door with her pistol pointed at him.

Paco put his hands up a little, indicating she had him. Alicia then stepped into the room clearing the doorway but keeping the pistol pointed at Paco.

Serena took another small drink of the champagne and then continued.

"Good-bye, Mr. Rivera."

He turned and gazed into her eyes. He expressed wrath, but she didn't back down from his stare.

Paco moved out of the hotel room with Alicia following him all the way to the door.

Repercussions from this incident came almost immediately.

The following morning when Serena entered her dressing room she found an envelope addressed to her sitting on the makeup table.

When she opened the envelope and pulled out the paperwork she found a copy of Alicia's contract.

On the contract were amendments canceling it. Paco Rivera's signature along with a witness accompanied the amendments to make the document legal.

A single tear erupted from her eye as she looked over the document. She then folded it back up and went to hunt Paco down.

She found him where she thought he might be, hovering around the dancers' dressing room.

"What is the meaning of this?"

Paco stared down at Serena with disdain.

"The meaning is exactly what the paper indicates. I'm canceling Alicia's contract. She didn't do as I asked her to do. That's an act of insubordination and a clear violation of her duties to the company. I don't need her anymore. You're in charge of the dancers Serena. She was your assistant, so it's your place to tell her."

Serena's face contorted with fury.

"You can't do this, Paco!"

He smiled, indicating she'd said just what he wanted.

"It's time you to learn who is in charge here, Ms. De La Rosa. I can do this. In fact, I can let all the dancers go if I want. The contracts are all written this way. You work for me, not the other way around. As I told you before, I'm very serious about 'my' business. You and this entire company are a part of my business."

His face became slightly strained and very intent.

"Now, Ms. De La Rosa, I'm in negotiations for a very lucrative contract in America. The weak link is your attitude. But I'll cover that with your contract, because if you do anything foolish, such as not honoring your contract with me, I'll dismantle your career; as well as Mimi's, and any other performer here that interrupts my business. All of you will be lucky to dance on the street for coins, if you or anyone else gives me problems. We can do this the easy way, or the hard way. It's up to you. Do you understand, Ms. De La Rosa?"

She stepped back and stared at him. He stared back. Finally, she said with a voice of contempt.

"I understand."

She turned and left.

Paco smiled as he closely watched her sashay away.

Later, in the hotel room, Serena held Alicia as she wept on her shoulder. Mimi stood by with tears running down her cheeks also.

"That pig. He can't do this, can he?"

Serena said nothing; she gazed over at Mimi though, indicating he could do this. She continued holding Alicia until she could cry no longer.

Mimi also remained in the room until Alicia calmed down.

"What are we going to do? We can't leave Alicia behind."

Alicia appeared a little unsettled when Mimi said this.

"We're not leaving her behind," replied Serena quickly.

She then seemed to be in thought. Alicia and Mimi sat watching her with apparent anticipation.

After a few moments, Serena began to lay out a plan to keep Alicia close by.

"We have the show tomorrow night and then we leave for London. We only have three shows there and the tour ends. I'll arrange for Alicia to travel in the same trains and ferries to London. Then I'll make sure she is in the same hotel. We'll keep you close Alicia. Just don't let Paco see you."

Alicia nodded and wiped her eyes again.

"It's not right. You just wait until everyone else hears about this. They're going to be mad as H E double L."

Mimi now became animated with anger; though she was a dainty little woman, she had a huge heart.

"You should calm down, Mimi. Paco will try to destroy anyone that gives him problems."

The young dancer acknowledged Serena and nodded. But Serena knew Mimi wouldn't stand by completely idle. She and Alicia had become like big sisters to Mimi and the young woman would be compelled to do something in defense of Alicia.

As the performers arrived for the last show in France, Mimi went from one performer to the next on a personal crusade for Alicia. By the time the show ended, she had the entire company fired up.

When the performers spoke to Serena she told them she couldn't say anything about the situation.

All the performers assumed correctly that Paco had made some type of threat to her.

The company packed up for the trip to London. On the train and then on the boat across the English Channel, Mimi continually moved about stirring the performers to action.

Though Paco didn't realize it, Alicia traveled with the company but remained hidden on a separate train car or the other side of the ferry. Serena and Mimi took turns checking on her as they moved closer to London.

From Mimi's actions the company became enraged about Alicia's dismissal. By the time they reached London a pact amongst the performers had been decided upon.

They all agreed to not perform the final three shows in London unless Alicia was rehired with a new contract. The performers presented their signed agreement to Mr. Cantelli.

After some thought, Mr. Cantelli sided with the performers. Although Serena told him Paco would try to destroy the entire company, Mr. Cantelli stated Paco had gone too far this time and he would personally deliver the ultimatum.

Later, Mr. Cantelli stood by as Paco finished looking over the signed paper.

"You're making a big mistake siding with the performers, Cantelli. You know all I need to do is put the word out and none of these people will work in the entertainment business again."

Paco held the paper in his hand and paced back and forth in front of the window. He appeared ready to pounce on Mr. Cantelli. But knowing he couldn't resolve the situation with violence he restrained himself.

"They've decided to take that risk and I'm standing with them on this Paco."

After turning to the window and gazing out, Paco continued.

"You stand to lose a lot of money if the company has to pay cancellation fees. Forty percent of those fees will come from your pocket."

"I realize that Paco. Money isn't everything though. Alicia worked as hard as anyone the last two years. Everyone feels certain she would do the same for any of them. I also believe she would. You had no right to do what you did, regardless of whether you have the power to do so."

Now Paco seemed unable to restrain his anger and shouted.

"No right? She pulled a gun on me, Torre! She's just lucky I didn't take it away and beat her senseless with it."

Mr. Cantelli expressed no fear and didn't move.

"It seems the issue is a matter of pride for you, Paco, not principle."

He then turned and left the room. As he left Paco shouted out.

"I'm not going to be pushed around by you, Cantelli. Do you here me? I'm not bringing her back!"

That evening Mimi sat in the hotel room with Serena. The young dancer had tirelessly traveled back and forth from the room Alicia remained hidden in, and Serena's room.

Seeming to fear for both, she would keep one company for a while and then go to the other's room.

"What do you think Paco is going to do?"

Serena had been in deep thought when Mimi asked this. She turned to Mimi. After considering the question she softly answered the young dancer.

"I don't know. I suspect he would like to dismantle the company and fire all the performers. However, this puts him in a bad situation altogether right now. If the three shows are canceled, he stands to lose a lot of money as well as prestige in the business. He'll try something to win, I'm sure of that. I just wish I knew what."

Silence prevailed for a while as the two thought about this. Then a hard knock came on the door.

Serena knew immediately who it was. She sat up and appeared to decide something within herself as Mimi looked at her.

Mimi stood up to answer the door, but Serena motioned for

her to stay put. She then moved to the door and cracking it open slightly found Paco in the hallway.

"Yes?"

He still appeared upset from his meeting with Mr. Cantelli.

"What do you have to do with this Serena?"

He held the paper up. She took a deep breath, as if she were about to dive into very cold water. Then slowly and with a soft voice she replied.

"I've not eaten yet. Do you know someplace we can eat? We can talk there."

Paco's face immediately became less contorted. He studied Serena as if she were playing a trick. Then he smiled a little but still appeared suspicious.

"Yes, I know a place we can go. But if you're a part of this mutiny Serena, this little truce won't last long. Do you understand?"

Serena remained stoic and showed no emotions.

"I understand. I need to get my cloak."

She shut the door and went to retrieve it.

"Who was it?" Mimi asked as Serena moved towards her room.

"It's Paco. We're going out to eat."

"You're what?"

Mimi stood up and followed Serena to her room.

"How can you do this? I can't believe it!"

Serena put her cloak around her and looked at Mimi tenderly.

"Then don't believe it. Just trust me. Will you do that?"

Serena placed her hand on the young woman's cheek, just as Olivia used to do to her.

Mimi smiled a little when she did this.

"I'll trust you. But I don't like it. He's a snake."

Serena walked towards the door; then turning as if to comfort Mimi she checked her small purse and replied.

"Yes, and if a snake enters a home, it shouldn't have the opportunity to bite the entire family."

Mimi seemed puzzled as Serena again moved slowly towards the door. When she reached for the doorknob Mimi took Serena's arm and replied in a soft tone.

"It shouldn't have the opportunity to bite even one member of the family."

Serena turned to Mimi and appeared touched by this keen observation but gave no reply.

She smiled slightly, though not a happy smile, and then slipped from Mimi's grasp and out the door to where Paco waited.

Paco took her to a very nice restaurant in London. She said little on the way there and once at the restaurant she also didn't volunteer conversation.

She sipped her wine and glanced at him occasionally. He seemed to be undressing her with his eyes from across the table.

When the food came, Paco ate with a methodical precision, bite after bite. Serena nibbled bits of hers but didn't eat much.

As Paco finished eating, he wiped his mouth, turned up a large drink of wine, sat the glass down and then focused his attention on Serena once again.

"So," he finally said. "What's your part in this mutiny, Serena?"

She turned her eyes up to him but not her head as she held her wine glass close to her chest; seeming to absorb the faint aroma of the wine.

"I have no part in that," she replied and then sipped her wine again.

He studied her suspiciously. She again turned her attention to the wine glass to avoid his gaze. After a moment of considering her response Paco continued.

"You're a beautiful and mysterious woman, Serena De La Rosa. I don't understand you and perhaps that's also something I find interesting about you. I don't believe you're lying about this, but I do wonder what side you're on and for that matter why you're here now. Can you give me some insight concerning this?"

Serena never looked at Paco as he said this. She smelled her wine and then as he spoke she took another sip. The waiter came by and filled her glass again. Still she seemed to pay little attention to him.

After a long moment of apparent thought, she responded to him, but didn't look at him. Instead she seemed to be speaking with her wine glass. She lifted it up once while speaking, as if gazing at the light through the wine.

"I'm here because I chose to be here. You continue to mention a deal with the Americans. Now the performers are threatening to close the shows down. I want to know what's going on, and where I stand in all of this. It seems you're the only one that can give me this information."

Paco leaned back in his chair. He picked up his wine and held the glass for a few seconds. Then he had another large drink before replying.

"That's a very neutral answer, Serena. You're very adept at being obscure. You've brushed off every attempt I've made to get better acquainted with you. But now you suddenly have dinner with me. This sort of behavior causes a man to wonder. In fact, I've considered the possibility that you're not interested in men at all. The way you kept Alicia and now Mimi around, this thought presented itself to me on several occasions."

He took another drink of wine before continuing.

"Actually, if that's the case, I would be glad to allow Alicia to return, as long as you girls bring me into that mix."

Serena turned her eyes to him just in time to see him smile and wink after this comment. She had a sudden urge to throw her wine glass at him, but she held her composure.

Then after another short pause he continued.

"No, I don't believe you could dance as you do without an interest in men; even if you're also interested in women."

With this crude attempt to stir an erotic connection between Serena, Alicia, and Mimi; it was as if he had poured a tankard of beer all over the beautiful friendship that had slowly developed between the three women.

She felt ill and wanted to leave. Instead she said nothing but had another sip of her wine; hoping to rid herself of the filth Paco had dished out upon her.

Finally, she responded with disdain in her voice.

"You've pursued me as if I were one of your Cancan

dancers, Paco. I find it insulting that you feel a few roses and some wine will be sufficient to get me disrobed and into your bed."

Paco smiled, and then responded casually.

"I know you're worth more, Serena, the roses and wine were just for starters. I would like to do more if you would give me a chance. I would love to dress you with diamonds and silk negligees."

Serena realized her self-dignity now teetered in a precarious balance. She tried to keep calm, but only anger-filled words seemed to find their way to her thoughts.

Finally, after a moment of unsuccessful self-restraint she said with a flat tone of contempt.

"Is that what you consider a compliment? Once again you treat me as one of your tarts. You present your intentions as noble and then toss sugar cubes and carrots at me as if I were a horse. Do you suppose I spent years learning to dance so I could be the source of someone's sexual fantasies, or the plaything for some, self-absorbed, semi-wealthy businessman? I find your pathetic mannerisms revolting and childish."

She then sat back into her chair and gazed into her glass again.

She felt much better, even though the hope of helping her friends now diminished in her mind. She considered drinking more wine and becoming drunk. Maybe that would help her forget this disgusting waste of time.

No, she quickly realized Paco would simply try to take advantage of her, even after knowing how she really felt.

She wouldn't bother to look at him. She felt sure he must be ready to leave now, and she could at least get away from him. She again sipped her wine.

She thought of her friends and considered the chance she had. Again, she knew she'd done the right thing; she wouldn't perjure her true nature to this man. She wouldn't lower herself to his level to do something good.

Now she wondered what he was doing across the table but refused to even give him a glance as the seconds slowly ticked by in a strained silence.

Serena tipped her glass up and finished her wine. Then sat the glass on the table in preparation for what she thought must surely be the last of their conversation.

However, she became completely surprised by the sound of Paco chuckling, somewhat under his breath.

She braced herself to not reveal an expression of surprise, but immediately turned up and looked straight at him.

He sat staring at her and smiling coyly as if he'd just caught her doing something naughty.

She again forced herself to make no expression, even though inside her mind confusion stirred as to what he now thought. She stared at him with the same blank stare she became accustomed to using with him.

He raised his glass to have the waiter come over and fill it, never taking his eyes off Serena or losing his strange smile.

The waiter filled his glass and motioned in question to Serena. She gingerly picked up her glass and he filled it also.

"You're cunning as well as beautiful. Everything is finally

becoming clear now. All this time I've been hunting bear with a slingshot."

Serena still had no idea what he meant. But she wouldn't reveal this to him. Instead she went back to the wine glass. She sipped the wine while she kept her eyes on Paco from the rim of the glass.

He continued as she studied him.

"You're not on their side, or my side, you're on Serena De La Rosa's side. You know very well you have the goods to fetch a high price and as you said, 'I've been throwing sugar cubes and carrots at you'.

"I apologize for that, Serena. But I'm on the verge of making a big deal Sweetheart. And when this goes through I'll be able to give you what you want. Believe me; this deal in America can make us both rich."

Paco tipped his glass up and after another quick drink continued.

"I realize now I've been short-changing you but stick with me and you'll get in on a big cut. I've been trying to get a deal with these people for years and never had the performer to make one. But now I've got you, and they've got an itch for you real bad, Serena."

She slowly began to understand the situation.

Somehow, in Paco's warped mind, where everyone is out to get the most money they can, and where you always judge the people around you by the financial value they hold, Paco had completely mistaken what Serena said as meaning she wanted more money and his advances were insulting due to the low financial value they represented.

Serena's mind raced as he spoke. She still had a chance. She straightened up and put her arms on the table just as Paco finished by asking. "What do you think of that?"

She gazed into his eyes with a keen expression of interest and then said in a sultry voice.

"You've finally gained my attention, Paco… tell me more."

He smiled with the expression of having just made a profitable deal.

Paco appeared to relax. He sat back and began to relate all the things she'd hoped for and more.

"America is where the real money is. Europe has been flat broke since the war. The problem is getting into the American market. You see, in America they have prohibition. It's the stupidest thing any government could have done, but it's good for the business we want into."

Paco leaned over the table to get closer to Serena.

"The Bootleggers and Rumrunners, along with the owners of the Speakeasies are all raking the money in hand over fist. And these people need quality entertainment. But they want people that will work with their program, and that's where you and I come in.

"I've been waiting and watching for someone with your talent to come along. I knew the Americans would be at the Madam Rouge the night you danced there, and I had to pull some major strings to get you in. But that little number you danced was the magic charm and now all that's left is to finish this tour and sign on the dotted line, Sweetheart. Then we'll be on easy street."

As Paco spoke of this, Serena felt cold and wanted to be somewhere else. But she continued to show interest in what he said, making mental notes on everything as Paco elaborated his plans for her.

"You'll love America. I'm telling you, once we get in good with these people we can kiss the meager pickings here good-bye."

She sat up even straighter and moved forward. This made her breasts more obvious and as she knew it would, caused Paco to gaze down at her chest.

"So, Paco, what about the rest of the performers; are they going to America as well?"

She tried to be more appealing to Paco, even though she wouldn't be deceptive and lie to him. After a close examination of Serena's chest, he replied.

"No, we don't need them. Besides, these Americans only want you. Believe me; they have back-up dancers running out of their ears. And don't even ask about musicians, they're so thick you can't wade through them. That's why it's so hard to get into the American market. They have tons of people in the entertainment business.

"The only problem they have is there aren't enough highly talented performers. No, I just need to decide what to do about this mutiny they're pulling on me. I would like to fire them all, but it's going to cost me to cancel these last three shows. Either way though, once I get this deal through they're all out."

Serena took another drink of wine. She had drunk more than she wanted to already and very much felt the effects of the alcohol, but she knew she needed to hold everything together.

She realized the less talking she had to do the better chance of not revealing her true feelings again.

Then, Paco looked at her as if she needed to comment. She took a deep breath and sat her glass down with an extra effort of feminine daintiness. Then, licked her lips in a seductive manner and said.

"It seems to me, fewer tickets to America, and less hotel rooms, will save us a lot of money."

Paco smiled when she said this.

"That's right! And exactly what I was thinking. I know why I've been so attracted to you now; you and I think alike."

Serena smiled as much as she could. She felt sick just having to sit at the same table with this man.

When the evening was done, and Paco walked Serena to her room, he tried to kiss her.

"Hey, don't think you're going to be getting any liberties just yet, Paco. It's easy to talk about big things. I'm a woman that needs to see the proof first." She pushed him away and he smiled coyly.

She opened her door and slipped in. Mimi was waiting directly inside, and Serena immediately fell into her arms.

"Bathroom," was all she could say.

Mimi helped her to the bathroom and Serena promptly began vomiting in the toilet.

Mimi stood outside the door with a towel and Serena's robe for what seemed like hours.

Finally, after she finished cleaning up, Serena reached out and took the robe and towel.

Then, when she came out, Serena put her hand on Mimi for support as they moved towards her room.

"Did you check on Alicia?"

"She's alright. Carla is with her now. She really misses you though, she asks about you again and again when I'm with her." Mimi replied as she helped the dancer.

"Alright, try not to leave her alone for long. She's always been with me; I don't want her to be alone for too long. Try to bring her here tomorrow so I can see her. Just, don't let Paco find out."

Mimi nodded as they moved towards the bedroom.

"Find Mr. Cantelli first thing in the morning. Tell him I need to meet him somewhere that we won't be seen by Paco. Don't mention my dinner with Paco to any of the performers do you understand?"

"You shouldn't go out in the morning, you're not well."

As Serena lay down in her bed she replied.

"I'll be fine, Mimi. Just do as I ask, please. It's very important that Mr. Cantelli is aware of the situation."

Mimi covered her up with the blankets.

"I will," she replied softly.

The following morning in a small coffee shop on a London side street, Serena spotted Mr. Cantelli sitting at a table. She quickly went to the table and sat down across from him.

"Good morning, Serena. I hoped you would remember this little coffee shop from last year."

Serena smiled, and a waiter came over to take her order.

"So, what's this about? Mimi said it was very important."

Serena pulled her sunglasses off and sat them on the table.

"You must contact Paco today. Let him know you wish to talk with him about the situation. Speak with him as early as possible today."

The waiter brought Serena some coffee.

Mr. Cantelli tipped his cup up for a sip as he considered what she said.

Serena glanced around, seeming concerned about someone seeing them in the coffee shop together. She then sipped her coffee and appeared to relax a little.

"The first show is three days away. I believe Paco will be contacting us soon. If he cancels these shows he'll have to pay hefty penalties. You know as well as I do Paco is all about money; he won't want to do that. He can hire Alicia back and pay three years' salary for what he would pay in penalties."

Serena took a deep breath and stirred her coffee. After seeming to think about what she wanted to say she began to speak.

"Paco is not at all concerned about Alicia, or you or any of the performers. In fact, I suspect he may cancel the shows at anytime, and that's why you need to make a deal quickly. He's almost ready to sign a contract with some Americans and the company is just a problem he needs to tie up before he signs the deal."

Serena took another small sip of her coffee and then continued.

"From what I've put together, he may want to cancel the shows, so he can fire all the performers and be done with their contracts. This of course may create problems for the performers finding work again, but he doesn't care about that.

"I also believe he's working on a way to dissolve the company and leave you to pay any outstanding debts since you sided with the performers. Then he'll present the situation with the performers as 'causing the cancellations' of the last three shows."

Mr. Cantelli sat back in his chair as if this information had deflated him a bit. They both sat in silence drinking their coffee and seeming to evaluate the circumstances.

Then Mr. Cantelli replied, "I know something of the Americans Paco wants to cut a deal with. They're connected directly to the criminal underworld; the gangsters are the owners of the illegal Speakeasies, as they're called. They're certainly Paco's kind of people but bad news altogether.

"The Company he's wanted to sign with for years now basically puts on a few legitimate shows here and there. They have some 'below grade' movie studios also that produce low-budget films. This is all done however for the appearance of them earning their money legally. Most of their income is derived from selling illegal alcohol and shuffling their performers around the Speakeasies, which I suspect are all over the country."

He then appeared to think of something.

"How is it you happen to know about his plans?"

Serena gazed around the small coffee shop again, seeming

284

reluctant to answer. Then she replied without looking at Mr. Cantelli,

"I went to dinner with him last night."

Now Mr. Cantelli sat up in his chair.

"Serena!" he spoke as a father might speak to his daughter and a bit louder than he may have meant to.

He looked around the coffee shop as if he wanted to continue speaking loud but realized others would hear. In a softer tone he continued.

"I know what you're trying to do. I know you may want to help us. But you're in more danger than any of us. Money can be replaced. New jobs can be found. He wants you as his plaything; his trophy. I don't care what he may have told you about this deal with the Americans. All he wants from you is a way in. Once he's in America and settled in with these people he won't think twice about selling you out if necessary."

Serena held her head down as a daughter might after being scolded by her father.

"I'm aware of Mr. Rivera's true nature. But if he's allowed to finish this, everyone will be hurt, and he'll win again. It's better for one to be hurt than all of us."

Mr. Cantelli sat up even more and leaned over the table a little.

"No, Serena. I won't allow you to do this. You don't have to take the fall for the rest of us."

Now Serena looked straight at him and with a firm voice replied.

"I don't plan on falling. If we work together, we may be able to get through this. But, I'm willing to take a risk for the others. There's no way I can get out right now unharmed. I'm locked into his plans and if I don't at least appear to follow them, he'll take great pleasure in crushing my career, along with all the others. If you and the others can get out; at least I can have comfort in that. I see no other alternative right now."

Mr. Cantelli thought of what Serena said with concern in his eyes. He again leaned back in his chair and gazed down at his coffee cup.

Finally, after a few moments of thought Mr. Cantelli replied with a softer tone.

"What do we need to do?"

Serena considered this question as the waiter came by and refilled their cups.

"You should approach Paco as if you feel he'll relent and hire Alicia back. When he expresses no plan to do so, you should appear worried and begin negotiations with him."

She took another sip of coffee and continued.

"Whatever you do, don't reveal that you have any idea of his true plans. Make a deal first to finish the tour and then all the performers be released from their contracts. Then I believe you should try to negotiate to sell your percentage of the company to him. Since you own forty percent of my contract, he'll likely be willing to do this to expedite the deal with the Americans. As it is, if he cancels the shows you'll have to pay forty percent of the fines, so this is also attractive to him."

Serena glanced around the small coffee shop as if to be sure no one could hear her. Then she went on.

"He wants a reason to dissolve the company with my contract intact and he may be able do such a thing if he cancels the shows. But, if you can make a deal with him at the same time you deal with the performer situation, it might tie everything up nice and neat, all at once for him. I suspect he'll be glad to do this. He can get out from under the other contracts and he'll own one hundred percent of my contract, which is the only one he really wants. He can also sign with the Americans right away before they leave Europe. Make sure every detail is in writing and signed before the shows."

After discussing the plans thoroughly, Mr. Cantelli left the coffee shop. After a few moments Serena also left and went back to the hotel in a different direction.

Later that morning Mr. Cantelli knocked on Paco's door.

"What can I do for you, Cantelli?"

"Can I speak with you Paco?"

He opened the door and Mr. Cantelli came inside.

"Please sit down," Paco motioned to a chair in the sitting area of his room.

"The first show is three days away Paco. Have you decided to bring Alicia back?"

Paco replied smugly.

"No and I was about to go downtown and cancel the shows before the close of business today."

Mr. Cantelli sat up, appearing shocked.

"What, you can't do that Paco! Why would you do such a thing? You can pay Alicia three years salary for what we'll pay in penalties!"

Paco now became more arrogant than ever. He smiled and replied,

"Let's just say it's a matter of principle, Cantelli. You may allow the performers to push you around, but I won't."

He stared at Mr. Cantelli who now expressed deep concern.

He said nothing for several minutes as Paco waited with glee; feeling certain he would win. Then Mr. Cantelli spoke with a timid voice.

"Let me talk with the performers before you do anything. Maybe we can still work something out."

Paco replied quickly.

"What you need to work out with the performers is who is in charge. That's why you've only survived in this business Torre and I've been successful. You allow your feelings to get in the way. It's a business and these people work for us, not the other way around."

Mr. Cantelli gave Paco a stare of contempt and replied coldly.

"I don't like the way you do business Paco. I never have."

He then stood up and as he went out the door said, "I'll be back later."

Meanwhile, Alicia and Mimi sat in the small sitting area of Serena's room. She lay back down immediately after returning from her meeting with Mr. Cantelli. The two women sat quietly with their thoughts while she slept.

When Serena came from her room, both women jumped up and went to her quickly to give her support. She appeared weak and pale.

She immediately smiled to Alicia when she saw her.

"You need to eat," Mimi said as they helped her sit down. "I'll go get you something."

She moved briskly out the door as Alicia pulled a small stool close to Serena. She sat across from her friend and studied her. She wanted to cry, but also knew she needed to be strong for Serena. She wondered where the dancer found her courage.

She reached out and took her hand and held it. Serena turned to Alicia and smiled again indicating this helped her feel better.

"I wish… we could just go home," Alicia finally said.

Then she remembered the long, difficult road Serena had traveled. She hoped her home was the same home as Serena's. This caused an unexpected surge of emotion. She could hold the tears back no longer and several erupted from her eyes.

"I'm sorry." She got up and turned away from her, feeling ashamed.

"I wanted to be strong for you," she mumbled sadly. "I didn't want to cry. I'm sorry; I know you don't need this right now."

Serena said nothing. Alicia wiped her tears frantically. She turned back and studied Serena who was gazing out towards the window. Finally, she wiped the last tear from her cheek and asked her.

"What's going to happen?"

Serena replied softly. "I don't know."

Soon Mimi returned with a plate of food. As Serena ate, Mimi spoke.

"I talked with Mr. Cantelli,"

She handed her a napkin. Serena grasped the napkin and looked at Mimi expectantly as she chewed her food.

"He said to tell you, he and Mr. Rivera will be negotiating this afternoon for a settlement."

Serena took another bite, then after chewing and swallowing her food she wiped her mouth with the napkin and replied.

"You should go talk with all the performers, Mimi. Tell them to trust Mr. Cantelli on the deal he makes with Paco. No matter what, they must trust his judgment on this, alright? Don't tell them I said this but tell them it's what Serena would do. They'll understand."

Mimi nodded and left her room quickly, as Serena continued eating.

"What do you need me to do?" Alicia appeared tired of sitting around. Serena smiled at her friend and replied.

"Stay close by me, and out of Paco's sight. I want us to make it home together."

When Serena said this Alicia almost began to cry again, but instead she laughed a little as she felt happy knowing Serena's home was the same as hers.

The sun had long set by the time Mr. Cantelli arrived back at Paco's room.

"Come in, Cantelli."

When he came inside the room a young woman came from the bedroom. She gathered her cloak and then left. Mr. Cantelli looked at Paco.

"One of my assistants," was his reply.

"Sit, please. I'll pour us a drink."

Mr. Cantelli sat down, and Paco poured two glasses of Gin.

"I hope you have something to tell me. If I must cancel two days before the show, we'll be paying a very high price. And forty percent of that bill will be yours."

Mr. Cantelli took a small drink and then held it in his hand as it rested on his leg.

"First, the performers will finish the tour, with the condition that you release them from their current contracts afterwards. Apparently, your iron-fisted management is not very popular with them."

Paco tipped his glass up for a drink and then paused before asking.

"Is that all?"

Mr. Cantelli seemed hesitant to go on, but after a few seconds continued.

"I want out as well. I'm offering you my shares of the business. If you're not interested, I'll sell to someone else, cheap if necessary, just to get out. Perhaps you'll have a better working relationship with who I sell to."

When Mr. Cantelli said this, Paco sat up a little, seeming to be concerned by the statement. He quickly recovered and went about as if he was not very interested.

For several moments Paco said nothing. He stood up and walked over to the window and gazed out. He went to his bottle and poured himself another drink and immediately turned the glass up. He moved back over to where Mr. Cantelli sat and finally replied.

"I'll give you the equipment for your shares. I'll transfer the office and storage leases in Naples to you as well."

Mr. Cantelli grimaced.

"I said cheap... I didn't say I would give my shares away! You'll get the liquid assets, company name and an established tour. I'll get some well used equipment, a large rental bill and no prospects or personnel to use it... What about the performer's contracts? A few may feel charitable enough to work on a percentage basis until I can get reestablished."

"I'm not finished yet," Paco replied.

"I'll release the performer's contracts if they finish the tour, but only on one condition. Serena's contract stays with me and I become full owner of it."

Mr. Cantelli quickly replied.

"The performers requested 'all' be released from their contracts, Paco. That's the deal!"

Now Paco became very animated.

"No, the deal is what I make it, Cantelli! I own the majority share, I make the calls! You and all the other performers are going to take the deal I give you or I'll cancel the shows and shut down the company. You'll pay the entire penalties since you sided with the performers and I'll keep Serena. You know damn well the courts will side with me on this."

Mr. Cantelli moved back in his chair, seeming to relent a bit to Paco.

Paco continued.

"The only reason I'm giving you a deal at all Cantelli is to save time. I don't care to bicker with the lawyers and I don't need to linger around to dispense with the equipment and costumes. You're getting a good deal to get anything at all. As for the performers, I would just as soon burn their contracts and make sure none of them ever perform in Europe again, after the treachery they've pulled. And I'll tell you this, Torre."

Paco now walked over and pointed his finger at Mr. Cantelli's face while he spoke.

"I've seen Mimi hanging around Serena's room. I'm sure she's trying to stir up trouble just like her friend Alicia. I'm tired of the problems these performers are making. Serena is going to America with me as soon as this infernal tour ends, one way or the other. The condition for me to release the other performers from their contracts is that until Serena sets foot in the United States, they'll still be bound by their contracts and I have the option to reject the entire agreement. I want no more problems from them, and if anyone interferes with me, I swear I'll make sure they pay. Is that clear?"

Mr. Cantelli sneered at Paco's remarks but said nothing.

"That's the deal, Torre. Take it or leave it."

After some thought Mr. Cantelli replied.

"I know who you're dealing with in America, Paco. They're in business with the gangsters. You're going to take a beautiful and talented woman like Serena and throw her into a snake pit, just so you can get into the American market. I'm aware of the entertainment provided at the Speakeasies. She doesn't belong on that sort of stage, Paco. That may be your kind of people, but Serena doesn't belong there."

Paco, who had ventured to the window, again turned quickly to Mr. Cantelli.

"You don't know Serena as well as you may think, Torre. And, it's no longer your concern what happens with Serena De La Rosa. But you can rest assured, in America she'll make the money she really deserves and wants. Regardless of how long she stays employed by me. Ms. De La Rosa will be among people that'll pay her what she should be paid. Unlike the petty change you've been giving her."

Mr. Cantelli took his glass and downed the last drink before replying.

"Regardless of what you may believe, money isn't everything, Paco."

Paco also finished his drink and said.

"I want a decision by tomorrow morning, Cantelli."

After leaving Paco's room Mr. Cantelli went to Serena's room, being careful that Paco didn't see him.

Inside her room the three women seemed to be waiting anxiously for something to happen. As he entered, Serena perked up, obviously glad to get any news on the situation.

Once he explained the offer to Serena, she considered it silently while the others sipped wine. Serena stood up and walked to the window. Then she turned and said.

"Accept the offer."

Mr. Cantelli expressed disappointment that she said this.

"Serena, the stipulation of you setting foot in America changes everything. Paco may be under the impression that you're agreeable to his plans now, but this stipulation is his insurance policy. One way or the other, he plans to have you under his control by the time the two of you reach America.

Believe me Serena; Paco will use force if necessary to subdue you. He's been waiting a long time to make a deal with these people and he'll be sure you're cooperative even if it takes fear to do so. We've got to try and renegotiate. You'll be alone with him all the way to America, and that's exactly what he wants."

Serena turned back to the window. By now it was getting close to midnight and she felt exhausted.

The streets of London below were almost void of traffic. She knew Mr. Cantelli was right about the situation. There seemed to be no other option though.

From the reflection in the window she could see Alicia and Mimi watching her. She studied their faces and considered trying to make an escape.

Perhaps she and Alicia could go back to Mexico and Paco would never find them. Then she realized something she'd never considered before this moment. As she studied the reflections of the two women that had become as sisters to her, Serena knew if she ran now, these two women would always fear men like Paco. They would always be timid and frightened by men that tried to take advantage of them.

If she ran now, she might save herself from Paco. But how would she live around the people she cared the most for, knowing she taught them to be afraid.

Serena took a deep breath as she gazed at the reflections of Alicia and Mimi. They were unaware that she studied them, and she wanted to somehow capture this moment; the love and concern in their faces.

She had no doubt now this was the family she'd always

longed for. She must be strong for them. She was aware of her chances with Paco; they were slim at best. She had few cards at her disposal to play.

It was certain Paco was more experienced at subduing women than she was at dealing with men such as him. Nevertheless, if everything failed, she would at least know the ones she loved could start new. She would do her best to avoid being a sacrifice for the others, but if that's what happened, she would rather it than running for the rest of her life.

She turned to the others as they sat awaiting her response.

"Paco isn't the first man I've had to avoid. All I need to do is avoid him until we reach America. The ship is very large, I can avoid him or make sure we're always in public areas. Once in America the deal will be final."

Mr. Cantelli again seemed to cringe. He stood up and moved towards her. Alicia and Mimi also stood up and positioned themselves behind him in a show of support.

"Even if you do make it to America safely somehow Serena, what then; if he suspects anything on the way he'll tighten the ropes even more. He's stacked the deck in his favor. He'll either make sure you're with him in this deal or he'll wear you down before you reach America. You've got to get away while you can."

All three were now standing in front of Serena with pleading faces. She knew they were concerned for her well-being and she also realized what she must do to move on from this point.

She looked at all three of them with a stern expression. Then with an assertive tone she began.

"Do not ask me again to run from a man such as Paco Rivera. I'll try to avoid him, but if he tries to force himself on me I'll fight him. He'll never win me over, even if he uses force. I'm stronger inside than Paco will ever realize. This is the path I must walk; to face Paco and I'll not waver from that. He'll lose this battle one way or the other, no matter how long I must fight him."

She moved forward a step and all three stepped back as she did so.

"Paco has a critical weakness. He's always had his way and has come to believe he always will. I mean to take advantage of that weakness, somehow. No matter how though, I'll find a way to fight him. If I run from this man now, I'll surely lose the person I am; I'll always run from men such as Paco and I'll always be afraid. I'll not allow myself to be swept aside by Paco's ruthless plans, so do not ask me again to run."

After hearing this, Mr. Cantelli, Alicia and Mimi appeared frightened by Serena's confident resolve. All three stood frozen with blank expressions on their faces.

Serena watched them closely and held them in this state for a few seconds. Then she turned back to the window.

In the reflection of the window she saw them look at each other and then walk to their chairs and sit back down. Obviously, she'd made her point.

Now she just had to survive the decision she'd made. As she thought of these things, a flash of lighting in the distance caught her attention. This triggered a feeling deep inside her; a feeling of being alone in a storm. She lowered her head and tried to brace herself for the struggle ahead.

The next morning Mr. Cantelli informed Paco he and the performers would accept the deal. Then they went to have the paperwork put together and both signed the agreement.

CHAPTER TWELVE:

The Closing Curtains

The performers worked quickly to make up for lost time as they prepared for the final three shows.

Once the settlement between Mr. Cantelli and the performers had been signed, Paco moved rapidly to secure his deal with the Americans. Before leaving for Paris however he stopped by Serena's room.

"What do you want Paco?"

He pushed the door slightly to move into Serena's room. Mimi quickly came into the sitting area, having heard Paco's voice. He looked at her and appeared a little disappointed at her being there.

"Can we talk in private?"

Serena looked at Mimi and then back to Paco.

"You fired my last assistant. Mimi has been filling in."

She again glanced at Mimi, "You can wait in the other room Mimi, thank you."

Mimi expressed reluctance to leave, but slowly moved to the other room where she remained close to the door, listening for trouble.

"I've finalized a deal with Cantelli. I now own your contract completely."

He watched Serena closely after saying this.

"Would you like a glass of wine, Paco?" She went to a table and began pouring a glass of wine.

"No, I have business to attend to."

Serena took a drink.

"So, we're finally going to America then?"

Paco seemed pleased with her response.

"Yes, I'm leaving for Paris right away. I'll have a contract by the time I return and as soon as the last three shows are finished we'll board a ship for New York."

Serena didn't act impressed. She came closer to Paco and he looked her over from top to bottom, as usual. She felt dirty when he did this but didn't turn from his gaze.

"You've promised much from this deal in America, Paco. I'm a woman that expects a man to keep his word."

Paco's mouth twisted down with anger at this comment, but he immediately regained composure.

"I believe, in America you'll begin to understand how well I run things. There have been too many distractions here."

After saying this he gazed towards the door that Mimi had went into.

"Yes, well I suppose since you own my contract now, I'll just have to hope you can deliver."

Serena said this rather nonchalantly. Paco smiled slightly and replied smugly.

"Don't you worry, I always deliver."

He then left Serena's room, indicating on the way out he would be back by the time the final show ended.

The London shows proceeded without interruption, but Serena continued to remain reserved and withdrawn from those around her.

Though Alicia and Mimi were constantly by her side, she spoke little and seldom smiled as the days crept by.

Ten days later, Paco approached Mr. Fedenza as the company packed up to return to Naples.

"Mr. Fedenza."

The assistant stage manager looked at Paco with apprehension but replied politely.

"Hello Mr. Rivera. What can I do for you?"

"I'm looking for Cantelli."

Mr. Fedenza gazed back down at his clipboard and replied in a cold monotone voice.

"He went to make some business arrangements. Maybe storage for the equipment, I'm not exactly sure. Is there anything I can help you with?"

Paco gazed around at the stage crew as they moved crates and stage props around.

"No, I guess our business is over anyway. How did the final shows go?"

Mr. Fedenza again responded without looking up as he seemed to be making calculations on his paperwork.

"Fairly well, considering how exhausted the company is."

Paco followed the assistant stage manager as he moved up to a large wooden crate and inspected it.

"Is Ms. De La Rosa around?"

Mr. Fedenza now stopped writing and glanced up at him. He then replied.

301

"I've not seen her this morning. Most all of the dancers have already left for Naples though."

Paco appeared distressed when he heard this.

"Alright thanks." He then hurried away.

Walking up to Serena's hotel room, he pounded on the door. Shortly after Serena opened it.

"Hello, Paco. How did it go in Paris?"

Paco was obviously relieved to see her and replied.

"Very good, we're all set. I've got us a one-year contract with future options. By the time we get to the United States all the arraignments will have been made for the engagements. Are you packed up and ready?"

Serena tried to smile but could only manage a small one.

"Yes, I'm ready."

"Good, our train leaves tomorrow at 8:00 in the morning. We'll board our ship tomorrow afternoon and leave port that evening. We should reach New York in ten to eleven days."

Again, Serena tried to smile but it seemed the best she could do was to not look unhappy.

"Don't worry. I'll be ready." She closed the door and went back into her room.

Inside the sitting area, Alicia and Mimi stood staring at her, seeming shocked now that the time was running out. Then, she noticed a tear run down Mimi's cheek.

Alicia spoke in a very firm voice. "We're not leaving you."

Several more tears rolled down Mimi's cheeks and she shook her head, indicating she agreed with Alicia's assertion.

Serena felt her heart well up with love for these two women

as they expressed their determination to follow her into a fire. She wanted to cry also. She wanted to hug them and welcome them along.

The prospect of not having these two dear friends by her side frightened her so much and it took all she had inside her not to breakdown at this point.

But, she knew that if she showed any weakness now, they wouldn't let her go alone.

She mustered all her strength to remain in control and putting her hand up to Mimi's cheek she wiped a tear with her thumb and caressed it the same way Olivia used to do so long ago.

She smiled lovingly and said, "I'll be alright. It'll only be ten days or so. I can manage for that long."

Mimi now reached up and grasped Serena's hand and held it tight to her cheek as another tear flowed freely down and over Serena's hand.

Alicia rushed forward and hugged Serena. This caused Mimi also to move forward and the three stood together in an embrace.

Now Serena could no longer hold back the tears and several rolled down her cheeks.

"You two go to Naples. No need to worry about anything, Mr. Cantelli will take care of everything."

Alicia mumbled through her tears as her head rested on Serena's shoulder.

"We won't leave you."

Mimi tried to say something also, but Serena couldn't understand her as she now wept as a child.

She felt as if she would fall apart right there. She wanted to cry with them and came very close to breaking down.

Her head moved in a straining fashion as she stared up at the ceiling, struggling to hold back a flood of emotions. Her mouth tightened in the effort to remain in control.

Finally, with a massive effort, she regained her composure enough to have them sit down. As they both wept, she reassured them again that she would be alright.

After calming down some, Alicia asked about the trip and Serena relayed what Paco had just told her. Then the two women seemed to slowly feel better and Serena said good night and good-bye. She again told them she would see them in Naples as soon as possible.

The following morning Paco picked her up from the room. She sat quietly in the cab as it raced to the train station.

Once on the train she sat with a book in her hands. She'd intentionally purchased several books to assist her in avoiding conversation with Paco.

He sat across from her and on one occasion she glanced up to confirm her suspicions that he was staring at her breasts. He seemed to regard them as if they were a dessert he would soon relish.

When Paco realized she'd looked up from her book, he simply smiled slyly. He did not however turn his gaze away from her. She managed something of a smile and returned to her book.

As she looked at the pages, pretending to read, she grasped for a plan to survive the trip unscathed. Eventually she decided she must keep up an impression that she agreed with Paco's plans, for as long as possible.

If he became too aggressive to manage, she would attempt and evade him until reaching New York.

There were no doubts about Paco's resolve to make sure she was on his side or break her in one way or another before reaching the United States. He was a controlling person and he would certainly make a move to do so either by alliance or fear, whichever it took.

As they began boarding the huge ship, Serena felt panic growing inside. Her thoughts raced with every step. She considered turning and running.

She could smell the ocean and the dark loneliness erupted within her stronger than ever.

Step by step she felt to be leaving a secure place and moving to a place where she had little control and Paco had almost all. She glanced back at him and he smiled with a new confidence and arrogance that reassured her of the thoughts she had being true.

He also knew well that every step they took removed her from her friend's ability to assist her and placed her more firmly into his grip.

She took a deep breath and struggled to keep her feet moving forward up the boarding ramp. Finally, they reached the deck and she took hold of a rail to steady her balance.

"Are you okay?" he asked with an unconvincing tone of concern.

"Yes, I'm alright. That's quite a climb."

Paco chuckled a little and taking her arm led her on into the ship's bowels.

When they reached their cabins, Serena felt some relief that he hadn't ordered one cabin for both. Instead he ordered his and her cabin side by side.

Considering this she decided he must know she was still the key to his plans in America. He would have had them in the same cabin, but should she become startled, she would still have an opportunity to make an escape before the ship left port.

This at least bought her a little more time and perhaps a fraction of security.

"We'll go to breakfast together in the morning," he said as she slipped into her cabin. She nodded before closing the door.

The weight of the situation now pressed down on her and she collapsed onto her bed exhausted.

When she awoke the next morning, the ship had slipped out of port and was far out to sea.

Initially Paco acted content to have her securely on the ship.

For several days Serena managed to fend Paco off with her stance on him proving his deal with the Americans was all he said it would be.

She tried to stay in her room and act as if she was not feeling well, or that she was reading a book.

For a while, Paco was easily distracted by the ship's entertainment and lounges. As he did so well, he flirted with women, gambled, drank and merely made sure Serena was always close by.

He would take her to eat with him once a day and make the usual advances. Serena would in turn remind him she expected results not promises.

Slowly however, and as the ship grew closer to New York, Paco became less and less inclined to be easily brushed off.

On the seventh and eighth day, Paco's demeanor began to change dramatically. Although it was not uncommon for him to pull a metal flask from his jacket pocket and take a drink, he now began to drink more than usual.

As they sat eating dinner on the eighth day, Paco finished off a large drink of wine and then told Serena, "The Americans will have some reporters at the dock to publicize their newest acquisition. Don't worry, I speak English, I'll do all the talking. All you need to do is stand there and be beautiful for the cameras. If any of the Americans, ask you a question just point to me."

He stared across the table at Serena. She saw something in his eyes now she hadn't seen before. He seemed to be losing patience and would begin asserting himself more and more.

She said nothing but simply nodded and continued to eat small bits of her food.

As she ate, and Paco had another drink of wine, several men approached the table. They all wore uniforms and one appeared to be the captain of the ship. He spoke with a strong British accent.

"Hello, it really is the famous Flamenco dancer, Serena De La Rosa. This is Serena De La Rosa isn't it?"

The man glanced at Paco when he asked this. Paco smiled and replied in English.

"Yes, this is Serena De La Rosa, the famous Italian dancer."

"Ms. De La Rosa, I saw your show in London a few weeks ago. I've noticed you here in the dining room several times and felt certain it was you. I'm Captain Hill, humbly at your service."

Serena said nothing but stared blankly at the captain.

"Oh, I'm sorry Captain." Paco said and then repeated what the Captain said to Serena in Italian.

Serena then said, "I'm pleased to meet you, Captain." She said this in Italian and Paco translated to the Captain who smiled and continued.

"Ms. De La Rosa, we have a stage here and I'm sure I could locate a guitar player among our crew; would you do us the honor of a dance? It would be such a treat for us." The captain said this to Serena, but then turned to Paco when she tipped her glass for a drink of wine, as if he were not speaking to her.

Paco then repeated the captain's request in Italian.

Serena glanced up at the captain. She casually smelled her wine and replied.

"I'm sorry, but I have nothing prepared on such short notice."

The captain turned to Paco for the translation. He didn't translate her words this time. Paco stared at her and when he didn't translate what she had said, Serena glanced up.

He appeared to be in thought. She watched him, and his disposition grew darker as she watched him. Then he said to her.

"You will dance for the captain, Serena."

"I told you Paco, I'm not prepared for a dance."

Paco turned to the captain and said in accented English. "Ms. De La Rosa will be glad to dance for you Captain."

"Oh, thank you Ms. De La Rosa, I'll have the guitar player come up straight away. Oh, this is splendid! We'll get the word out and I assure you there will be an audience waiting anxiously."

The captain and his men then left to make the preparations.

Serena stared at Paco. She took another drink of her wine. Now she knew the end of the rope was close. She'd stretched it out as far as she could. Paco wouldn't allow her to go much farther without his control over her. This was the beginning of his total dominance over her, just as she knew would be coming sooner or later.

She turned her gaze into the wine glass.

There was only one person she could dance for now, only one love strong enough to overcome the storm around her. Serena could only dance for her mother.

She realized the moment had finally arrived. As Paco stared at her from across the table, she knew the time had come. It must be now, because it was the only dance left for her in this pale situation.

Gazing into her wine glass, she wondered if this might be the last performance. Once again Paco was in a position to win. Though Serena didn't love Paco as Olivia had, he was now poised to rip the dancer from her soul, just as he had done to her mother so long ago.

The time had finally arrived for her ultimate expression of

the art, and possibly it would be the swan song of Serena and Olivia both. Perhaps this would be the last performance between the two as master Flamenco dancers.

She turned up the last sip of wine, sat her glass on the table and turned to Paco. He'd never turned his gaze away from her as she considered these things.

"I'll get dressed." She stood up.

Paco smiled.

In her cabin she pulled her mother's picture from a suitcase. She studied the picture lovingly. This time there were no tears. She ran her fingers over the glass, as if she wished to connect with Olivia somehow.

She sat the picture on the table and pulled a dress from her luggage. It was a beautiful Spanish style dress that was like the one her mother wore in the picture. For this reason, it was one of her favorites.

She slowly put the dress on as she gazed at her mother's picture. Then, she sat down and put her hair into the exact same style as Olivia had hers in. The tiny bows on her dress were adjusted carefully to appear the same as those on Olivia's dress.

When Serena was finished, she sat on the bed and stared at the wall.

Soon, Paco's hard knock came on the door. Serena opened the door.

"They're ready for you."

She nodded and walked towards the lounge.

Inside the expansive lounge, a large audience had

assembled. The captain and his crew had done an efficient job in spreading the word of Serena's dance.

She went to the low stage where a guitar player sat at the corner.

Before stepping onto the stage, she slipped off her dancing shoes. If this turned out to be her last dance, it would be like no other she had ever performed.

When Serena stepped up onto the stage and walked over to the guitarist she could tell he was very nervous.

She spoke in Italian and asked the man if he knew a slow Spanish song to play.

"I'm, sorry Ms., I don't speak Italian." He replied with a British accent.

Now the guitar player appeared even more nervous and obviously had been prodded into this by the captain.

Serena spoke softly in English for the man.

"Can you play something slow and in a Spanish style?"

The guitar player nodded. "Yes Ms., I believe I can do something. I have several Spanish songs I've worked on. I hope it will be good enough, Ms. De La Rosa."

Serena tried to smile.

"I'm sure it'll be fine."

She stood in the center of the small stage and lowered her head. The guitarist began to play. She thought of her mother and began to dance from her heart.

The moves were subtle and delicate. She flowed gracefully about the stage; without any effort. This wasn't a Flamenco dance or a Fandango dance. This was a dance all her own. She moved as her heart told her to move.

Everyone in the lounge became hushed as she drifted to a place that only such a dancer as Serena could find. She took the audience with her as she gracefully moved to recreate her heart's deepest desire on the small stage.

Serena felt she was now in the eye of the violent storm. And now in this calm place, this refuge inside her, Serena realized she had at this moment become the dancer her heart desired, the one in the picture that Olivia had shown to her in that tiny back room of the Cafe Flamenco. She had finally transformed into the dancer that had pulled her from the darkest place and gave her hope and love.

In this strange violent mixture of fear all around her and love for her mother, Serena merged the dancer Olivia had hoped to be as well as the dancer Serena had become, into one.

Now, at this moment, she met her destiny as a dancer and the resolution lay before her on this tiny stage. She grasped it with her soul and embraced it just as she had done everything, for her and her mother.

As this occurred the spell reached out over the room and lay upon the audience as a mist might settle on delicate blades of grass in the morning.

She expressed her desire to see Olivia once again, and though the audience only saw the graceful moves and her dress swaying lightly around her, inside Serena was reaching out through the distance and capturing the love and memories of her beautiful mother.

The guitar player now glanced up as he could also not resist the magic that was somehow turning his crude strumming into a masterpiece.

His heart filled with emotions and he dedicated himself to play as long as this beautiful woman wanted to dance. He would do anything she asked now. She had graced his music as a beautiful woman graces an artist's canvas. He knew he would remember this moment for all his life.

When the song ended, Serena stood with her side to the audience. She slowly turned but did not look at the audience this time. Instead she gazed out over the top of them.

A single tear rolled down her face. She turned and slowly walked off the stage. The silence gripped the room so tightly now that it was almost unbearable. This was the only time she'd not released an audience.

She moved gracefully through the lounge and on towards the doors while the audience sat quietly.

Only Paco had a heart cold enough to resist the magic; as she passed by him and reached the doors he began to clap. This seemed to break the spell and the room erupted in applause as she moved quickly towards her cabin.

Now the tears fell freely down Serena's face as she held her hand to her mouth and raced to the safety of her room. Once inside she fell to her bed and wept.

She had poured her heart out in the dance for her mother and now the feeling of being alone was stronger than ever.

After many tears, she slept that night in her dancing dress as she had no strength to take it off.

The next morning Paco knocked on her door to take her to breakfast. As they sat at the table, several people came by and complimented her on the previous night's performance. She nodded and thanked them in Italian.

"I've never seen you dance that way."

Serena glanced at Paco when he said this.

"You see, Serena, if I'd not made you dance, the captain and all the others would have missed that. It's as I've always said, you need a man such as me around. I can help you achieve those things you may not think you could otherwise."

Serena thought of his comment for a few seconds as she picked at her food without much zeal. Then she replied but didn't bother to look at Paco.

"Mr. Rivera, your ability to, 'make me dance,' is equal to the ability of you spreading your arms and summoning a tempest. No one has ever made me dance… and no one ever will."

This immediately made Paco angry. His face twisted a bit as Serena now glanced up at him. He said nothing because another admirer approached and complimented Serena on her dance.

She knew well the eye of the storm had passed and the violence would soon come. She looked back down to her plate and again picked at her food.

Paco's intense stare remained on her until after breakfast. He went to the lounge and Serena went to her cabin. Now Paco's wrath was stirring. She must prepare herself. She rubbed her hands as she sat on the edge of the bed and considered this.

After dinner that evening, Paco followed her to the cabins. In previous days he would go somewhere to gamble or drink maybe, she cared little where. Now he stood hovering over her in front the door.

"Good night, Paco."

He pulled a flask from his pocket and downed a large drink. He then placed the cap back on and put it into his pocket.

"I said good night, Paco," this time she said it with a more serious tone.

He smiled what she considered to be a very devious smile and then replied.

"It's time we take this relationship to the next level, Serena. We're a team now. We need to strengthen the bond."

"Paco, I'm not one of your Cancan dancers. You've got to do more than just say this deal is great. I need to see it for certain."

She tried again to discourage him, though this had become of little leverage lately.

Paco moved in closer to her as she said this, causing her to be pressed against the door. He maneuvered to a position that would keep her from escaping. Smiling down at her, he replied.

"That's not going to work any longer, Serena. When you had all your little friends around it worked, but now it's just you and me. It's high time you stop playing the 'hard to get game.' You're a woman, I'm a man, it's simple chemistry.

"You just need to relax and let me be in charge. I'll take care of everything for you."

He moved in even closer. She could smell his breath as he spoke. She knew what he wanted, and he'd decided not to wait any longer for it. He continued as she turned her head away from his and tried to melt into the door.

"Serena, you're going to a place where you don't speak the language; you don't know anyone and you're an ocean away from home. You need me Serena, and it's time you understand that. It's time for you to let go and let me run things. I only want to help you, Sweetheart. Just let go and we'll take America by storm together."

He reached down to take the key from her hand. She realized this was his next move to take control. He would take her key and then take everything else he wanted.

Panic stirred inside her. She felt trapped. Once they were inside her cabin, there would be no escape, and this was exactly what Paco wanted. She searched desperately for any way out.

Just then, a man came from around the corner and walked towards them. When he saw Paco he asked, "Mr. Hernandez?"

As Paco replied, "I'm not Mr. Hernandez," she darted under his arm and ran as fast as she could away from him.

"Hey!" Paco shouted and chased after her.

As she rounded a corner she saw him fall, likely from taking too many drinks from his flask.

She quickly darted through passageways and doors until she had become lost herself.

Frantically she searched for a safe place. Paco would surely go to great lengths now to secure her before the ship docked.

When she located an isolated nook on the deck, she pulled a deck chair over and sat, watching nervously for any sign of Paco.

A door behind her proved to be locked and obviously unused for some time, so Serena felt she could remain unseen if he should look along the deck area.

The salty ocean air drifted past her face. Night crept in and she relaxed some. She lay back in the chair as rain began to fall.

She watched the deck in front of her become wet from the growing storm. Though she was not directly in the rain she still became damp due to the partially covered shelter of her hiding spot.

Lightning and thunder began to accompany the rain in earnest. Serena pulled her cloak around her as much as possible as she slowly began to drift into sleep.

"Help me, please!"

She could see Gina in her life vest, floating in the darkened sea. Serena seemed to be hovering over the stormy seas as the young woman she used to be floated helplessly in the rain and wind.

"Help, please!"

Serena tried to understand. She looked around her and now she sat in a very small boat, wearing a fancy Flamenco dancing dress.

The ocean pushed the tiny boat about violently. Serena became drenched from the storm.

"Gina," she called out as she grappled in the boat to pick up a small oar.

She quickly began to paddle towards the young woman. She could see her and hear her.

"Please… help me!"

Serena tried to paddle harder as she spotted Gina raising her hand out in desperation.

"Gina, I'm coming. Gina!"

She shouted now and tried to reach the young woman in the water, but the harder she paddled the farther away Gina floated.

"Gina...!" Then, she could barely hear Gina call out.

"Help me..."

Serena could no longer see her as the wind and rain whipped the small boat about.

She sat in the small craft gazing out over the stormy ocean. She realized her breath could was expelling as a mist and the cold began to penetrate her wet body. She began to shiver as the raindrops fell rapidly onto her face and hair.

She stared out to the ocean, still hoping to see Gina, but there was no sign of her.

As she felt unbearably cold and wet, something odd happened. The water became calm in the area around her small boat.

She felt warmer and her breath could no longer be seen. As she sat in the dark, calm sea; her dream came to an end.

When she awoke, the rain had passed, and the sun crept up over the horizon. She considered the strange dream for a few moments.

Then, she realized a blanket lay over her. She inspected the blanket briefly, then stood up and peeked out to the deck.

There was no one to her left but gazing down the deck to her right, she saw a crew member cleaning. He must have covered her up she thought.

Sitting back down in the deck chair she considered what she might do. Paco would be searching for her; she had little doubt of that.

Pulling the blanket up around her and watching the sun rise into the sky, she felt hungry. Just as hunger was about to force her to abandon her hiding spot, a crew member walked past. After seeming to notice Serena he stopped, and in a thick British accent asked.

"Uhm, would you care for some toast and coffee, Madame? I have some extra here and I hate to throw it out."

Serena gazed up at the man holding a covered tray.

"Yes, that would be wonderful," she replied.

The man put the tray down beside her.

"I'll pick the tray up later, so don't worry about that." He then strolled off as Serena thanked him.

The food and coffee did wonders, and she began to feel better, though still very frightened as she wondered where Paco might be.

After the small meal wore off, she decided to chance a move. She got up and slowly wandered around the ship.

Carefully she moved closer to her cabin in the hope she could get cleaned up and change clothes.

Ever so cautiously she made her way to the hallway close to her cabin, she peeked around the corner and when no one could be seen she quickly and quietly strolled up to the door and inserted her key; then slipped into the room and closed and locked the door as gently as possible.

When she had finished getting cleaned up, she located a small box of chocolates and lay on the bed. As she began to nibble on one of the chocolates Paco came to the door. He knocked very hard.

"Serena, are you in there? Open up, I just want to talk."

She slid to the side of the bed and then moved off it and into the small space between the bed and the wall.

"Serena, I know you're in there. Open up."

Carefully, she pulled the blanket from the bed to cover herself as Paco twisted the locked doorknob back and forth, and then finally left.

She finished off the chocolates and slept that night in the small space beside her bed.

The next morning Serena was awakened by another knock on the door. She peeked up from her hiding place beside the bed and listened.

This knock didn't sound the same as Paco's. She waited, and the knock came again.

She began to move out of her spot, but then she thought, this might be a trick of Paco's.

She lowered herself back down and barely peeked over the bed in the direction of the door. After another knock the person at the door moved away.

As the hours ticked by, she could no longer endure the pains in her stomach due to hunger. She examined the empty chocolate box in a vain hope one last chocolate might appear. She knew it was not safe in the room either. If Paco decided to check her cabin, he could find a way in.

Around noon, she decided to venture out and find food and water.

She walked to the door and put her hand on the knob, but then hesitated a few more seconds, as if something might happen to spare her from taking this risk.

Once she confirmed to herself again she must find food, she slowly opened the door and peeked out. When no one could be seen, she darted out and locked the door.

Making a brisk pace down the hallway, she maneuvered through doors and passages in a long route to the dining room.

In the large dining area, she stopped a waiter as he passed by.

"Could you bring me some bread, or something I could carry to my room please?"

The waiter appeared puzzled by the woman standing close to the wall and speaking to him as if she were hiding from someone.

"Excuse me, Madame?" The waiter spoke English but also with a strong British accent. Serena asked her question again in English now.

"Do you have any bread, or some food that I can take back to my cabin and eat?"

The waiter expressed a loss at what to say.

"If you would like, I can find you a table Madame and I can bring you something."

Serena scanned the dining room apprehensively.

"No, I just need something to take back to my cabin. I'm not feeling well."

The waiter, still seeming unsure replied. "Yes, well, if you'll come with me I'll see what I can find."

Serena followed the waiter to the kitchen door.

While the waiter searched in the kitchen she watched the dining room.

Suddenly, Paco came into the large dinning area.

Serena squatted down immediately and leaned to an angle that enabled her to watch him.

He scanned the dining room, obviously trying to find her. Just then the waiter came out the door.

"Are you alright, Madame?"

Serena looked up at the waiter.

"Yes, I just needed to sit for a moment."

The waiter now asked her with concern.

"Do you want me to fetch the ship's doctor?"

She peeked out at Paco as the waiter said this. He had fortunately been looking around the dining area and didn't seem to be searching in the direction of the kitchen.

"No, no I'll be alright. Could you get me a glass of water though?"

"Yes, certainly," He then turned to go into the kitchen but realized he still held part of a loaf of bread.

"Oh, I brought this for you," he handed the loaf down to her.

"Thank you."

She immediately took a small bite as she continued to watch Paco.

Once he had searched the dining area over, he left, and Serena slowly stood back up.

"Here you go, Madame." The waiter handed her the glass of water and she downed half of it quickly.

"Thank you," she said after catching her breath.

"I'm glad you're feeling better."

"Yes, thanks. I'll leave the glass in my cabin."

Serena quickly made her way out of the dinning room with the half loaf of bread and half glass of water.

She went back to the small nook on deck and sat eating the bread and sipping the water. Now she began to feel much better.

She remained hidden for several hours.

Then, she noticed something on the horizon and realized the ship was approaching land. She stood and went to the rail, to get a glimpse of the United States. She'd not seen America in over eight years.

She stepped back into the nook. There was no time to reminisce. Maybe, just maybe, she would make it. She waited until the ship came closer to land.

She needed to get to her room and gather her things. If she could get her stuff together and find a place to hide, maybe she could get off the ship safely.

Moving around corners and cautiously down hallways, Serena maneuvered back to her cabin.

After checking the hall where her cabin resided, she slipped to the door and tried to open it quickly.

Just as she got the key in, someone came around the corner. She became startled and tried desperately to open the door.

As she fumbled with the key she realized the person wasn't Paco but rather one of the ship's crew. The young man in uniform moved swiftly up to her when he saw her.

"Excuse me, Ms. De La Rosa?"

Serena stopped before going inside.

"Yes?"

"Ms. De La Rosa, are you alone?"

Serena appeared puzzled. She glanced around and replied.

"Yes, why do you ask?"

The crewman replied in a soft voice.

"I have a telegram for you, but it came with specific instructions that it only be delivered to you while you were alone.

"It actually came in yesterday and I've been hoping to get it to you before we docked."

She eyed the young man suspiciously but took the piece of paper from his hand.

"Thank you," she said and went into her room quickly, then locked the door behind her.

Inside her cabin she opened the telegram and read it.

"Everything is set. See you soon, TC."

Serena smiled and sat the telegram on a small table. She then began to gather her things.

Outside her room, Paco had approached the hall to their cabins when a young crewman called out, "Ms. De La Rosa?"

He moved up to the edge of the hall quietly. He peeked around the corner and saw the crewman talking with Serena as she stood in front of the door to her cabin.

The crewman then handed her a piece of paper and she went inside the cabin and shut the door.

Paco smiled contemptuously as the young crewman walked down the hallway and past him. He had her now. His blood had become hot as he'd searched the entire ship for her.

Walking up to the front of her cabin, he considered what to

do. If he found someone to open the door, Serena would escape again.

He pulled the shinny metal flask from his coat pocket and took a drink as he paced back and forth in front of the door.

The more he paced the angrier he became. She was trying to play him for a fool. She had something going on and he must put a stop to it before the ship docked.

After pacing for several minutes, he downed one more drink and placing the flask back in his pocket, he looked down the hall both ways, to make sure no one was close by.

With one swift move, he kicked the cabin door open.

Inside, Serena almost fell over from shock. Paco entered quickly and then pushed the broken cabin door shut.

"Hello, Serena. Surprised to see me?"

He instantly noticed the telegram on the table and picked it up.

"What do we have here? 'Everything is set. See you soon, TC,' well, well, very interesting that you should get such a telegram from our old friend Torre Cantelli."

Serena had slowly backed up and now stood in the small doorway leading to her tiny bedroom.

"Get out, Paco," she tried to sound brave.

Paco laughed and moved closer to her.

She stood frozen in the small doorway, trying not to move closer to the bed.

Paco crept even closer, seeming confident he now had her cornered. She watched his eyes scan her up and down hungrily.

"I don't know what game you're playing. But it stops now."

She reluctantly gave inches away and was now inside the small bedroom.

"Get out, Paco, I'll not tell you again. I'll scream, I swear."

He continued to move towards her until the back of her legs were against the bed.

"We'll be docking soon. But I believe we have just enough time."

She sneered at him and replied sharply.

"What are you talking about; time for what?"

Paco reached inside his coat and pulled out a large handkerchief. He began to wad the handkerchief into a ball.

"Just enough time to teach you who's in charge."

Seeing him wad the handkerchief up she knew immediately what he had in mind.

She raised her right hand to hit him. He grabbed her wrist and held it tight. She began to scream and hit him with her left hand. Paco moved quickly and efficiently, as if he'd done this before.

He crammed the balled-up handkerchief into her mouth and fell onto her at the same time. As they fell onto the bed, his weight caused her to struggle for breath instead of trying to spit the handkerchief out.

Her left hand became pinned by his arm. Once she caught her breath, she tried to spit the handkerchief out but he now pushed it farther into her mouth until it became lodged and she couldn't get any leverage against it with her tongue.

The handkerchief was so far into her mouth she could

barely breathe from her nose. She gagged and struggled more, but this simply increased her need for air.

Paco quickly grabbed one of Serena's scarves from a small table by the bed and pulling her wrists together tied them.

She continued to struggle but between the inability to breath and his full weight on her she quickly became exhausted.

She attempted to calm down and focus on pulling air into her desperate lungs. As she struggled more and more to breathe, she felt her heart would give out.

The realization of there being no escape began to sink in. Paco's breath smelled of alcohol and his eyes had fire in them as a wild animal.

"This should have happened a long time ago, Serena. You just need to learn your place."

He groped her breasts and began to kiss her neck roughly. She'd never been with a man before and now the man she despised pressed himself between her legs and seemed intent upon forcefully taking her virginity.

She felt herself going into some type of shock as she struggled in vain for air.

Her eyes strained for an escape route as she stared up at the ceiling. She wanted to cry but couldn't.

Deep inside she'd known this might happen. She'd walked into this just as she had done so many years ago. She gambled and now it seemed certain she would also lose Serena De La Rosa, just as she'd lost Gina.

As the room became darker and air became harder to obtain, Serena realized she could never be the same person once he had forced himself into her.

These thoughts raced through her mind as he began ripping at her dress and trying to reach the virgin skin of her breasts.

How could she ever dance as before once he had taken her by force?

Wasn't this time different though? She gambled for the others, not herself. This time she didn't get onto the ship in a vain gesture for self-gain. This time it was a gamble for the ones she loved.

Yet once again she was losing herself. The person she'd spent years rebuilding was sinking into another violent ocean of despair.

Surely the act of selfless love would be worth the price, wouldn't it? Somehow this mattered little as everything began to grow darker.

As Serena stared at the ceiling, she realized she was dying. Death approached her rapidly as the restriction of air due to the cloth in her mouth, along with the weight of Paco allowed for little air into her withering lungs.

She began to feel as if she were floating in the ocean again. A storm raged, and the rain and wind whipped against her.

She was Serena, not Gina and she realized she had no life vest on this time as she slowly began to sink into the violent ocean. Her arms were spread out, but she couldn't move them.

Helplessly, she sank farther and farther into the storm-swept sea until her face began to go under water.

Once again, just as happen so long ago, she stared into the grim face death. Once again, she resigned herself to this death and felt there was not hope of surviving the storm.

As the last bit of air in her lungs slowly lost its power and her hand slipped underwater, someone grabbed it. Someone began to pull her up.

Serena came out from the water gazing into her own eyes, yet they were the eyes of the young woman that fell into the ocean so long ago.

Gina stared at her with no expression on her face. She pulled Serena up and now took her other hand as well.

They held hands while silently gazing into each other's eyes. Serena could barely believe what she now saw.

For so long she'd searched for Gina. She'd wanted to apologize to her. But she couldn't find her. Now, somehow in these last few seconds of her life, Gina had found Serena.

She examined the sweet young face of the girl she had been. Nothing needed to be said as they had finally found each other again.

They began to slowly spin in a circle, as if dancing together while the storm all around them grew stronger.

Faster and faster they spun around. The ceiling of the cabin now grew faint and only the dance with Gina could be seen in Serena's mind.

Her eyes slowly closed as death began to take her.

Childhood memories and memories of the Cafe Flamenco merged into one beautiful painting on her soul.

Death was no longer as frightening as Gina and Serena had finally become one and the same now.

As she faded away, Serena finally felt a quiet peace inside her soul, now that she would die a whole person.

Something changed.

A tiny bit of air rushed into her lungs and she opened her eyes enough to see some light.

She sensed Paco leaning off her as he reached down to pull her dress up. This allowed her just enough air to recover slightly.

He'd already torn her dress on top but couldn't get through the material to reach her breasts.

Now he seemed to want more than her breasts and would waste no more time to get it.

As he searched for the bottom of her dress Serena again pulled a little bit of the life-giving air into her lungs.

Just as her senses began to slowly come back, she saw something hit the back of Paco's head and heard a dull thud sound.

He fell onto her and the weight of his body almost pressed the tiny amount of air from her lungs again.

She strained to get more air as darkness once again began to overtake her eyes.

Then, through her slight vision she saw hands pulling on Paco.

He was rolled off her and the beautiful sight of Alicia and Mimi came into view. They were both working feverishly to completely remove Paco from the top of her.

Once he was off Serena, Alicia quickly said, "I told you, we'll not leave you."

Serena's heart leapt with joy when Alicia said this in a manner as if she were getting on to her.

Now the flood of tears came suddenly and as Mimi pulled the handkerchief from her mouth Serena let out something crossed between laughter and crying.

As she wept and gasped for air, the two young women untied her.

She grabbed them both and hugged them, crying without restraint.

Now all three wept as the realization of her close call became apparent.

A few moments later, she sat stoically on a small chair, desperately trying to regain her composure. She wiped her eyes and face with a cloth.

"We're docking," Alicia said as she peered out the portal.

Mimi had been sitting and staring at Paco on the bed. She finally asked what must have been on her mind for some time.

"Is he dead?"

Serena looked up, and then at Paco on the bed. She realized she must be a leader again, regardless of how she felt.

She stood up and walked over to Paco. Noticing the shinny flask in his pocket, she pulled it from his jacket and held it up to his nose. She could see the metal fog up.

"No, he's still alive."

She laid the flask on his chest. Stepping back, she thought of what they must do now.

"Quickly, help me get changed."

She began to take the ripped dress off.

"We've got to get off this ship as soon as possible; before he wakes up."

After changing and gathering her stuff together, Serena quickly moved to the door with Alicia behind her.

Mimi however, paused. Possibly feeling she wanted to do a bit more, she walked over to Paco and cautiously twisted the cap of the flask until it began to leak very slowly onto his chest.

She then smiled with satisfaction and turning quickly caught up to the other two women.

By the time the ship was ready to off-load, all three women were first in line to disembark the ship.

Once off the ship and through designated channels, the three were met by several well-dressed men.

One of the men held a publicity photo of Serena and they both appeared to be watching for her.

"Ms. De La Rosa?"

Serena stopped and looked the men over with suspicion. The shorter man beside him glanced at the photo and said.

"Yeah, that's her."

"Do you speak any Italian?" The shorter man asked.

The taller man turned to his partner with apparent aggravation.

"Do I speak any Italian? Do you speak any Russian?"

He then turned to Serena and asked again slowly and using his hands to help him in his attempt to communicate.

"Where is Mr. Rivera?"

Serena said nothing, but slowly pointed back to the ship.

"Well, the reporters are waiting," the tall man continued anxiously. "I guess we can wait a few minutes for him."

When Serena heard this, she began walking at a brisk pace

away from the ship with Alicia and Mimi following close behind.

The two men, being obviously surprised, took off behind her with the tall one saying, "Or, I guess we can go see the reporters and maybe he'll catch up."

As they moved farther away from the ship the women slowed down a bit and the two men caught up and directed them to where a group of reporters were gathered around a small platform.

Seeing that Paco had still not arrived, but the reporters were waiting with apparent anticipation, the two men decided to continue with the announcement.

The men stepped up on the platform and the tall man began to speak. As he spoke several flashes from cameras went off and then the reporters prepared to take some notes.

"Alright everyone, I suppose we'll get this started. You've been called here as a courtesy of Crown Stone Entertainment Company. We'll be officially announcing a great new acquisition."

He then gestured for Serena to step up to the platform and once she had done so he continued.

"This beautiful woman is the famous Italian Flamenco dancer, Serena De La Rosa. We've recently signed a one-year contract with her manager Paco Rivera. We've already prepared for an extensive tour and we're thrilled to have her onboard."

Serena paid little attention to the tall man as he spoke. Instead she scanned out past the reporters until she spotted what she was looking for.

Behind the reporters and rushing towards the group she saw Mr. Cantelli with four men who appeared to be bodyguards.

As soon as she spotted Mr. Cantelli she stepped up beside the tall man and held her hand up indicating she wanted to speak.

"Well, um, it seems Ms. De La Rosa wants to say something. Does anyone here speak Italian?"

A muffled laughter could be heard amongst the reporters.

When the tall man finished saying this however, Serena began to speak loudly and although with a slight Spanish accent, she spoke plainly in English, so all could understand.

"I realize you're all here to report on my employment with Crown Stone Entertainment Company."

When Serena began to speak English, the two men beside her became surprised. The reporters also perked up; realizing this may be more than a routine story.

More camera flashes went off as she continued.

"There's been a new development and I've made a decision that has changed the circumstances. Some time ago, my assistant Alicia Banes was fired and her contract canceled because she defended me from unwanted advances by my manager Mr. Rivera.

"In the contract Mr. Rivera owns however, there is a stipulation on page three, section five. This stipulation states that should my assistant Alicia Banes be released from her contract for any reason, I'll have the option to nullify my obligations to the contract and dissolve it."

Now Mr. Cantelli came in behind the reporters and the four men moved to clear a path for him. Serena continued.

"On our trip here from England, Mr. Rivera again became aggressive and subjected me to unwanted advances. Therefore, I'm invoking the stipulation of my contract and from this point forward have no more obligations to Mr. Rivera."

After stating this, the reporters became very excited and the two men from Crown Stone Entertainment Company stepped back in obvious embarrassment.

One of the reporters then asked.

"Ms. De La Rosa, what are your plans if you're not to be employed by Crown Stone Entertainment Company?"

Serena motioned to Mr. Cantelli as he continued to edge his way to the small platform.

She replied.

"I'm very glad you ask that. My former Manager, Mr. Torre Cantelli, arrived here a few days ago. After receiving a telegram from me and becoming aware of Mr. Rivera's continued aggressive behavior, he has put together a contract and I'll be happy to sign this new agreement here today."

Mr. Cantelli stepped up to the platform and began to speak with a rather strong Italian accent.

"As you can see, I've employed a number of security personnel for the specific purpose of protecting Ms. De La Rosa from Mr. Rivera. I've also prepared a new contract for Ms. De La Rosa and while you're all here, this new agreement can be put into affect."

Mr. Cantelli quickly pulled the paperwork and a pen from

his satchel. Using the back of one of the security personnel, Serena signed the contract, followed by Mr. Cantelli.

More camera flashes accompanied the signing.

"Thank you, Ms. De La Rosa."

Mr. Cantelli then turned to the reporters and said, "Thank you also for documenting this occasion for us. I would now like to get Ms. De La Rosa to her hotel room so she can get some much-needed rest."

After this, Mr. Cantelli, Serena, and the others all moved quickly to waiting automobiles that sped away as soon as they got inside.

The two men from Crown Stone Entertainment still appeared to be in shock. They slowly began to move towards the dock in the hopes of finding Paco.

Though most of the reporters followed Mr. Cantelli and the others in a vain effort for more information; one reporter keenly followed the two men at a distance.

Realizing he may be able to get a scoop; the reporter quickly reloaded his camera.

Following unseen, he crept closer and closer until he shadowed them.

Meanwhile on the ship, Paco had awoken in the room. He sat up and the empty flask fell from his chest without him noticing.

He rubbed his head and felt the sore place where Alicia had hit him with a large, heavy ashtray.

Stumbling up, he gazed out the portal to realize the ship had docked. He then moved quickly out of the room in search of Serena.

After making his way off the ship he was met by the two men from Crown Stone Entertainment Company.

"Mr. Rivera."

Paco stopped. The reporter now slipped in closer as he saw what he'd hope for.

"Yes, what's going on?" Paco asked the two men.

As they came closer, the shorter man smelled the strong aroma of the alcoholic contents from the flask. He stepped back a little and then the tall man also smelled Paco and waved his hand a bit as if to ward off the alcohol smell.

"Mr. Rivera we've been looking for you. You've put our company into a very embarrassing situation."

Paco appeared puzzled. "What do you mean? Where's Serena?"

"Ms. De La Rosa has used our press gathering to announce her departure from contract with you. She has also signed a new contract with a 'Mr. Cantelli'."

Paco began to rub his head in confusion. This caused his hair to become a mess.

"She can't do that. I'll sue her for breach of contract. She'll never work again after I get through with her."

The two men now appeared aggravated by Paco.

"Mr. Rivera, maybe you should spend less time drinking and more time reading your performers' contracts."

Then the short man added with a strong tone.

"You'll be hearing from our lawyers first Mr. Rivera, but they'll not be the last you'll be hearing from us."

The tall man added.

"Goodbye, Mr. Rivera."

The reporter in hiding now realized he had the scoop he'd hoped for. Right before the two men moved to leave, he stepped from his hiding spot and quickly snapped a picture of the three men.

The two executives were caught with a surprised expression, but Paco stood in a state of confusion rubbing his head and his hair standing up. He appeared to be completely inebriated and having just awoken from a drunken stupor.

The reporter then dashed off.

The two executives turned and stared at Paco with increased anger as they knew well an embarrassing story would be surfacing.

Paco still appeared to be at a complete loss as to what had transpired. The two men left him alone and astonished by the recent events.

One Destiny, Two Women

The following day, Mr. Cantelli, Serena, Alicia and Mimi, as well as the four security men and several other associates of Mr. Cantelli, all gathered in a large room of an upscale hotel.

They were enjoying a small, low-key celebration of the new contract and of the perhaps lesser-known "freedom" for all the performers formerly under Paco's control.

On a table lay a news article with the embarrassing photo of the three men. Paco had a dazed expression in the photo; his hair standing up and altogether appearing drunk and disoriented.

The headline over the picture read "Sassy Italian Dancer Derails Drunken Manager along with Crown Stone Entertainment."

Suddenly, Paco stormed into the room.

Quickly realizing the dangerous situation, the security men closed in on him and pulled revolvers from under their coats.

Alicia, Mimi and Mr. Cantelli also closed in behind the security men in a gesture indicating Paco would need to go through them as well to reach Serena.

"I just want to talk with her. Where is she… Serena!"

He was obviously intoxicated as he struggled in the security men's hold.

A silence settled over the room as everyone seemed to be in a mild shock from his sudden entrance.

From behind the others Paco heard Serena's voice.

"Let him speak."

She then moved towards him and the others stepped aside to allow her through.

When she came into view, Paco almost didn't recognize her. She seemed to radiate elegance and was more beautiful than he'd ever seen before.

Being free from his grasp, she no longer endured the burden of dressing drab and conservative to dull his advances.

This was a new woman, a whole woman; complete and confident in her surroundings.

She held a glass of wine close to her chest. She said nothing to him but stopped about ten feet away and stared at him without expression.

"Serena, you can't do this to me!"

Paco pleaded, then after glancing around and expressing a dislike for speaking with so many around; continued in a more reserved voice.

"You don't double cross these people and get away with it, Serena. This could destroy me."

Serena appeared unmoved upon hearing this. She continued to stare at him for several seconds before commenting. Then, after deciding what she wanted to say, she spoke in a slow deliberate voice.

"I'm quite certain this will destroy you, Mr. Rivera. You have no friends. But you've cultivated many enemies over the years.

"After the Americans take you down, those enemies will come from far and near to ensure you stay down. There'll be no one that will risk trying to save you."

Paco stepped back a little, seeming shocked by her bluntness.

"So, was that your plan all along? You just wanted to destroy me?"

His eyes flamed now as he grew angrier. It seemed he wanted to strike out at Serena, but the security men kept a tight ring around him.

She again replied without emotion.

"I'm a dancer, Mr. Rivera. You're the one that makes plans. You're the one that decides what is best for those around you; based solely it seems on the dictates of what pleases you. You're the one that demands complete control, even if that requires violence or harm to the ones you seek to control. No, Mr. Rivera, I don't plan such things. I'm a dancer, that's all. I'm only in control of my dancing, but perhaps you now see, it's something that cannot be controlled by force."

Paco's face contorted as he appeared to search for another answer. The truth was unsavory and as he grasped for something other than the truth he lashed out with a loud tone.

"I brought you here to help you, Serena. I planned big things for you. I wanted you to be successful in the United States and you turn around and do this to me?"

With this comment, Alicia noticed Serena's eyes lower to half open and the dancer's head lift slightly with an expression of contempt. She knew well Paco had said something that finally touched a nerve in her friend and she also knew the pain would soon come for Paco.

Serena's voice became lower and a tension could be heard, as if she was doing all she could to hold back a flood of wrath upon him.

"I once listened to a man such as you, Paco Rivera. I trusted him when he said he planned to help me and make me successful.

"That decision cost me everything, even the person I might have been. I fell into an ocean of despair so deep, I felt I would never stand on my own feet again.

"But someone helped me learn to walk again. This person knew what it meant to lose everything, because she too had lost everything. She is the same as me Mr. Rivera. She's also a dancer."

Serena now moved slowly closer to Paco.

"This dancer made a mistake when she was young and at the peak of her dancing skills. The mistake she made was to fall in love with a man. She gave her love freely to this man and he in turn cast that love aside as if it were worthless.

"Heartbroken, she became almost completely empty. She even lost the ability to dance as she once had. And though she was left with almost nothing after this man broke her heart, she realized there was one love inside her that the man could not destroy, the love of dancing.

"She began to teach others to dance and slowly began to love again. She gave love to those around her; to her students and family, and love came back to her, so she grew strong again."

Serena paused a few seconds as if to allow Paco to absorb what she said. Then she continued before he could make a comment.

"I'm one of those people this woman gave her love to, Mr. Rivera. I was without anything or anyone and she showed me compassion and love. She taught me not only to walk again but to dance. She gave me strength inside where I thought there would never be any again.

"That same love is inside me today and helps me survive ordeals I might not otherwise survive. This woman I speak of is my adoptive mother, Mr. Rivera. Perhaps you remember this woman? You are, in fact, the man that cast her love aside as if it were an old rag. Her name is Olivia Frisco."

When Serena said this, Paco's face instantly went pale.

Alicia and Mimi both turned to Serena in amazement as they suddenly realized the actual depth of the situation.

Without allowing Paco an instant to recover, Serena moved even closer to him and spoke with a new ferocity as he struggled with the weight of her previous revelation.

"It's her love that enables me to dance as I dance. It's her love that gave me the strength and foundation to be who I am today.

"So, it seems to me Mr. Rivera, you're faced with only two options. You can blame me for your destruction. But to do this you must also accept that the same love you cast aside as worthless, in fact, had the power to break you completely.

"Or, you can blame your own arrogant indifference to those around you. Either way Mr. Rivera; when you find yourself completely alone in the ocean of life, you'll be forced to face yourself, I'm quite certain of this. And this is when you'll see the person you truly are. And when you know the true Paco Rivera, I believe the only thing that will remain for you, is a sea of regrets."

Paco appeared ill. His mouth moved slightly as if he wanted to say something but couldn't get the words out. His eyes searched hers. He wanted some other answer, one that made him right. In vain he grasped for an escape.

Serena held him with a stare straight into his panicked soul.

Alicia watched her friend wield this power from somewhere deep inside; it had been cultivated over the years, and now, at this very second, she demonstrated her true mastery over it.

She wouldn't let Paco break away until the truth had been

branded upon his soul. He became sweaty and trembled as she held him for what seemed a very long moment.

Then, she released Paco with her final words to him.

"The dance is over, Mr. Rivera, good-bye."

Paco almost fell back as he became liberated from her hold. He stepped back, frightened and appearing wounded, then stumbling to the door he left quickly as a stray dog might, escaping the wrath of an angered housewife.

A New Dance Begins

Almost nine years to the day that Gina had washed up on the beach of Mexico, the door of the Cafe Flamenco opened.

Light streamed in against many lovingly framed pictures of Serena, all along the walls.

Some were pictures from her time in Vista Cruz and others were from Europe.

Inside, several patrons sat at tables, eating and drinking. They all watched as a young girl of around thirteen stood up on the stage in a pretty white dancing dress.

Olivia was at the bottom of the low stage; facing the young dancer and giving her instructions.

"Maria, you must use your left leg when you turn at that point. Remember, your left leg."

Olivia stepped forward and tapped the girls left leg, but her student made no move.

"Are you listening, Maria?"

Olivia now looked up at the young girl.

Maria had a blank expression on her face. Her mouth had

dropped open and her eyes were wide, fixed upon something behind Olivia.

Then, one of the patrons to Olivia's right slid his chair out and turned towards the door, also seeming surprised as he stood up.

To her left, several patrons slid their chairs out and as Olivia turned she watched them stand up to face the door with an astonished expression.

Olivia slowly turned around to face the door.

There stood Serena with a small entourage behind her. She was dressed eloquently and could have stepped straight off the fashionable streets of Paris.

Directly behind her, on one side and the other, were Alicia and Mimi, also dressed beautifully, and behind them stood Mr. Cantelli with his warm smile.

To the right, a guitar player sat his case down as he gazed around the cafe.

Several other assistants also sat baggage down as they examined the establishment curiously.

Tears began to flood Olivia's eyes as she strained to view her daughter through them.

Her hand trembled as she put it to her mouth in disbelief of who stood in front of her.

Serena had already begun to cry as soon as she walked in and saw her mother teaching Maria.

"My child," was all Olivia could get out of her trembling lips.

"Mother," was the only thing Serena could say.

They quickly moved to embrace each other. They both began to weep tears of joy without restraint.

Alicia and Mimi turned to each other and smiled.

The little girl from Jacksonville had finally found her way home.

The End

We hope you enjoyed A Tempest Soul. You may be interested in other books by Oliver Phipps. We've listed some of his other works here for your convenience.

Spyder Bones

We've heard the tales. The eternal struggle between good and evil. Many religions are based on the concepts. God, Satan, angels and demons; ideals interwoven into our very existence.

Most all have chosen a side, whether they admit it to themselves or not. Many have at least a basic understanding of what is happening. Some have even discovered secrets beyond the veil of what we see. However, there are a few, who not only understand the war, but are in the very thick of it.

This is the story of Spyder Bones, a mystic warrior.

It's the summer of 1969 and Aaron Prescott is a seasoned soldier. After serving one tour of duty in Vietnam as a cavalryman, Aaron returns for a second tour as a combat medic.

Aaron's life revolves around the love of his Vietnamese girlfriend, the danger of combat and his passion for music. It's not an overly complicated existence. But that's about to change.

Aaron, or Spyder as he is known to his friends, suffers a near death experience during combat. He is subsequently trapped in a comatose state for months. During this time, he is exposed to an unseen war. A spiritual struggle that most only have a vague awareness of.

Aaron must make some difficult decisions. But, regardless of anything else, he knows his life will never be the same.

Tears of Abandon

In this haunting adventure, several friends from college put together a plan to kayak down an Alaskan river during the summer break.

Soon there are five young people headed for the Alaskan wilderness. Things go great until they discover an unusual sound and begin to follow it, eventually finding something long lost and almost forgotten.

Twelve Minutes till Midnight

A man catches a ride on a dusty Louisiana road only to find out he's traveling with notorious outlaws Bonnie and Clyde.

The suspense is nonstop as confrontation settles in between a man determined to stand on truth and an outlaw determined to dislocate him from it.

"Twelve Minutes till Midnight will take you on an unforgettable ride."

Ghosts of Company K

Tag along with young Bud Fisher during his daily adventures in this ghostly tale based on actual events. It's 1971 and Bud and his family move into an old house in Northern Arkansas. Bud soon discovers they live not far from a very interesting cave as well as a historic Civil War battle site. As odd things start to happen, Bud tries to solve the mysteries. But soon the entire family experiences a haunting situation.

If you enjoy ghost tales based on true events, then you'll enjoy Ghosts of Company K. This heartwarming story brings the reader into the life and experiences of a young boy growing up in the early 1970s. Seen through innocent and unsuspecting eyes, Ghosts of Company K reveals a haunting tale from the often-unseen perspective of a young boy.

Diver Creed Station

Wars, disease and a massive collapse of civilization have ravaged humans of a hundred years in the future. Finally, in the late twenty- second century, humanity slowly begins to struggle back from the edge of extinction.

When a huge "virtual life" facility is restored from a hibernation type of storage and slowly brought back online, a new hope materializes.

Fragments of humanity begin to move into the remnants of Denver and the Virtua-Gauge facilities, which offer seven days of virtual leisure for seven days work in this new and growing social structure.

Most inhabitants of this new lifestyle begin to hate the real world and work for the seven-day period inside the virtual pods. It's the variety of luxury role play inside the virtual zone that supply's the incentive needed to work hard for seven days in the real world.

In this new social structure, a man can work for seven days in a food dispersal unit and earn seven days as a twenty-first century software billionaire in the virtual zone. As time goes by and more of the virtual pods are brought back online life appears to be getting better.

Rizette and her husband Oray are young technicians that settle into their still new marriage as the virtual facilities expand and thrive.

Oray has recently attained the level of a Class A Diver and enjoys his job. The Divers are skilled technicians that perform critical repairs to the complex system, from inside the virtual zone.

His title of Diver originates from often working in the secure "lower levels" of the system. These lower level areas are the dividing space between the real world and the world of the virtual zone. When the facility was built, the original designers intentionally placed this buffer zone in the system to avoid threats from non-living virtual personnel.

As Oray becomes more experienced in his elite technical position as a Diver, he's approached by his virtual assistant and forced to make a difficult decision. Oray's decision triggers events that soon pull him and his wife Rizette into a deadly quest for survival.

The stage becomes a massive and complex maze of virtual world sequences as escape or entrapment hang on precious threads of information.

System ghosts from the distant past intermingle with mysterious factions that have thrown Oray and Rizette into a cyberspace trap with little hope for survival.

Where the Strangers Live

When a passenger plane disappeared over the Indian Ocean in autumn 2013, a massive search gets underway.

A deep trolling, unmanned pod picks up faint readings and soon the deep sea submersible Oceana and her three crew members are four miles below the ocean surface in search of the black box from flight N340.

Nothing could have prepared the submersible crew for what they discover and what happens afterward. Ancient evils and other world creatures challenge the survival of the Oceana's crew. Secrets of the past are revealed, but death hangs in the balance for Sophie, Troy and Eliot in this deep-sea Science Fiction thriller.

The House on Cooper Lane

It's 1984 and all Bud Fisher wants to do is find a place to live in Madison Louisiana. With his dog Badger, they come across a beautiful old mansion that was converted into apartments.

Something should have felt odd when he found out nobody lived in the apartments. To make matters worse, the owner is reluctant to let him rent one. Eventually, he negotiates an apartment in the old historic house but soon finds out that he's not quite as alone as he thought. What ghostly secret has the owner failed to share?

It's up to Bud to unravel the mysteries of the upstairs apartments, but is he ready to find out the truth?

Bane of the Innocent

"There's no reason for them to shoot us; we ain't anyone" - Sammy, Bane of the Innocent.

Two young boys become unlikely companions during the fall of Atlanta. Sammy and Ben somehow find themselves, and each other, in the rapidly changing and chaotic environment of the war-torn Georgia City.

As the siege ends and the fall begins in late August and early September of 1864 the Confederate troops begin to move out, and Union forces cautiously move into the city. Ben and Sammy simply struggle to survive, but in the process, they develop a friendship that will prove more important than either one could imagine.

A Life Naive

Life for twenty-seven-year-old Hershel Lawson has been relatively uneventful and that's the way he likes it. When his grandmother passes away, leaving him her car and a last wish of him taking her ashes to L.A., his life takes a turn and it will never be the same again.

With his new task and grandmother's ashes, Hershel sets out

from St. Louis Missouri in the spring of 1962. He travels unimpeded along scenic Route 66 for two days but is suddenly and unexpectedly relieved of two important things, his car and wallet.

Sally is a sassy and street-smart young woman on her way to Hollywood. She's determined to prove everyone wrong in the "one horse town" she left and make it as an actress in California. Through mishaps of her own, Sally comes across Hershel. Though neither one realizes it, the real journey is about to begin.

Take a seat and journey with Hershel and Sally along historic Route 66 during its heyday. Laugh and maybe shed a tear or two as they struggle against the odds, and often each other, to make it a few more miles down the highway

The Bitter Harvest

The year is 1825, and a small Native American village has lost many of its people and bravest warriors to a pack of Lofa; huge beasts' humanoid in shape but covered with coarse hair. The creatures are taller than any normal man, and fiercer than even the wildest animal.

Rather than leave the land of their ancestors, the tribe chooses to stay and fight the beasts. But they're losing the war, and perhaps more critically, they're almost without hope.

The small community grasps for anything to help them survive. There is a warrior on the frontier known as Orenda.

He's already legendary across the west for his bravery and honor.

Onsi, a young villager, sets out on a journey to find the warrior.

Orenda will be forced to choose between almost certain death, not just for himself, but also his warrior wife Nazshoni and her brother Kanuna, or a dishonorable refusal that would mean annihilation for the entire village.

The crucial decision is only the beginning, and Orenda will soon face the greatest test of his life; the challenge that could turn out to be too much even for a warrior of legend.

*

Made in the USA
Coppell, TX
18 November 2020

41565278R00197